The Succubus

Adele walked through the woods and ran her hands through her long, tangled hair. Something strange was happening to her. Was it superstition or was the demon really haunting her, making her lose control of herself – making her think about sex all the time? It frightened her, but somewhere, deep in her subconscious, it excited her, too. Perhaps that meant it was too late. Perhaps the succubus had already claimed Adele as her own.

The Succubus

ZOE LE VERDIER

BLACK
lace

Black Lace novels are sexual fantasies.
In real life, make sure you practise safe sex.

First published in 1998 by
Black Lace
332 Ladbroke Grove
London W10 5AH

Typeset by SetSystems Ltd, Saffron Walden, Essex
Printed and bound by Mackays of Chatham PLC

ISBN 0 352 33230 1

For Chris K.

Chapter One

Jamie's body was aching. That wasn't unusual in itself, he always ached after class. The ritual daily torture of the job had been effortless at the age of twenty, but was getting harder to cope with now he was nearing thirty. But today, and every day since he'd come back from Germany, there was another ache to add to his collection; more of a longing, grumbling hunger from somewhere deep inside him.

His eyes weaved through the mass of sweating, tired limbs sprawled across the studio floor. There she was, standing at the barre, absorbed in stretching her wonderful muscles and, it seemed, completely unaware of the effect she had on him. He smiled as he watched her. Adele was still as conscientious as when she had joined the company five years ago. Students fresh from ballet school were expected to be keen, but in most cases that eagerness to impress quickly wore off. It was touching to see her, still striving to improve her body while most of the other dancers, exhausted from a tough class, were lounging around, chatting and laughing. Jamie didn't know why she bothered, her body was perfect.

Adele had grown into a beautiful young woman. Her

shape was no longer that of a typically skinny ballerina. Although her limbs were toned, she was curvaceous, whereas most female dancers resembled sticks, and had about as much sex appeal. Her legs were long, well proportioned and lightly muscular. Her firm, round buttocks caught his eye, as did the feminine arc of her belly, an unbearably gentle upward curve which Jamie wanted desperately to kiss. Where most ballerinas had flat chests, Adele's breasts were full, pert and beautifully rounded, slightly upturned where they came to soft points at her large nipples. He had to stop himself from staring at her in class, her shape tantalisingly obvious beneath the sweat-stained fabric of her leotard. Her luscious, wavy brown hair, glinting with streaks of summer gold, fell below her shoulders in thick layers. When she wore it up, wispy curls snaked at the nape of her neck, teasing Jamie, making his fingers twitch as he longed to release her hair, to watch her shake it free. Her elegant, long neck drew the eye to her gently sloping shoulders and down to the soft curves of her cleavage. Her face was strikingly attractive, with strong cheek-bones, smooth, sun-kissed skin, a fine nose and small, Cupid's bow lips. But it was Adele's eyes that had kept Jamie awake from time to time since he'd been away: large, framed with long, thick lashes, and with deep green irises rimmed and flecked with brown, they always betrayed her feelings. He had never forgotten the look in her eyes the night he had kissed her.

Lifting one leg up on to the smooth wooden pole, Adele flexed her foot. Stretching her aching calf muscle she leant her taut body over her thigh. Sweat trickled in a warm rivulet down the furrow of her spine. She had pushed her body that little bit further until she felt a welcome ache in her limbs, the signal that she had worked harder than usual. Motivation was elusive; the constant pressure to push her body, force her muscles, to strive for improvement during the daily class was often a grind. But during the last week, Adele had found a new impetus. She looked in the mirror at him and shivered despite the muggy heat in the packed studio. He was watching her.

Adele flinched inside and averted her eyes as Jamie set off across the wide studio towards her. Oh God, she thought, he's coming to talk to me. I won't know what to say. Everyone will see me turn bright red and stammer, like some pathetic teenager.

He stopped in the centre of the studio as Jessica appeared from nowhere, and a mixture of relief, disappointment and envy mingled inside Adele's mind. Jessica didn't have any problems where men where concerned. Jessica didn't blush, or stammer, Jessica got what she wanted. She might have some competition where Jamie Butler was concerned, though. Not only was he an accomplished dancer, but handsome, too – admired by every woman in the company, and some of the men. He had only been back in the National Ballet a week having left, years ago, to take a principal contract with the Munich Ballet, and already gossip and rumour flourished regarding his sex life. 'He isn't with anyone,' they whispered eagerly in the showers. 'He's got his eye on someone in the company.' The company, Adele thought, certainly had its eye on him.

As Jessica cajoled him into practising some lifts with her, sixty adoring fans avidly watched the contours of his tall, muscular frame as he flexed and stretched. Sixty adoring fans followed the path of his fingertips as they traced deliberate, expansive patterns in the muggy air. Sixty adoring fans admired his wild blonde curls flopping over deep blue eyes, his smile friendly and nonchalant. Like an Arab sheikh with his harem, all he had to do was turn, point and beckon at any one of them and they would fall willingly into his long, strong arms.

'He still fancies you, you lucky cow.' Nadia's insistent

3

chirruping broke Adele's reverie. An Australian, Nadia was loud and friendly, with a cheeky, pixie-like face, her sharp features framed with dark, wispy curls. She was pale and thin apart from her heavy breasts, which jiggled constantly as she never stood still, always hopping about from foot to foot as if at any moment she might think of something better to do and run off.

Adele sighed hopelessly. 'Jamie can have any woman he wants, Nadia. He's hardly likely to want me.'

'I wouldn't be so sure,' added Carmen, Nadia's ever-present sidekick. The two were inseparable, and could usually be located by following the sound of raucous laughter. Carmen's accent was thickly Spanish, as were her looks. Small and strong, she was robustly built with tiny hands, feet and breasts. Adele envied her olive skin and dramatic, dark auburn hair. Her deep blue, almond-shaped eyes flashed with their usual fire. 'He still watches you in class,' she whispered conspiratorially, 'like he always used to do.'

'Is that why you've been working so hard lately?' There was a knowing smirk in Nadia's dark eyes, and a wicked edge to her voice. 'Are you trying to impress him?'

Adele snapped, her friend's gentle taunting having hit its target. 'The only person I'm trying to impress is the ballet master. Why can't you two just leave me alone?'

Carmen shook her little hands dramatically and spoke slowly for emphasis. 'If we left you alone, Adele, your pathetic sex life would be non-existent.'

Uncomfortable with the truth, Adele busied herself with her hair. As usual, several soft curls had eased their way out of her bun, and now clung untidily to the back of her neck.

'Jamie always had the hots for you,' Nadia insisted. 'And I seem to remember you were pretty keen on him. If you don't stop acting like such a wimp, Jessica will sink her claws into him.'

Carmen nodded. 'It looks like she already has.'

Jessica was dancing in front of Jamie, flaunting her lithe body and fluttering her pale eyelashes. She extended one perfect long leg high to one side, her determined strength allowing her to balance for what seemed like eternity, then suddenly, she sank effortlessly into a demi plié for a split second before whizzing into four quick pirouettes. Jamie laughed at her audacity, and before she finished spinning, grabbed her tiny waist and hoisted her high above his head. She arranged her limbs into a glorious position, legs stretched into the splits, arms flung back over her head in an expression of abandon. Adele wondered what pose she would have taken if Jamie had lifted her, an ungainly one probably, an uncomfortable, silly position that would have made the situation embarrassing. Gently, Jamie lowered Jessica to the floor, his strong forearms supporting her as her slender body slowly slid through his grasp. He held her for a moment and they laughed, a friendly, easy laugh.

Adele cursed, everything was so easy for Jessica. It was so unjust, that one woman should be blessed with more than her fair share of talent, looks and confidence. And now, it seemed, she had set her sights on adding Jamie to her list of lovers. Hot tears stung Adele's eyes and her face reddened with the sickening realisation that once again, Jessica would beat her to the prize. She swapped legs, raising her other foot to the barre and bent her body over until her face rested on her knee. Ignoring her friends, she closed her eyes and in the darkness, sheltered from the world.

Her attention was lifted again as David Renfell, the company's director, swung through the double doors. Since the announcement after class of an emergency company meeting, a low, murmuring rumble had filled the high studio. Rumour and speculation had spread quickly, each dancer with their own theory about the reason behind this hastily convened gathering. Were there going to be redundancies? Was the theatre closing or, worse still, was the best director the National Ballet had ever had about to announce his retirement?

The humming and buzzing died down as he strode to the front of the studio. Sixty pairs of anxious eyes left Jamie and followed David, his movements still as fluid and graceful as when he had been a dancer himself, the first real star of the National Ballet. He was a handsome man in his mid fifties, with close-cropped grey hair and a penchant for linen designer suits which skimmed ten years from his age.

'Erm, right. Thanks for coming everybody, sorry to have kept you in suspense. Now, I've got very bad news and very good news.' Someone muttered at the back of the studio and a small giggle broke the tension, but Adele's eyes never left David's serious face.

'As you all know, the National Ballet is highly dependant on Arts Association funding. The bad news is, the venerated members of the Association's board have decided they're giving too much money to London-based companies, and our grant has been slashed. I've begged and pleaded with them, but they won't budge. We therefore cannot afford to stage *Swan Lake* next season.'

The room erupted with worry. *Swan Lake* was a classic, a big favourite with the public, the balletic equivalent of a best-selling novel or a blockbusting film. If they couldn't afford to stage the production, the National Ballet Company would not raise the revenue it needed to sustain itself, and that would mean redundancies for sure, if not complete closure.

David raised his hand. 'I have good news too.' Silence fell like a cushion. 'Some of you may be aware that we are very lucky to have a group of dedicated private sponsors who, every year, make up the shortfall in our funds.' He ran his fingers through his close-cropped hair. 'I have this morning received a phone call from our most

6

generous patron, a reclusive millionaire who wishes to remain anonymous. He knows of our current predicament, and is willing to fund our entire next season, in return for a personal favour.'

Intrigue filled the room. 'Our benefactor, whose name is Rafique, is holding a party for a group of his friends in two weeks' time. He wishes to celebrate in his favourite way, by watching the ballet. However, rather than coming to us, the National Ballet is to go to him. He's chosen the dancers, the choreographer, the music and the story for his ballet, and those selected to perform for him are to have a week's rehearsals here, and a week in his manor house, as his guests.' David's eyes raked the room, scanning his dancers' faces for approval. 'I wouldn't normally ask you to do charity work, but the future of the company depends on it. And by the sounds of it, those chosen by Rafique will be treated like royalty while they're under his roof.'

David unfolded the piece of paper he had been clutching. 'The choreographer is Richard Chandler, and rehearsals are to begin at once. Will the following people please go to Studio four immediately. You are obviously excused from all other work for the next fortnight. Jamie Butler, Jessica Sharpe, Alexei Kabarovich, Nadia Brookes, Carmen Carreno and Adele King.'

Adele's eyebrows shot up at the mention of her name. She was thrilled. She was never picked to do anything exciting, and now she had a chance to save the company.

Jamie was at her side as she hoisted her heavy bag, crammed full of pointe shoes, leg warmers and several bars of chocolate, on to her shoulder. Together, they made their way along the dingy corridor to Studio four. He grabbed her hand and squeezed it, voicing her thoughts.

'Isn't this exciting? I wonder why Rafique has chosen us?' He lowered his voice, and his breath brushed against her neck. He let go of her hand, and rested his palm in the small of her back. Adele winced, aware that her leotard was damp with sweat. 'I hope we get to dance together, Adele,' he admitted. 'You won't be able to avoid me, if you have to dance with me.'

Adele and Jamie were the last to arrive, and as soon as they entered the small, sun-filled studio the choreographer clapped his hands loudly.

'OK darlings, now we're all here I'll fill you in, as it were. Adele, sweetie, come and sit on my cock. Did I say cock? I meant my knee. I want to tell you a story.'

Adele rolled her eyes surreptitiously and reluctantly perched herself on Richard's spacious lap. For the past two years, Richard Chandler had delighted in making her feel uncomfortable with his constant touching and sexual innuendo. His favourite hobby was embarrassing the more repressed members of the company with his depraved sense of humour. He was a beautiful man, very tall and extremely black, with a shiny bald head and wicked, dark eyes so well-soaked in sex that they made Adele flinch and turn away whenever she caught his gaze. The muscles of his extraordinarily long limbs were extremely well-developed and always shown off in skin-tight clothes, and his huge hands punctuated his speech with expansive, camp gestures. Aged thirty, he was an established though avant-garde choreographer, on loan to the company from the San Francisco Ballet. He was gorgeous, and very, very gay.

'Right my loves, listen up,' he drawled. 'A mysterious package arrived here ten minutes ago by courier.' Richard smirked, highly amused by this scenario. 'It contained a cassette and a letter, which I'm going to read to you now, in the hope that it will shed some light on this little venture for you.' Richard draped a heavy arm around Adele's waist and began to read in a comical, falsetto voice.

'My name is Rafique, and you have been chosen to be

my guests at Rantree Manor, near York. The ballet I have commissioned from you is about a myth that was made known to me when I moved to the Manor, and which has fascinated me ever since. In medieval times, Rantree was thought to be haunted by a female demon, a "succubus", who gained her strength and pleasure by having sexual intercourse with sleeping men. According to legend, Rantree's succubus was insatiable, and she took pleasure from female guests too. Some say the Manor is still possessed by the spirit.'

Richard paused to raise an eyebrow, silently passing judgement on Rafique, whom he obviously thought more than a little eccentric.

'Richard Chandler will choreograph my ballet.' His dark eyes looked around the room with a knowing smile, making the dancers giggle. Chandler was renowned for his overtly sexual style, and was the obvious choice for such a ballet.

'Alexei, Nadia, Jamie and Carmen are to play the demon's hapless victims. Jessica is to be the understudy, in case of injury during rehearsals. Adele King,' Richard paused for effect, 'will play the succubus.'

Oh God. Adele's eyes widened as this amazing news sunk in. A sexual demon? Her? Surely Rafique had made a mistake? Mortified, she glanced involuntarily at Jamie. He grinned at her, nodding encouragement.

Richard got up and Adele slid off his lap and stood facing the other dancers, her eyes fixed to the pale wooden floor to try and hide her hot embarrassment. She could feel Richard's powerful body behind hers as he hugged her, resting his chin on top of her head. 'Any questions?'

'Yes.' A thin, whining voice came from the corner. It was Jessica. 'How on earth is Adele going to play a sex maniac? From what I hear, it isn't exactly type-casting is it?'

Adele seethed and bit her lip until she tasted blood. What a bitch, she thought. She had to say something.

Richard got there first. 'No, dear, if it was type-casting Rafique wanted, I'm sure he would have picked you. Although from what I hear, a guy would need to be asleep to fuck you.'

Adele's hand flew to her mouth to smother a vengeful chuckle, as Jessica's face coloured violently. She savoured the moment, it wasn't often that Jessica Sharpe was rendered speechless. It served her right.

Jessica had been spiteful to Adele since the first day they had met at the London Academy of Ballet, the prestigious school which took pride in supplying top class dancers for the National Ballet Company. Carmen and Nadia had insisted that the root of her bitchiness was jealousy, although Adele could never understand why. Jessica's conventional good looks meant she was rarely without a lover for very long. A skinny, wispy ballerina, she had long legs, pale, straight blonde hair that fell half-way down her back, and icy blue eyes. Unlike Adele, her body was made for ballet, and technically she was a good dancer, although Adele always found her interpretation cold and emotionless. However, her assertiveness meant she always got to tackle the juicy soloist rôles that Adele longed for, instead of the insipid good fairies, kind sisters and spurned lovers that seemed to have become Adele's forte. No wonder she was furious at being snubbed as the understudy. Both women knew that it was Jessica, not Adele, who should be playing the demon.

Richard moved languidly to the tape deck. 'OK folks, give me ten minutes to get a feel of the music, then we'll get started.'

As the first few bars of music played over and over again, Nadia and Carmen ran across to join Adele at the front of the studio. Adele tried to listen as the rich sounds of the orchestra filled the room with dramatic, sensual harmonies. She didn't recognise the composer, and yet the music sounded so familiar. Was it Stravinsky? No. Debussy maybe. Now it sounded like Ravel.

Nadia's harsh voice broke the spell. 'This is going to be a scream! I've never stayed in a manor house before, have you? I wonder what this mystery man looks like. Rafique sounds French, or maybe Indian, or Arabian. What do you think?'

Adele shrugged. She liked Nadia but she could do without this conversation. She wanted to concentrate on the music. 'I don't know, but whoever Rafique is, I think he's got the wrong person. Jessica would be far better as a – a "succubus".'

Carmen scoffed. 'Bull shit. Jessica is a bitch. You are a far better dancer than she is. She is just jealous because Rafique is obviously an admirer of yours. You will be a wonderful demon.' She tutted frustratedly at Adele's reticence.

Nadia jumped about excitedly, whispering in time with her movements. 'I hope I get to dance with Alexei!'

Adele looked across at Alexei as he lounged against the barre at the back of the room, lazily circling a foot. Alexei Kabarovich was the most dramatically good-looking man she had ever seen. He was Russian, and had joined the company six months ago from his native Moscow Ballet, causing a thrill among the ranks of the National Ballet Company. Thickset, with huge, rippling muscles, he was a powerful presence both on stage and off, his unwavering dark grey eyes peering out from beneath strong eyebrows and thick, floppy dark hair, giving him an intense, brooding air. Adele could understand Nadia's desire to be partnered by him. Just the thought of his huge hands, effortlessly lifting and turning her, was enough to make the muscles of Adele's sex tingle and quiver. She realised with a mixture of delight and dread that as the succubus, she would be sure to dance with him. Alexei was famous for having affairs with his partners, and she hoped he wouldn't try it on with her. His laid-back, overt flirtatiousness scared her, and she had hardly spoken to him since he'd joined the company. She didn't want to have to start now.

As Adele tried to put Alexei out of her mind he lifted his head, dragging his eyes languidly away from his foot, as if it was an immense effort for him to look at anything but his own wonderful body. He looked up to find three young, attractive women admiring him, but wasn't surprised. Women had always admired Alexei. His eyes locked with Adele's, teasing her, and a lascivious leer began to twitch at his lips. He too, was thinking about who he would partner in this ballet.

'Right, guys.' Richard switched off the tape with a flourish and turned to face his cast. 'Nadia, you'll dance with Alexei. Carmen, you go with Jamie. Jessica, you learn Adele's part. I'll listen to the music properly at lunchtime, but let's get started with some ideas.'

The first rehearsal went quickly. The dancers got on well together, apart from Jessica, who sulked at the back, but no one took any notice of her. Richard worked at breakneck speed, his inspiration overtaking him as he used his hands-on approach to bend and mould his material, the dancers' flesh, into the quirky, sensuous shapes that were his trademark. As usual, he began by working on themes: passion for Alexei and Nadia, hesitant romance for Jamie and Carmen, and unadulterated, predatory raunchiness for Adele. And as usual, Adele struggled to twist herself into his vision – she felt awkward, uncomfortable and frightened by the idea of playing a sex-crazed she-devil. At the end of the day, when the others left for the showers, she stayed behind.

She only rehearsed a couple of steps before giving up. Dismayed by the incongruous sight facing her in the mirror, she trudged slowly to the back of the studio and sat slumped against the wall. Her reflection in the mirror opposite was distorted, she looked small and thinner than usual and felt pathetic.

In the warm solitude, she tried to make sense of the butterflies that chased each other in her stomach. On one hand, she was undeniably thrilled to have been chosen as the succubus, flattered to imagine Rafique, the enigmatic balletomane, admiring her dancing from afar. And yet the idea of playing a rampant demon scared her to death. She could barely let herself go in bed, even with a sensitive, caring lover like her last, and suddenly she was faced with the task of performing simulated balletic sex, not only with her friends and two of the most handsome men in the company, but in front of an audience too! It was a nightmare, the sort of frustrating dream she often had, where mid-performance she looked down to find herself naked, and everyone laughing; the cast, the audience, the stagehands. But she couldn't wake up and make this nightmare go away.

'Can I give you a lift home?'

She jumped. She hadn't heard Jamie come in. Fervently, she hoped he hadn't been watching as she had clumsily tried to grapple with her steps. 'Um no, thanks. I'm going to stay for a while. I need to get my head round Richard's choreography.'

'You shouldn't work too late. Your muscles will be tired now, you could easily strain something.' He strode loudly across the studio, the soles of his heavy boots squeaking on the lacquered wooden floor. Flinging his tatty rucksack aside, he squatted down in front of Adele. One lean knee poked provocatively from the rip in his jeans. 'Come on, let me give you a lift. Do you still live in Barnes?'

'You've got a good memory.'

'I never forgot anything about you, Adele.' He paused, and the intensity in his face made her shudder. 'I never

13

forgot that night at my farewell party, when I kissed you. Do you remember?'

Adele wished she didn't. She had tried to smother the recollection, to dampen its intensity, but that kiss had haunted her. She had never felt so stupid. Unable to formulate a word in reply, she enveloped herself in silence.

'I always wanted to ask why you ran off.' He reached out, and gently touched her bare shoulder. His long fingers felt cool on her skin.

Adele blinked rapidly. She struggled to hold his gaze, weighed down as it was with emotion.

'You knew how much I liked you, Adele.' His fingers trailed softly down her arm. 'I wanted to spend my last night in England with you.'

Adele flinched from his confession and scrambled to her feet, neck flushed, palms sweating. She had never told anyone why she had fled from that party, why she had escaped, panicking, into the comfort of the dark night. The desire she had for Jamie, the longing he had awakened with that tender kiss, had been crushed by the realisation that she couldn't stay, couldn't let him find out that she was still a virgin – probably the only one left in the company – at the age of nineteen. What a joke that would have been. The uneasy memory came flooding back, unwelcome.

'What's the matter?' Concerned, Jamie rose to his feet and moved towards her.

'I – I don't feel very well,' she muttered. Snatching her bag, she dashed for the safety of the dressing room. Ripping off her damp practice clothes, she stumbled into the shower, where the hot water mingled with the salt of her tears.

By the end of the week, the short ballet was finished. Adele had forced her body into the rôle, but as yet, her mind lingered behind. Unable to let go, shocked by the unabashed sexuality of the part she had to play, her cheeks were constantly coloured. She avoided eye contact with each of her partners, switching off her tortured mind as Alexei's thick fingers gripped at her hips, as Jamie's muscular thighs locked with hers. She tried to ignore Jessica's disdainful looks, her sure movements skilfully shadowing her own in the mirror. Richard had been patient with her, but Adele was aware that the real struggle was yet to come. Now she knew the steps, she would be expected to act the part.

Still, relieved that the first week was over, she finally accepted Jamie's repeated offer of a lift home. Despite her efforts to keep him at a distance, he had continued to be friendly, if a little hesitant towards her, and Adele felt she owed him an explanation.

As he drove her home to Barnes across Hammersmith Bridge, a thick silence expanded between them. Adele felt her heart racing with anticipation at the knowledge that she had to break it. He was waiting for her to speak.

She turned to him, his eyes glazed as they sat motionless in the traffic jam. 'I'm sorry about the other day, running off like that. You must think I'm pathetic. It's just that I was so worried about this rôle – still am. I really don't think I can pull it off.'

He turned to meet her worried face, an unexpected wickedness playing at the corners of his eyes and lips. 'Of course you can. I can't think of anyone better to play a sex demon.'

Adele's brow furrowed slightly and she looked quizzically at him. 'What do you mean?'

'In my experience, shy girls always turn out to be wild in bed and, well,' he hesitated, 'I've never met anyone shyer than you.' His eyes danced.

Adele knew she was being teased. She huffed angrily and looked out across the Thames, where a lone canoeist was training in the dusk. She wanted to get out of the car, to perch on the bridge's railings and dive into the dappled water, to let its murky green coolness envelop her, and never to have to come out again into the real world. It would be so much easier. 'I wish I could be more like Jessica,' she muttered to the river.

Jamie snorted. 'Jessica! Why on earth would you want to be like her?'

'Why not? She's pretty. All the men in the company fancy her. She's so sure of herself. She's not afraid of anything.'

Jamie turned the engine off. A bus had broken down further along the bridge and they weren't going anywhere for a while. 'I wish you'd stop this ridiculous obsession with Jessica. I know you two have been competing with each other since ballet school, but honestly Adele, she can't touch you. You're a better dancer, you're far better looking, and believe me, if the blokes in the company had a choice between you or Jessica, they'd go for you every time.'

Adele felt her breasts warm and swell at the compliment, but she didn't believe it. Jessica hadn't been without a boyfriend since the age of sixteen, whereas Adele hadn't lost her virginity until three years later. Even now, she'd only slept with four men, despite receiving many more offers. 'Really?' she asked, incredulous.

'Sure. The guys think Jessica's a – well, let's just say if someone wants a quickie, they go to her. You're different. It's your knickers they'd really like to get into.'

Adele's clitoris tingled, and she shifted in her seat. The hard seam of her jeans pressed against the tenderness of her bud as she moved, and she gently squirmed in delight. 'How do you know?'

'We discuss these things in the changing rooms. I know it's politically incorrect, but that's the way it is. In fact, when I was younger, we gave you all marks, to decide who was the most fancied woman in the company.' He fixed her with his limpid blue gaze. 'You came top.'

Adele felt a glow of confidence spreading up her spine like warm satin. She would never reach Jessica's level of self-assurance, but she found comfort in the realisation that she had admirers. Her lovers had told her she was attractive, and one had insisted she was beautiful, but she had never been convinced. The thought that men had discussed her, watched her, coveted her body, seemed to finally give her some certainty. Deep inside, a bloom of self-belief began to unfurl its bright petals.

'Flattery will get you nowhere,' she lied, laughing.

'Then I'll have to try something else.'

Adele's sex clenched involuntarily when she recognised the seriousness of Jamie's expression. Her eyes widened, like a creature caught in his headlights, transfixed by his earnest gaze. Part of her wanted to turn and run, but the other part kept her still, held her firm. She was mesmerised by her need to be crushed by his love, which was bearing down on her with the force of a speeding car.

'Adele, you know how much I like you. It was selfish of me, coming on to you when I knew I was about to leave the country, but I thought it might be my only chance to be with you.' He rested his hand on her thigh, and her muscles tensed beneath his warm palm. 'Now that I'm back, I'd give anything for another chance.'

Her mouth opened but she couldn't make a sound. The world began to turn in slow motion as Jamie's gaze flickered to her lips, then up to her eyes, then back again. He leaned towards her, and her eyelids slowly fell. With an aching tenderness that echoed in her heart, their lips touched, and her body succumbed. Their heads swayed in unison as he nibbled softly at her mouth, his kisses gathering urgency until his tongue gently parted her lips. Gently they explored each other, tongues entwining in an exquisite, slippery embrace. Adele lost her fingers

17

in Jamie's unruly hair, savouring its feel as it curled at her touch like tendrils of ivy, wondering what it would feel like to have him inside her, the man she had wanted for so long, the man who had wanted her. His wide palm cradled the back of her head, holding her gently but firmly, as if she was a vision who might at any moment evaporate into the summer night. They seemed to kiss forever, and with each passing moment, Adele lost herself further in the sweet passion he had once again ignited inside her.

Jamie's lips left Adele's and when she opened her eyes he was looking at her like no man had ever done before. Her breathing was deep and slow, and she was conscious of her breasts rising and falling under the soft material of her T-shirt, her nipples stiff within the white lace of her bra.

Horns blared behind them and his concentration returned to the road ahead. Frantically, he started the car and drove across the bridge, the traffic now clear. Out of the corner of her eye, Adele watched his hands, his long fingers gripping the steering wheel so tightly his knuckles were white.

There was silence as Jamie pulled up outside Adele's flat.

'Are you going to invite me in for a coffee?' he asked, at last.

Her body screamed, yes, yes! Every nerve ending hummed, her blood fizzed in agreement. Yes, she thought, come inside, undress me slowly, touch me, kiss me where it aches. Press your body into mine. Make me feel like a woman. Make love to me.

Instead, she said, 'No.' She watched her hands mauling each other nervously in her lap. 'Not tonight. I've a lot to do before we leave. I have to sew some ribbons on my pointe shoes and I've loads of washing –'

'OK, OK.' He held up his hands in surrender, and

immediately she felt like a fool. His polite kiss burned her cheek. 'I'll see you tomorrow, then.'

She escaped, rushing up the path to her front door, conscious of her breasts jiggling as she walked. For a moment the key wouldn't fit in the lock, then she was inside, safe in the familiarity of her cluttered hallway.

In the car, Jamie watched her disappear from view before starting the engine again. He fidgeted in his seat, his penis uncomfortably hard with the memory of her lips and the sight of her beautiful breasts, bouncing gently beneath her clinging T-shirt as she escaped.

'Adele, Adele, Adele.' The mantra of her name sounded sweet on his tongue. 'What are you so afraid of?'

Chapter Two

'*A*dele. Adele. Adele!'

She awoke from her dream to find that for once, reality was even better. The drab concrete of the motorway had metamorphosed into the lush green hills of Yorkshire. London's pollution was far behind; here, the air was clear, the clouds had been washed and hung out to dry and they glowed pink, orange and purple in the dramatic sunset. The undulating countryside was criss-crossed with quaintly uneven dry-stone walls, and fluffy, black-faced sheep munched nonchalantly on the grass, disinterestedly watching the minibus as it passed. Jamie's smile was as warm as the sunshine.

'Time to wake up, we're nearly there.' He squeezed her knee. 'Are you looking forward to this?'

She smiled coyly and looked out of the window. Butterflies of anticipation had been fluttering at her heart ever since he'd kissed her, and waking up to find him beside her again set their silken wings brushing against other, more sensitive parts of her body. 'I know I'm going to hate rehearsals, and I'm dreading the performance.' Turning to face him, she fell headlong into his deep blue eyes. 'But there are some things I'm looking forward to.'

'You're looking forward to dancing with me, darling, I can tell.' Adele looked up at Alexei as he loomed at their side, draping a powerful arm over the headrest of the seat in front. 'I haven't partnered you before, have I?' His accent was as Russian as vodka.

'I – I don't think so,' she faltered.

'You would remember it,' he winked. He leant across them and pointed out of the window, his elbow brushing against Adele's breast. She flinched and pressed herself back into her seat. 'We're here,' he announced unnecessarily.

Adele watched as the twelve foot high gates slowly opened up, letting the excited group of dancers through the only visible gap in the forbidding, wire-topped wall surrounding Rantree Manor. She assumed there must be a hidden camera in the trees, because there wasn't an intercom. The crest on the ironwork drew her attention, its design suiting her mood. It was an abstract, swirling pattern with dramatic, entwining whorls of dark, exotic colours, not like a traditional family crest at all. She frowned slightly. The design seemed familiar. It disturbed her, somewhere deep in her sub-conscious, but like the ballet's music, she couldn't quite place its origin.

As the gateway silently closed, she shuffled uncomfortably in her seat. There was no going back now, no escape. Not only was she going to have to perform the most demanding rôle of her career here, but she was going to have to stop acting so pathetically with Jamie. This week was the ideal opportunity for them to begin again, in the romantic setting of the Manor. Tonight, the dancers would go out to the pub or congregate in someone's bedroom, as they always did on tour – usually in Jessica's room – and she knew exactly what she had to do. She must dilute her nerves with alcohol, allow herself to relax in his company, and invite him into her bed.

'Adele, look!' Jamie touched her shoulder as gasps filled the minibus, and she turned to discover the cause of the commotion. They were poised at the top of a narrow zigzagging track that traversed a steep, thickly wooded hill. The trees, a mixture of ancient, gnarled oaks, thin beeches and wide firs, cut out the fading daylight and turned the winding lane into a dark, fluttering green tunnel. Through gaps in the lush foliage Adele could see horses grazing, their eyes flashing darkly as the handsome animals looked up at the intrusive diesel chug of the dancers' vehicle as it progressed downwards. At the bottom of the slope the trees parted to reveal a small lake, its miniature island alive with the distant flutter of birds' wings; and behind the lake, was the Manor.

Adele added her own gasp to the collection in the small coach, at the stunning sight of the building as it stood waiting for them. Unlike the others, her reaction was not rooted in delight. The Manor inexplicably threw a dart of panic into Adele's heart, as if it was a huge, wicked animal, luring her near so it could swallow her whole. A sense of foreboding crept over her, and she had to concentrate to force her lungs to expand and take in air.

Rantree Manor was menacing in its grey, Gothic splendour. Its sharp corners were only softened slightly by the purples, pinks and oranges it bathed in as the sun set behind it. Built from dark, weathered stone, it was irregular in shape, with its steeply-pointed gables, some tall and wide, others short and narrow, as if the architect had been in a confused, drug-crazed frenzy when he designed the building. Three corners of the house sported high octagonal towers, and a surfeit of heavily mullioned windows glared darkly at Adele, like a cluster of insects' eyes, black and unfeeling. Wide balconies

22

hung beneath the double windows on the first floor. Off-centre to the left, steep granite steps led from the lawn to the huge oak door, which was studded with black metal fleur de lys, and crested with the same strange design as on the Manor's gates. A flutter of terror manifested itself in a nervous tic at the corner of one of Adele's eyes. It was easy to imagine this place being haunted by a she-devil, a succubus.

There was an eerie silence among the small group as the minibus halted, and the six dancers and their choreographer moved to the front door as it opened from within. Adele felt feverish, hypnotised by the Manor's haunting glory. Hesitantly, she followed her colleagues as the immaculately dressed butler waved them into the gloomy, high-ceilinged hallway.

'My name is Foster, and may I welcome you, ladies and gentlemen, on behalf of all at Rantree Manor.'

Adele clung to Jamie's arm. It was hard for the butler to hold the attention of the small group, whose eyes were wandering upwards along the imposing stone staircase with its ascending line of Gothic candle holders, and dark, crackled portraits. Foster coughed politely.

'The Master wishes me to convey his apologies to you. He wanted to personally welcome you all, but unfortunately he is busy at present.'

Carmen was giggling with Nadia at some private joke, but Foster remained unfazed. He licked his lips, reminding Adele of an ageing lizard, cool and scaly, with his thin grey, slicked back hair and a heavily wrinkled, pallid, almost transparent complexion. His eyes darted from side to side, never looking at anyone directly, and he rubbed his hands dryly as he spoke.

'Before I show you to your rooms, the Master wishes me to make you aware of certain rules which must be obeyed while you are guests at Rantree Manor.' The dancers glanced suspiciously at one another, and Carmen's laughter stopped abruptly. 'You have each been allocated a bedroom, and there is to be no swapping or sharing of rooms. Visiting each other's bedrooms is strictly forbidden, as is leaving the grounds. Apart from the theatre, the dining room and the gardens, you are not permitted in any other parts of the Manor. Anyone caught breaking these rules will be dealt with according to the Master's wishes.' He paused for effect. 'Now, you will please follow me. Your luggage will be brought up presently.'

Adele and Jamie followed their friends as they trailed behind Foster up the steep staircase. The group was unusually quiet, and Adele assumed they were all sharing her uneasy thoughts. What had happened to their director's promise that they would be treated like royalty at the Manor? It now seemed they were going to be treated like children.

Frustration flared in Adele's eyes as she realised she would be unable to sleep with Jamie while they were guests at the Manor, unless she broke the rules. How dare Rafique spoil her plans with his petty regulations!

But anger was swiftly replaced by a blush of foolish embarrassment. She was here to dance, to save the company from closure, not for her own selfish pleasure. How could she even think about Jamie when the company was in danger? The National Ballet was relying on Rafique's generosity, and she was already considering disobeying his requests. He was obviously an eccentric man, maybe he was elderly, and very old-fashioned about people sleeping together under his roof. Perhaps he felt responsible for the dancers, and didn't want them leaving the grounds in case something happened to them. Anyway, it was none of her business. Jamie had been away for five years, and another week apart was a small price to pay for the sake of the company's future. She had to put Jamie out of her mind, and get on with her job.

Yet, as Adele climbed the stairs, she couldn't resist a

sidelong glance at him. She watched his buttocks strain beneath his well-fitting jeans, the taut muscular globes pumping him effortlessly up the steep staircase, and she longed to clutch them, to clasp at his smooth flesh and pull him down on top of her. The short golden hairs at the back of his neck glinted in the shards of light which pierced the gloom from the high, narrow windows above. She ached to touch his hair, to grab his neck and kiss him hard. His arms, long and well muscled, were lightly tanned in warm contrast to his pure white T-shirt and as she watched them swing at his sides she imagined grabbing his hand, raising her top and pressing his fingers to her breast. In a flash, she saw herself holding him, pulling him into one of the tall, shadowed alcoves that dotted the walls of the hallway below, freeing his penis from his jeans and pushing it inside her right there. She craved the feel of his hardness parting her tender lips and sheathing itself in her moist flesh while the others watched, her lust for him taking control. She needed to feel his long, hot manhood, thrusting deep inside her, pulsing as she clutched at him with her sex. As she mounted the stairs she moved closer to Jamie, hoping to brush against him, to feel his warm skin, just for a second, against her arm. Wetness cloyed between her legs and goosebumps rippled down her neck and forearms, and she felt her nipples erect and brush against the rough lace of her bra. She felt as if every hair on her body had become a tiny, hungry clitoris, and she could shimmer in the heat of a million minute orgasms, if only she could touch him. She had to touch him, now.

Adele paused as she reached the top of the stairs, blinking wildly, a thin film of sweat clammy on her spine. What was wrong with her? She felt confused and ashamed by the rush of lust that was pouring in a torrent over her body. An inexplicable force was urging her on from deep in her psyche, taking over, making her think about Jamie and his lithe body, when she had to concentrate on her work. For heaven's sake, she had a ballet to perform in six days time – a ballet in which she must take the lead. Her rôle was a challenging one to fulfil, and she had to dance it well, not only for the sake of the National Ballet, but for the sake of her pride. Rafique obviously had faith in her talent, and she had an obligation to him, to herself, and to the company, to repay that faith. There would be plenty of time with Jamie when they got home.

Adele pressed her trembling fingers to her temples and tried to compose her thoughts. It was the long journey from London; combined with the stress of the first week's rehearsals, it had tired her and made her dizzy. Her imagination was running riot, as it often did when she felt off-colour. She took a deep breath and quickened her pace to catch up with the others.

The corridor leading from the stairs was long and dim, coolness rising up from the grey tiled floor like curling smoke. The high walls were papered in deep navy blue with a dull gold *fleur de lys* motif, each one staring at Adele like a tiny glinting eye. Perched along the walls were wrought iron sconces, their candles unlit, the grey gloom only alleviated at each end of the passage, where tall pointed windows shed trapeziums of summer light on the floor. As the dancers followed their guide to one end of the dark tunnel, a fierce draught rushed at Adele's feet, as if a door had been opened behind them, and she spun to look for its source. There was nothing there, although the gloom was so dense between the windows that someone, or something, could have easily hidden in the shadows. Adele wanted to run to the window, to fling it open and bathe in the warmth of the sunset, to inhale the fresh green scent of the lush gardens outside, to escape from this oppressive blackness. No wonder her mind had clutched so fervently to thoughts of Jamie, yearning for his body, wanting to engulf herself in his warmth. The atmosphere in the Manor was far from welcoming.

Adele shivered violently as sweat dried cold under her T-shirt. She realised with a shudder that her misgivings about her forthcoming rôle would not be calmed by this house. It was so cold, so dark and gloomy, aptly symbolising the fear that had gripped her when she first learnt she was to play the succubus. Rantree Manor was more than a mass of stone, metal and timber. It was an animal; a huge, evil beast luring Adele deep inside its guts, licking its lips lasciviously as it began to pick at her vulnerable soul.

One by one, Foster showed the dancers to their rooms. Jamie was the first to be ensconced, flicking a friendly wave at Adele as the dark oak door was closed behind him. The corridor must have had twenty unmarked doorways, dotted among the blue walls seemingly without pattern or symmetry, and yet Foster knew exactly where each member of their small party was to go. Adele tried to memorise each person's location, but it was hopeless and she gave up as Alexei was shown to his room. He winked at her and then he was gone, and she was left alone with the lizard at the opposite end of the passageway to Jamie.

'Miss King.' Foster slithered around her disconcertingly. 'This is your room. I hope everything is to your satisfaction. Please, take a little time to rest after your journey. Dinner will be served presently, and I will return shortly to escort you to the dining room.' With a dart of his dusty hands, he ushered Adele inside and closed the door noiselessly behind her.

She sighed loudly with relief as she surveyed her domain for the next week. It was beautiful. Where the hallway and corridor had been dank and depressing, the bedroom was airy, bright and uplifting, making her forget her worries. The dark wooden floorboards were almost entirely covered with thick rugs, and she slipped off her shoes to enjoy their comforting feel on the soles of her feet. The walls were adorned with paintings; colourful landscapes, sleek, glossy-coated horses and ancient portraits in faded gilt frames. Tall windows flooded the room with the coloured glow of the setting sun, dappling the faded, yellow-papered walls with warm oranges and reds, and Adele was delighted to find they led onto a wide balcony, with an ornate Gothic parapet and a panoramic view over the grounds. Running to the adjoining room, Adele squealed with delight at the sight of a huge, sunken bath with a gold velvet canopy, as well as a shower, toilet and basin all hidden cleverly amidst dark wood panelling. She loved to soak after rehearsals, but her bath at home in the flat was tiny. This one was enormous. Perhaps she would enjoy her stay here after all.

Feeling suddenly cheerful, Adele almost skipped back into the bedroom. She danced around excitedly, savouring the space and opulence, which was such a contrast to her cluttered flat. Although decorated in authentic Gothic style, the room held all the conveniences of modern life, cunningly disguised so as not to ruin the effect. Maybe Rafique wasn't as weird as Adele had imagined. He certainly had good taste, or at least knew an interior designer who could provide it for him.

A tall, ornate cupboard with elegant spires concealed shelves of crystal glasses, a kettle, coffee and tea, and fine, gold rimmed china. Beneath the shelves a rack was stacked with expensive red wines, and beneath this a small fridge contained jugs of freshly squeezed fruit juices, milk and bottles of white wine. Hidden in a small bedside cabinet was a miniature stereo system, already loaded with a tape of the ballet's music. Adele searched and discovered the speakers, encased in walnut pinnacled surrounds, positioned high up on a wall to provide the best sound possible. This would be very useful. She could learn the music thoroughly and rehearse her part in private, practising Richard's difficult movements. She flicked on the cassette player, and climbed on to the huge four-poster bed.

The bed was so comfy, so soft and cocooning, that Adele wondered how she would manage to get up for rehearsals every morning. It was such a wide expanse of luxury in comparison to her narrow bed at home. Rolling on to her side, she stroked the dark wood of one of the posts, which felt smooth and cool beneath her fingers. She then flopped on to her back, admiring the opulent cream and gold of the bed's canopy, matching the tasselled bedspread. She closed her eyes, and let the exotic ballet music sprinkle over her like a tepid shower of rain, savouring the warmth each note aroused in her body.

Rocked by the lilting, haunting melody of the music's slow beginning, Adele felt her body relaxing again after the journey. She rehearsed the ballet in her head, watching Jamie and Carmen in their pas de deux, the prelude to the succubus's first devilish appearance.

As she imagined the couple moving harmoniously together, her thoughts lingered over Jamie's lithe body, his supple limbs gracious and sure in their movements, a sweet tenderness in his face and hands as he partnered Carmen, his nubile young lover. With every stretch of his long legs, every arch of his proud neck, every bend of his narrow waist, Adele yearned for him. On the bed, her skin prickled to imagine him on top of her, sliding in and out of her pliant flesh, creating a delightful friction between their two willing bodies, his handsome face racked with joyful agony above hers. As her hips began to gyrate in time with the music's sensuous rhythm, she unbuttoned her jeans and slid a hand inside her warm knickers.

In her mind's eye, Jamie made love to her. Her fingers foraged around at her damp sex, she breathed deeply and arched her back slightly, thrusting her breasts upwards towards Jamie's imaginary mouth. She wanted his lips at her nipples, gently sucking at first, then nibbling, then biting her into a frenzy. Vividly, she saw his head bow to her breasts, and she cupped a hand to a mound of flesh and pinched one of her nipples into eager stiffness. She could almost feel Jamie's hair brushing at her neck.

Then suddenly, the image of Jamie was gone. He was replaced by Carmen, who sat naked astride Adele, licking and nuzzling at her swelling breasts. Instead of Jamie's curly hair tickling her skin she now felt Carmen's silky locks brushing enticingly at her ribs. Instead of Jamie's hot, velvet prick inside her clasping sex, Adele felt Carmen's sex, soft and wet, kissing hers. Instead of a taut, flat chest pressing at her stomach she felt Carmen's breasts, small and delightfully soft, and her fingers ached to touch them, to cup their delicate shapes in her gentle palms. As Adele's fingers parted her own silken labia and delved inside, she imagined it was Carmen's sex she was exploring, Carmen's sex that was writhing at her touch, Carmen's clitoris that was stiffening into an angry, hungry peak. Adele rolled her bud between index finger and thumb and pressed her head hard into the pillow, imagining Carmen's head, rolling with unrestrained pleasure as Adele teased her nipples and tweaked her beautiful clit into a roaring, thunderous climax.

'No!' Adele jerked back into consciousness as the music paused, the sudden silence pulling her rudely from her semi-slumber. The sunshine that had warmed the room before was gone, and she shivered with cold. Putting a hand to her throbbing head, she found it drenched in sweat as it had been on the stairs. She walked shakily to the bathroom to wash her face, to wash away the awful, wonderful vision that had left her hand wet with dew, and her body shivering with confusion.

Drying herself on a fluffy, comforting towel, Adele

came back into the bedroom and perched on the edge of the bed. She rested her head in her hands. What on earth was going on? First she'd wanted Jamie so strongly on the stairs, and now this! Why was her mind filling with images of sex?

Adele rocked herself slowly. She concentrated on regulating her breathing, and gradually her palpitating heart returned to its normal rhythm. Wetness gathered between her legs once again as she relived her fantasy. Her vision had aroused her intensely, and yet she felt guilty.

It was the rôle Carmen had played in her imaginings that disturbed her. Carmen was a friend, a colleague whose nakedness Adele saw every day in the changing rooms, and her body had never elicited such feelings before now. Why had her thoughts turned to Carmen for pleasure, instead of Jamie? This was very confusing. Adele had never looked at a woman in that way before, or at least she couldn't remember it if she had.

Adele sat up straight and gently rolled her neck, trying to ease the tension that was now bunched in her shoulders. She was tired. The seven hour minibus journey from London had drained her and made her feel queasy. This, combined with the deep-seated and growing worry about her daunting rôle in the ballet, was making her feel unwell. That was the only explanation. She would feel better after dinner.

Adele ignored the tapping at first, thinking it to be the creak of an ancient floorboard. But it persisted, and as it grew louder she padded to the door. No sooner had she opened it, than Nadia ran inside and jumped on to the bed.

'Nadia, you're not supposed to be in here!' Adele admonished her friend. 'You heard the rules. We'll get into trouble!'

'Oh really, Adele.' Nadia was rolling on the bed, grinning cheekily. 'What on earth is Rafique going to do to us? Visiting each other isn't a crime, and anyway, he needs us here to perform for him.'

'Foster said we'd be punished if we broke the house rules.' Adele tried to look disapprovingly at Nadia, but her friend was ignoring her, suggestively stroking one of the poles on the four-poster bed.

'Your room's nicer than mine.' Nadia lunged at Adele and grabbed her hand. She opened the door a crack and peeked out before turning back to whisper conspiratorially, 'Come on, let's go and break some rules.'

Carmen's bedroom was lovely, but Adele was glad it wasn't hers. The colour scheme was a rich, bloody crimson that suited Carmen's volatile temperament. It was striking, Adele thought, and very sensuous, but she preferred the sunny golden yellows of her room. She doubted whether she would be able to sleep in this incredible red. It would probably encourage even more vivid fantasies than the one she'd just had.

As Carmen and Nadia bounced around childishly on the bed Adele smiled and shook her head resignedly. This was typical. If there was a rule, these two could be relied upon to break it. This must be a record though, the dancers had only been in the Manor half an hour. Adele felt a little guilty. As the lead dancer in the ballet, she had a responsibility to Rafique, and she should not be a party to this rebellion. If Foster discovered them, he would surely be angry. He would be coming upstairs soon, to fetch them to dinner.

'I'm going back to my own room. We shouldn't be doing this.' She felt like a strict elder sister to these two, although they were both slightly older than her.

'Don't be so stupid.' Carmen shook her head. Her dark auburn hair flicked around her face, and it seemed to glow deep red, taking on the dramatic colour of the room. 'The rules of this house are childish and ridiculous. We're adults. Relax.'

Adele could not relax. 'I know Rafique's rules are strange, but it's his house, and his money that's saving the company. I'm going back.' Adele didn't want to admit it, but her recent fantasy was also playing a part in her discomfort. She felt uneasy around Carmen, as if she had violated her friend in some way by imagining her naked, writhing in ecstasy on top of her.

Adele turned to the door before the renegades could stop her. But Foster was already there, and her breath was violently trapped in her throat at the sight of him, cold and pale, framed in the dark doorway.

Foster glared at each woman in turn. His eyes flashed evilly, and Adele's heart jittered at his obvious anger.

'I'm sorry, Foster, I was just asking Carmen for a headache tablet. I've got a pounding head, and I . . .'

He slammed the door in her face, and her excuse was rendered pointless. The space where his white head had been a moment earlier was replaced with dark, equally unfeeling oak. All three stared in horror at the door handle, as they heard the unmistakeable noise of a key grinding in the lock.

Adele banged her fists on the door. 'Foster! Foster, let us out! We won't do it again. Please, this isn't fair! Foster!' Her voice was filled with remorse. Something in its pleading tone must have struck into Foster's coldness like a warm dart, because he returned, sliding open a small hatch near the top of the door.

'Please let us out Foster,' Adele begged, as his face reappeared. 'I was only getting an aspirin, I promise it won't happen again.' Adele searched his eyes for pity, but there was none. They were as cool and hard as granite.

'You have broken the rules,' he hissed. 'I will inform the Master. You will be punished.' The hatch slid shut, and he was gone.

Adele rested her forehead on the door and cried softly. This was too much. With bitter irony, her lie to Foster came true and her head started to pound. She tasted nausea. They had been here half an hour, and already they had incurred the wrath of their eccentric patron. They would probably be deprived of dinner. The company director would no doubt be told about their disobedience, and they would be sent back to London in disgrace. Jessica would get to dance the lead rôle, as she should have done all along.

'Come and sit down.' Nadia put her arm around Adele's shoulders and guided her on to the bed, where they sat in line like naughty schoolchildren.

'I wonder what will happen to us,' Carmen mused, a tinge of apprehension blurring the edges of her normally confident voice.

'We'll be sent home,' Adele snapped. 'I won't get to dance, and we'll all get into trouble for letting the company down. Why couldn't you two just behave for once?'

'I'm sorry, Adele.' Nadia stroked her hair, and there was genuine sadness in her eyes. 'It's all my fault, I didn't mean to get you into trouble. As soon as we're out of here, I'll go and explain to this nutcase Rafique, that it was nothing to do with you.' Nadia squeezed her shoulder. 'Don't cry, you look so sad when you cry.'

Adele looked up at her friend and managed a vague smile. In the scheme of life, this set-back was not so important. But to Adele, it was disastrous. Silently, she made promises to Foster, to Rafique, to anyone who would listen. If she could be given a second chance, she would obey every rule for the rest of the week. She had to be allowed to stay, to play her rôle in the ballet. She needed to make a success of it, for her own self-esteem.

Two hours passed, and Adele concluded that the punishment Foster had threatened was the deprivation of dinner. She got undressed and climbed beneath the blood-red covers of Carmen's bed, determined to get

some sleep in case they were allowed to join the rehearsals tomorrow. She shuffled to one edge of the mattress
and told the others to join her. They did, and all three
lay in a row, the wine they had drunk making them
giggle like teenagers at the absurdity of their situation.
The dim light from a bedside lamp illuminated the
crimson velvet canopy above their heads.

'This is like being inside a womb,' Nadia commented.
'It's so ... red!' Above the heavy bedspread, Nadia's
bare breasts wobbled as she laughed. Adele knew she
shouldn't look, but she couldn't help herself; they were
so full, so pale and heavy, with dark brown areolae that
looked like juicy, ripe berries ready for picking. Adele's
thighs twitched and she rubbed her legs together, aston-
ished at the sensation of her clitoris, slowly stiffening.

'It's not a womb, Nadia,' Carmen cackled from the
other side of the bed. 'It's a pussy. Warm and wet and
... mmmm.'

Adele looked across at her and gulped, trying to
swallow her rising confusion. Carmen's hands were at
her breasts, circling her nipples into peaks of pleasure.
One of Nadia's hands was similarly engaged with her
own flesh. The other hand was hidden beneath the
covers, but Adele was in no doubt about its occupation.
An undulating ruffle under the bedspread, accompanied
by a noise like cooing doves emanating from Carmen's
open mouth, told Adele all she needed to know.

She tried to close her eyes but could not escape the
images flooding her mind, and she immediately opened
them again. She was transfixed by the look on Carmen's
face, the same look she had seen earlier, in her mind.
With growing unease, Adele acknowledged the alarming
wetness at her pussy, and her own hand moved beneath
the counterpane as her eyes strayed from Carmen's
small, delicate breasts to Nadia's generous mounds of
flesh, and back again. This was incredible. What on earth
was happening to her?

Nadia's free hand moved underneath the covers and Adele flinched as it came to rest on her thigh. There was a look of sisterly concern on her face. 'Adele, have you ever made love with another woman?'

Shock, mingled with bewildered arousal, formed a strange expression in Adele's eyes that answered Nadia's question.

'Carmen and I always share hotel rooms when the company is on tour.'

'I know,' Adele whispered. 'But, I didn't know – '

Nadia smiled and an eyebrow twitched wickedly. Her hand strayed towards Adele's yearning sex. Her fingers lightly brushed the tangle of hair that nestled at the top of her thighs. 'You should try it Adele, you'd like it.'

Adele wanted to try it. She wanted to pull the covers back and watch Nadia's hand as it caressed and probed at Carmen's succulent flesh. She wanted to feel Nadia's fingers at her own sex, gently parting the satin moistness of her labia and dipping inside. She wanted to cup Carmen's breast in one hand and Nadia's in the other. She wanted to feel lips at her nipples, at her clitoris; soft lips, female lips. She opened her legs, and gasped as Nadia's hand fell into the gap she revealed. She could feel her clitoris eagerly thrusting from its hood in anticipation of the touch of a friend, the touch of a woman.

'Get back to your own rooms immediately!' Foster was at the open door again, fury flaring in his pale eyes. Adele jumped from the bed, ashamed more by the fire kindling between her legs than by Foster's gaze on her naked body. She grabbed her clothes from the floor with shaking hands and began to struggle into them with difficulty.

'I said, get back to your rooms. Now!' Adele looked up to find Foster's icy glare at the dark golden triangle of hair that shielded her aching pussy from his view. Disgust curled at his lips. Had he been watching through the hatch in the door? Could he see the dew of her desire glistening on her inner thighs?

She didn't bother to ask. Pushing past Foster into the gloomy corridor, she clutched her clothes to her breasts, hiding as much of her body as possible from his piercing gaze. Her buttocks were bare though, and as she passed the butler he landed a smarting blow across her cheeks. She ran down the corridor to her own room, closely followed by Nadia, looking back to see him staring savagely at her naked, pink behind.

'Pervert,' she muttered, when she was safely back in her own territory.

The room was dark apart from a tall candle on the bedside cabinet, perched in an ornate, carved candlestick. The flame flickered in the slight breeze from the open balcony doors, and as it danced it created ever-changing patterns on the wall behind. Beneath its light, a small tray held supper, and Adele threw her clothes on a chair and fell to her knees in front of the cabinet. Like a naked nun, she worshipped before the altar of food, grateful that she was not to be deprived of dinner after all.

As she demolished her meal, Adele's hunger subsided and was gradually replaced by a now familiar feeling of growing discomfort. On the tray in front of her was a single orchid in a bud vase. It resembled a woman's sex – soft, silky, pink, inviting – and it reminded her of the inexplicable, unquenched desires that still simmered inside her, bubbling so close to the surface of her skin that even the sight of a flower could bring her close to boiling point. Adele stroked the outer petals, delighting in their feel on her fingertips, then she caressed the open centre, the sex of the exquisite bloom. She sat back on her heels and moved her knees apart, arching her lower back provocatively, dropping her hand to the open flower that lay unfurled between her legs. Her behaviour this evening had been extraordinary, and her arousal at

37

the sight of her friends was baffling. She wanted to suppress the feelings that had stirred within her, and yet as her labia opened to welcome her fingers the image of Carmen once again infiltrated her mind, joined this time by Nadia, in a whorl of writhing, feminine sensuality. Adele stroked the inner edges of her petals and she moaned. The noise covered the footsteps approaching behind her.

'Tell me what you're thinking.'

Shock waves skidded between Adele's shoulder blades. Someone had been waiting for her in the bedroom. Without a sound, he had watched her eating, naked. Now he was standing behind her, and she could feel his knees, hard against her back.

'Who are you?' she snapped, eyes wide, her warm desire suddenly cooled.

'My name is Rafique, but you must call me Master, because while you are under my roof, that is what I am.'

Adele let out the breath she had been holding captive. The Master's words were stern, but behind them lurked a voice with a reassuring tone, its timbre rich and relaxing, like a good cognac on the palate, or warm oil smoothed into aching limbs.

'Tell me what you're thinking,' the Master repeated.

'I was thinking about the ballet,' Adele blustered, suddenly very aware of her nudity. 'I was thinking about my rôle, and how difficult it will be for me. I – I want to be convincing as the succubus, but I don't think I can do it.'

The Master shifted his weight behind her, and she felt the soft material of his trousers brushing against her buttocks. 'You can do it, Adele. You are a very talented dancer. Believe me, once you have completed this week's rehearsals, you will be eager to perform as the succubus.' He paused to stroke her hair. 'However, I am not stupid. You were not thinking about the ballet. Tell me what you were really thinking.'

Adele was silent. She couldn't possibly reveal the thoughts that had been clouding her senses. She would have to think up another lie.

Her buttocks quivered as a shoe poked between her open legs and touched her gaping vulva. The hard leather was cold on her sex, and despite her fear she found the sensation incredibly exciting, sending ripples of nervous energy up her spine. Her clitoris seemed to cry out as the Master's toe touched the hub of her lingering lust.

'Adele, you are treating me like an imbecile. My shoe is wet where your sex has kissed the leather. I can smell your delightful musk from here. I watched your antics with Nadia and Carmen, through the hatch in the door. Now, tell me what you were thinking.'

'I can't.' A sob caught in her throat as the humiliation of her situation overwhelmed her. 'I can't.'

'Adele, you have broken my rules.' Leaning over her shoulder, the Master extinguished the candle with a forceful puff. He pulled her to her feet and turned her round to face him. His movements were firm but they hid gentleness beneath, as if he cared about her. 'You must be punished. Now speak.'

His voice was beautiful. Hypnotised by its satin richness, Adele conceded. The darkness was her friend, hiding her embarrassment as it flushed at her cheeks.

'I was thinking about Carmen and Nadia.' Silence. She continued. 'I was wondering what it would be like to – to touch their breasts.' In the sudden darkness, Adele could see nothing, and she jumped when warm, large hands cupped her breasts. 'I was wondering what it would be like to feel the shape of their breasts with my fingers.'

The Master began to trace the edges of Adele's breasts with his soothing fingers, discovering their full, pert shapes, brushing the areolae with the sides of his thumbs. Every word Adele uttered was a tiny, sharp nail, pinning down her shame, opening up her soul so the Master could peer inside. And yet, she was enjoying herself. She had felt unusually horny all day, and now she was getting her release, in the most bizarre way imaginable. This was no punishment, this was a game. One that she could control.

'I wanted Carmen to lick my nipples.' The Master enacted her wishes, and as Adele's desire grew beyond her control, so did her courage. 'I wanted her to suck them, gently at first, then hard.'

The Master's lips fastened over a large areole, and his tongue flickered over her stiff nipple. Gradually, tenderly, as if he was prising the nectar from a bud of honeysuckle, he tended to Adele's needs, slowly sucking the tip of her breast until it was engorged with blood and it ached for pain. Lightly, he began to nip at her stiffness, with gentle teeth and lips that seemed designed for the purpose. Adele's breath shuddered in her lungs. She was amazed, as much by the sensation at her breasts, as by the warm feel of his hands as they cupped her shoulder blades. She opened her legs.

She continued to describe her deeply troubling desires to this stranger, and his movements echoed every word. While one hand stayed at a breast, fondling, rolling, pinching her flesh, the other hand ran over the slight curve of her stomach. A skilful finger prised the lips of her sex open and tentatively poked inside, wetting the tip with her juices. Adele could smell her musk, heady in the air, as the Master circled her erect nipples with the same fingertip, moistening them with her honey. He bent his head and sucked again, then he moved his lips to Adele's to let her taste herself. His tongue wrapped itself around hers. It felt long, thick, strong. She knew what she wanted next.

It was a struggle now to give voice to her cravings. She had to plunder depths of inner strength, previously untapped, to find the power to form the words she needed. But the force of her longing was screaming out to be satiated, and she only hesitated for a second before telling the Master what she was thinking.

He fell to his knees, and Adele was convinced that his need was as great as hers. His palms pushed at her hip bones and his fingers spread at her belly. Her pussy lips were open, wet, ready. She wanted his tongue so badly, she felt she was being stifled by her own lust.

And then he was inside her. Poking deep inside, his tongue thrashed and writhed, reaching every inner inch, searching for her pleasure. The lips of her sex, swollen and heavy with dew, kissed at his lips as he plunged so far in that she felt he licked at her womb. His head swayed from side to side, and his hands grasped, craving more of her, pulling her further into his face, pushing himself further inside her. His fingers gripped her juddering thighs and pushed her legs wider apart. Sliding his palms upwards again, his thumbs hooked at her outer lips, and he opened her still wider to his probing.

He wants my soul, Adele thought, and he can have it.

Her cries were ferocious as his attention turned to her heavy, engorged clitoris. As he had done with her nipples, he spread her juices over the stiff little bud and began to suck it into dizzying ecstasy. His kissing was interspersed with nibbling and then biting, and Adele gasped and cupped her breasts, pushing the mounds together, squeezing her own flesh. The sensation at her crotch was too much. Two fingers were inside her sex, then three, thrusting hard, and she pushed her hips into his face, in time with his mesmeric rhythm. His other hand delved into the cleft between her buttocks, and Adele was torn between tilting her hips forward to his face, or backwards to his hand. Suddenly she was still, as a finger, lubricated with her own arousal, pushed inside her tight anus without warning or preparation. She was impaled on his touch, magnetised to his lips, a prisoner of her own incredible passion.

The overwhelming sensations bursting from every pore forced Adele to stay still while the Master brought her to climax. A finger pushed in and out of her anus, which sucked and pulled greedily as he thrust. Three fingers moved rapidly inside her crimson pussy, and her inner muscles clutched at him as if to keep him within her forever. His teeth pinched her aching bud and his tongue lapped at the bundle of sparking nerve endings that sent messages of orgasmic delight throughout her body. She was coming. She gripped her nipples and a tear ran down her cheek. At the moment of climax, every orifice, every pore, every corner of her soul was open to him.

Afterwards, they sat together on the edge of the bed. Adele was breathless, astounded by her reactions to the Master; a stranger, their patron, a man whose face she still had not seen. A man who had now dragged her to the brink of ecstasy, and pushed her over the edge. His title was apt, he was indeed her master tonight, and she was his willing slave as one by one he pushed his fingers into her mouth and she licked them clean.

She wanted to spend the night with him. She was desperate to look at him, to touch him, to give him the pleasure he had allowed her. But it wasn't to be. When Adele had finished sucking her juices from his fingers he stood and moved silently to the door, pausing before he closed it behind his tall silhouette.

'I hope I won't have to punish you again, Adele,' he whispered. 'It's not a task I enjoy.'

Chapter Three

*A*dele watched the droplet of sweat on its journey from Carmen's neck into the low-cut back of her turquoise leotard, where it added to an ever-growing damp patch. The parallel tubes of muscle on either side of her spine glistened with effort, and Adele could see them tense and relax as Carmen unfurled her leg into a perfect arabesque, her toes pointing towards Adele's cleavage. The music coming from the tinny tape recorder trickled to an end, the exercise finished and Carmen brought her leg down, closing her foot into a perfect fifth position. With a loud groan, she relaxed her small body over her thighs, and as she stretched, Adele noticed that sweat had also gathered in the cleft between her muscular buttocks. She straightened up and turned to face Adele, ready to repeat the exercise with her other leg. Beneath her delicate breasts, half-moons of perspiration emphasised her shape. Adele blinked guiltily; her leotard was as dry as when she had put in on.

'Adele! Wake up!'

She turned at the sound of Richard's voice, gripped the barre and prepared to begin the slow, controlled adage exercise again. Eyes glazed, she worked on autopilot, bringing her toe slowly up to her knee before raising her thigh and unfolding her leg high in front of her face. She held it for a moment before gratefully dropping her foot and resting for as long as possible before starting again, this time lifting her leg to the side, her toes in line with her eyes. She turned to look at her foot; her arched insteps were a blessing, especially when she was feeling lazy. So was her suppleness – it meant she could still produce pleasing lines, without really trying.

Strong male fingers grabbed her buttock. It wasn't tense, as it should have been, and her flesh filled Richard's grasp. He flicked at the hand that was gripping the barre, and she lost balance. 'You're a cheat, Miss King,' Richard snapped from behind her. 'You shouldn't be leaning on the barre.' He moved so close she smelt his after-shave. 'You don't fool me for a minute,' he whispered. 'I bet you fake orgasms, too.'

'Sorry, Richard. I'm not feeling myself, today.'

'Then feel someone else,' he hissed. He pressed his lips close to her ear and circled her waist with his hands. 'Just don't waste my time in class.'

She tried, but for once her body refused to respond. Avoiding Richard's disapproving gaze, she wafted through the rest of the morning class, assuming a concentrated air. But it was impossible to focus. Her mind was full of confusion.

Jamie noticed it too. After he and Alexei had dismantled the portable barres and put them back in the wings, he joined her at the side of the tiny stage as she half-heartedly stretched.

'Are you all right? You seem tired.'

'I am,' she said, avoiding his eyes as he sat down beside her. 'I didn't get much sleep last night.'

'What happened? We missed you at dinner. Rafique told us you'd broken the rules and would be eating in your rooms.'

44

She looked up, a little too quickly. 'You met Rafique? What's he like?'

'He's charming, intelligent and witty and very knowledgeable about the arts.'

'And?' she urged. 'What does he look like?'

'The man is gorgeous.' Jessica sat down between Adele and Jamie and slipped her long legs effortlessly into the splits. She raised her hands above her head, and her pointed nipples poked out sharply from beneath her leotard. 'Tall, slim, olive skin, big hands – sexy hands.'

Adele's innards twitched as she remembered how those hands had felt, moulding her breasts, gripping her pelvis, pulling her to his hot mouth. 'What else?'

'Ooh, let me think,' she mused, ignoring Adele and turning to look at Jamie. 'Mid-forties, wavy black hair, dark, dark brown eyes. A beautiful mouth. He's got a faint Spanish accent, and – ' she paused, smiling lasciviously, 'he wants me.'

Jamie snorted disdainfully. 'What makes you think that?'

Without using her hands, Jessica twisted her hips and turned away from Adele and Jamie, settling into the splits in the opposite direction. Slowly, she arched her spine until her head hovered above her back leg. Flaunting her incredible looseness, she turned to Jamie. 'He couldn't take his eyes off me at dinner,' she smirked.

Adele felt her cheeks begin to take on the deep burgundy of her leotard, and she hid her face in her towel.

'He may have been looking at you,' she heard Jamie say, 'but he was talking about Adele.'

Tentatively, she emerged from her embarrassment. 'What did he say?'

'He said you were a beautiful dancer, but that you needed to let yourself go on stage.'

'Oh.'

Jessica sat up. Skewing her body again, she moved

into perfect side splits, facing Adele. 'Don't let it upset you dear, he's not telling you anything you didn't already know.' Her mouth twisted cruelly. 'You must admit, you are a little frigid. On stage,' she added, as an afterthought.

'Jessica, I'll put this politely.' Jamie gripped her bony shoulder with his long fingers. 'Go away.'

Anger hardened in her eyes as she stood up. 'Jamie, I'll put this politely.' Jessica bent her body towards him, sticking her neck out like a chicken about to peck. 'Go fuck yourself.'

Jamie raised an eyebrow and watched her stalk over to where Alexei was lying. 'Is she always that nasty?'

'That was nothing,' Adele chuckled. 'Wait until you catch her in a bad mood.'

'She's very jealous of you.'

'I can't think why.' Already, Jessica was sharing a joke with Alexei. Her sharp cackle and his booming laugh echoed across the small stage.

'I can.'

His smile was full of longing, and it stirred a seed of guilt deep in the pit of Adele's stomach. What would Jamie have thought, if he had seen her last night, her shyness overwhelmed by the Master's touch?

'So, what did you do that warranted missing dinner?'

'Nadia and I were in Carmen's room,' she muttered, fiddling nervously with the ribbons of her tattered ballet shoes.

'Was that all? That's a bit harsh isn't it, Foster?'

Adele looked up. Silently, the butler had appeared on stage bearing an ornate silver tray loaded with cans of soft drink, fruit and chocolate. His eyes were dead as he bowed, waiting for them to take what they wanted.

'I don't make the rules,' he lisped. 'Besides, I believe Miss King had a very enjoyable supper in her room.'

She almost dropped the two bars of chocolate, but

Jamie seemed unaware of her discomfort. He was watching the butler.

'He gives me the creeps,' he whispered, as Foster moved on to Alexei and Jessica. 'In fact, the whole house gives me the creeps. Have you ever seen a theatre like this one?'

She hadn't. The company toured a lot, and she had lost count of the number of stages they had danced on. The view from this one was quite disturbing. If the architect had been under the influence of hallucinogenics when he designed the Manor, then the theatre was a bad 'trip.'

The auditorium was tiny, and at a guess, it seated a hundred. Not on the usual red velvet seats, though; these high-backed, wooden chairs were upholstered in black, and they rose steeply so that the back row was higher than the stage. Behind them, enormous mirrors lined the far wall, and from a distance their reflections were distorted. This was bad enough during class on the small stage, but it would be very disconcerting during the performance. Accustomed to looking out into darkness, using the familiar fluorescent green exit signs to focus on during pirouettes, the dancers would have to contend with the reflection of the stage lights and the warped images of themselves while they danced at Rantree Manor.

The theatre walls seemed to slope inwards claustrophobically as they rose towards the ceiling. Tiny boxes, just big enough to seat two, hung precariously from both walls, although they weren't symmetrically arranged; there were three on the right, and four on the left. Carved from wood that had aged almost to black, the balcony edges were adorned with Gothic pinnacles, between which hideous gargoyles peered with bulging eyes towards the stage, their sharp tongues pointing and wide mouths grimacing. The twisted little characters were obviously not riveted by the performance, because their gnarled bodies were otherwise engaged. Knobbly penises stabbed at distended anuses which pouted eagerly like lips, and clawed fingers pinched at pointed nipples and curled cruelly around over-developed, wart-ridden testicles.

From the ceiling, delicate chandeliers lit the way for the audience, but above their beauty another horror awaited anyone who glanced upwards. There, a rudely painted fresco depicted lovers, sleeping peacefully on soft pink clouds, bodies entwined. Above them hovered a huge demon with purple eyes, rats' tails for hair, and blood dripping from her cruel mouth. She was naked; the nipples on her pendulous breasts were wide, unblinking eyes, and between her legs, lips gaped hungrily, sharp teeth visible where the soft flesh of her pussy should have been. Her fingers were clawed talons, reaching longingly towards the lovers beneath her. Her forked tail twisted twice around her heavy thigh before inserting its pointed tip into the vagina of the nearest sleeping girl. Adele could almost hear the demon's laughter as it racked her powerful body.

'That must be the succubus,' Jamie concluded. 'Well, you were right about one thing.'

'What's that?' she asked, puzzled at his grin.

'Jessica would be better suited to the part.' He raised his eyes to the ceiling. 'Those two could be sisters.'

Adele chewed on her lip, humming persistently as she danced in an attempt to drown out Richard's deep, incessant drawl. While she rehearsed her first solo he constantly cajoled and criticised, goading her into the rôle as if she was a stubborn cat refusing to go into a basket. He was right, of course. In the back of her mind, audible above the music, her humming, and Richard's gathering roar, an insistent little voice told her that sooner or later she would have to relent. With the performance only days away, now was the time for

Adele to let go of her inhibitions and begin to take on the characteristics of the succubus. As yet, she was showing no sign that she could perform the rôle as he envisaged it, and it was driving Richard wild.

'Adele, for fuck's sake!' He turned off the music and boomed at her from the front row of the audience, his huge hands clasped on top of his bald head in exasperation. 'How many times do I have to tell you? You're a sex-demon. You're ravenous. Nothing can fill your appetite. You've got to look like you'd fuck the whole audience, given half the chance. The way you're dancing, you look like you'd rather have a nice cup of tea and a sit down.'

Adele tried to muster a smile. The corners of her mouth flickered, but her eyes showed hurt and frustration. The other dancers were sitting in the audience a few rows behind Richard, witnessing her humiliation. Jessica was sniggering, loudly.

'Darling.' Richard lit a cigarette, took a deep puff and rubbed his neck with one huge hand. 'Haven't you ever seduced anyone?' Adele was silent but Jessica answered for her, with a loud snort that reverberated up Adele's spine and made her cringe. She had never made a move on a man, except in her dreams. 'Don't you enjoy sex?'

Richard's taunting wasn't usually so cruel, but Adele could see he was completely exasperated. His frustration was understandable; he gave everything to his choreography, and expected his dancers to do the same. Adele loved her work, and the last thing she wanted was to ruin his ballet, but it just wasn't possible for her to perform for him, not today. Her mind was being pulled by too many other forces.

He shook his head slowly. Spreading his arms wide, his whole body shrugged at Adele. 'Come on, girl. Try and remember the last time you had a good fuck. You're acting like a virgin. Act like a slut.'

Tears sprung at her eyes. Richard turned his back,

avoiding her hurt Labrador expression. He wafted a hand in her direction. 'Take a break, Adele. I'll work on Alexei and Nadia for a while.'

She stumbled gratefully into the gloomy wings at one side of the stage, pressing herself against the cold stone wall, pleased to be hidden among the shadows. She held back until she was out of sight, then allowed her tears to flow in the backstage darkness that was so familiar and now so comforting. Alexei and Nadia appeared on stage and she closed her eyes, but the ballet's music was still there, and Richard's voice targeted her in the gloom with the deadly precision of a heat-seeking missile. She pushed herself further into the wall, hoping that if she stayed still and quiet, he would forget about her.

She jumped as the wall gave way behind her and she tumbled backwards into the light. Breathless with shock, she cursed at the grass, still damp with morning dew. A small green stain now marked one of her clean pointe shoes. 'What sort of place is this?' she muttered. 'Sexual punishments, obscene paintings, secret passages . . .'

As the door slowly closed itself, the sun reflected on the bright red and white 'Fire Exit' sign. She smiled ruefully. Nothing sinister about that.

The sun dried her tears and she began to follow the path that led into the woods. It was warm outside, and smelled of summer. Richard had told her to take a break and she would, as far away from the theatre as possible.

Soon, the trail plunged her into darkness. It was still warm beneath the trees, but the lack of sunlight made her nipples harden in her leotard. Further on, the foliage grew so densely that the track became difficult to follow, and she had to look down at her feet to make sure not to trip over the twisting roots that snaked across the ground. Damp leaves slapped at her bare shoulders and wet her skin, a thorn caught at her tights and laddered the pale, flimsy fabric, high up on her thigh.

'Damn,' she whispered, freeing the branch that clung to her leg and inspecting the row of holes it left.

'Oohh.'

She froze at the faint, low moan. Her heart raced and blood pounded in her ears, but it was unmistakeable.

'Ooohhh.'

Shaking uncontrollably, her fingers flew to her open mouth. Slowly, so as not to make a sound, she turned towards the noise and peered into the trees.

'Mmmm.' It was getting louder. 'Aaahhh.'

Adele swallowed, it didn't sound human.

'Oh. Oh. Oh!'

A twig snapped behind her. 'Who's there?' she screamed. More twigs snapped followed by frantic rustling and rapid footsteps. Terrified, Adele blindly fought her way through the bushes, unsure in her panic of which way she was heading. Noise surrounded her, leaves and branches gripped at her flesh, conspiring to trap her but she pushed on. When she emerged into the small clearing she was covered in a film of cold sweat.

She stood still until the fear stopped gushing in her eardrums and she could hear again. Only when she was sure that whoever, or whatever it was had gone, did she move towards the open door of the small, rickety hut.

Standing in the doorway, it took a long moment for her eyes to acclimatise to the gloominess. When they did, she immediately wished they hadn't. The scene before her brought to mind *Lady Chatterley's Lover*, except this was shocking. Along one side of the hut, a narrow mattress was half-covered in a grimy blanket. The floor was dark earth sprinkled with wood shavings, creating a pungent, organic perfume. A paraffin lamp swung from the roof, and a row of candles stuck out of beer bottles along the thin wooden window-sill. A wispy curl of smoke pointed out the one that had only just been extinguished. The small window was caked in dirt. Covering the walls, so that not one inch of wood showed through, were pictures of women. Pornographic pictures; large breasts, buttocks, spread for the camera, pussy lips, open and swollen with desire, faces contorted in a show of ecstasy. On the bed, a magazine lay open – beside it, sticky on the blanket, was a fresh, unmistakeable stain.

Horrified and yet fascinated, Adele crept inside. Her fingers trembled as she picked up the magazine, pondering over who had been there, masturbating in front of the anonymous women on the glossy pages. They looked so false, prostrating themselves for the lens, and yet something about their openness aroused her. She dropped her head. Her gaze fell down the deep valley of her cleavage, and she wondered whether he – whoever he was – would have been as excited by her breasts.

Footsteps approached and she dropped the magazine. Unable to move, she waited as discovery grew inexorably nearer.

'I thought I made it clear, I didn't want to have to punish you again.' His words were stern. 'You're out of bounds.'

Jessica was right, he was gorgeous. For a long moment, Adele stood in silence, allowing the details to slowly ingrain in her memory.

Everything about him spoke of confident masculinity. His rich black hair was all one length; he wore it casually swept back from his face, its slight waves falling in line with his strong jaw. His nose was Roman, his cheekbones well-defined. His skin had a luscious Mediterranean tone, dark and smooth except for the scar on the ridge of his cheek. His mouth was sensuously wide. His tall, slim frame was draped all in black; well-cut trousers and a designer polo shirt, open at the neck where a few dark hairs curled suggestively. His seductive brown eyes smiled, and she realised he was waiting for her to speak.

'I – I'm sorry, Rafique, I went for a walk. I heard a noise, and –'

'I also made it clear that you were to address me as "Master."'

'I'm sorry, Master,' she whispered. He nodded slowly in approval. His gaze was so intense, she had to escape it. Reluctantly, she went back to studying the unconventional wallpaper. 'What is this place?'

'My groom insists on living here. He has his meals at the house, but he won't sleep there, not even in winter. When it gets too cold, he sleeps in the stable with the horses. Joe's pretty wild. Wilder than my stallions.' He followed her gaze downwards to where the magazine lay crumpled on the mattress. Gracefully, he stooped to pick it up. 'What do you think of all this?' His hand circled the tiny shed.

'I don't know. I've never seen anything like it.'

He opened the magazine and nonchalantly flicked through its well-thumbed pages. 'Does it embarrass you?'

'Yes.'

'You shouldn't be embarrassed about sex. Everyone does it.' Tilting his head, he cursorily glanced at the centrefold. 'Men like to look at women.' Slowly, his eyes travelled from her face to her feet and back up again, lingering lazily over her breasts on the way. 'You're even more beautiful in the daylight.'

So are you, she thought.

'But I'm still going to have to punish you.'

The magazine fell from his hands. Its pages fluttered in time with her wildly beating heart. Her breath quickened as he moved closer, and it stopped altogether as his hands cupped her shoulders. Sliding his thumbs beneath the straps of her leotard, he pulled them over her arms. Blinking sleepily, as if intoxicated, he stared at her exposed breasts. She knew without looking that her nipples were stiff.

'Kiss me,' he commanded.

She raised her face to his. Her eyes began to close but opened again as his hand pushed her mouth away.

'Not there.' He smiled at her bewilderment. 'On your knees.'

She gasped. Roughly, he bore down on her shoulders until her knees thudded into the soft floor. Eyes widened as his deft fingers released his penis and it unfurled before her, springing as it slowly hardened. Adele was stunned by its savage beauty.

'Adele.'

Wrestling her eyes away from his groin, she looked up at her Master. 'Yes?' she breathed.

'Do you know what I want?'

'Yes.' It was pretty obvious, even to someone as naive as Adele.

'I want you to kiss my cock,' he confirmed. 'Suck me, Adele. Lick me until I come.' His hand clasped around the back of her neck and pulled her head towards him. 'I want to feel my cock inside your pretty mouth.'

Her clitoris throbbed as she raised her hands and stroked his velvety smoothness. His prick bobbed and tensed further at her touch; her own body quivered, gratified to discover his manhood was as long and dark as the rest of his body. Her fingers closed around his girth, and as his erection gained its full length its swollen, purple head thrust violently from his foreskin. Wetting her lips, Adele pressed her face to his penis. Above her, he grunted with satisfaction as she lapped away the bead of moisture seeping from the tiny, blind eye. Her trembling tongue traced the bulging vein that ran along his hardness and she breathed in deeply, inhaling his musty, musky odour until it filled her lungs. She was amazed by the desire his sweet smell aroused in her as it coursed through her veins, traversing the electrically charged nerve-endings that sent scorching signals throughout her body, making her scalp writhe as millions of hairs tensed and erected. Slowly, Adele licked his full length, making him harden further at the sensation, all the while a hand mauling and squeezing at the twin bulges between his legs. She drew his purple head between her eager lips, alternately sucking, licking and flicking with her quick tongue until hunger overcame her and she could bear the teasing no longer.

Fastening her lips tightly around him, she sucked his long, rigid cock into her mouth as far as it would go, barely leaving room for her tongue. The Master's breathing rasped as he gave way to the sensations flooding his body, and his hips began to thrust involuntarily. Adele grasped the base of his splendid, delicious phallus, preventing him from moving. She wanted to control this. It was for her as much as for him.

The Master pushed with one hand against the wall, and his other hand clasped her neck. His grip told of hidden force, force he was using to hold himself still and quell his natural desire to ram himself into her warm, wet mouth. Instead he let Adele set the pace, gentle grunts catching in his throat as she sucked voraciously, teasing with her tongue as her lips moved greedily up and down his slippery rod. She drew his strength from him, delighted to feel his legs jerk when she ran her thumbnail between his tight balls, pressing hard, sucking harder and faster, savouring the feeling of power she gained from holding him in her mouth. Squeezing his width tightly, she lost herself in a frenzy of lust, forgetting all her self-doubts as she succumbed to her primal urges. His fingers twisted in her hair as his body jolted and with a violent thrust of his pelvis his buttocks clenched, his yielding hardness touched the back of her throat and his seed filled her mouth. He held her head still while he shuddered into her, although there was no need; she wanted to be there, to taste his salty release as it slithered down her neck. She swallowed, savouring his sweetness, her spine tingling as she imagined his delicious juices sliding down into her stomach like liquid silver. She felt strong, happy, calm.

Pulling out of her mouth, he fell to his knees. She just had time to see his penis pointing accusingly at her before his face filled her vision and his lips pressed to hers. Holding her shoulders, he thrashed around her mouth with his tongue, searching hungrily for a taste of himself inside her. His kiss was voracious.

Their faces parted and they stared at each other while their breathing slowed. Despite having given him pleasure, Adele felt strangely grateful to the Master. He had shown her the power of lust, the joy of abandoning herself to her senses. It was as if a tiny part of the succubus had taken control of her. If she could only capture the feeling she had when she was with Rafique, she thought, she might be able to tackle Richard's rôle and do it justice.

The Master's eyes showed gratitude too, deep within their darkness. His fingers shook slightly as he touched her mouth. 'You're going to make a wonderful succubus,' he said, reading her mind.

A breeze swirled into the open doorway. Adele shuddered as it caressed coldly at the dampness between her legs. The shock brought her back to reality. 'Oh God,' she murmured, scrambling to her feet, 'rehearsals.'

She rushed out into the clearing. In her panic, she was unable to find the path until the Master parted the bushes and revealed the way. The meaning behind his smile was a mystery until she arrived in the hallway, and realised her breasts were still on show.

Adele forced herself to slow to a walk down the long corridor to the theatre annexe, as she tried to bring her lungs under control again. But as she pulled open the heavy door at the back of the auditorium, the sight that greeted her stole her breath away completely.

The small theatre was full of music. It was a theme

56

she recognised immediately – the eerie, haunting melody of the succubus. Each note was like a spider crawling over her skin, as she watched Jessica dancing in her place. She was half way through the pas de deux with Jamie. He was kneeling in the middle of the stage, head bowed as if asleep, his body swaying as the succubus whirled maniacally around him. Suddenly, the music crashed and changed and Jessica began to stalk towards her prey, picking out the violin's rhythm with the precision of her movements. Circling Jamie, she changed the choreography slightly, throwing in some quick pirouettes before coming to a dramatic halt in front of him. Leaning forwards, she held Jamie's shoulders and kissed him, her leg high behind her head in a stunning arabesque. Then she let go, controlling her balance as her leg swivelled from the back, to the side, to the front. Finally, she brought her foot down, hooking her leg around Jamie's shoulder and pulling his face towards her groin. As the music rose to a crescendo their hands clasped, their bodies shuddered together in a theatrical show of ecstasy, Jessica's head fell back and she laughed audibly.

She was still laughing when Richard's applause finally stopped. Jamie got to his feet, smiling sheepishly as Jessica flung her arms around his neck and kissed him again. His grin disintegrated when he saw Adele; Jessica's deepened.

Richard turned to find the source of their reactions. 'Adele! Where the hell have you been?'

'You told me to take a break. I went for a walk.'

'I meant five minutes, not forty-five.' He wagged a finger at her.

Her eyes flickered to the stage, and Jessica. 'What does it matter? You obviously didn't miss me.'

He draped a heavy arm over her shoulder, and turned her away from the stage. 'Look, I didn't know where you'd gone, I thought you'd stormed off. We've got less than a week, Adele. I had to carry on rehearsing.'

Adele looked up into his beautiful, black face. 'She's good, isn't she? Much better than I am.'

'She's good,' he admitted, lowering his voice so Jessica couldn't hear. 'Being a slut comes naturally to her.'

'Why don't you put her on in my place?'

He shrugged. 'This is Rafique's party. He wants you, Adele.'

She huffed incredulously and wriggled out from underneath his arm. 'Thanks! Thanks for the vote of confidence!'

'Lunch is served,' Foster rasped from the doorway.

'Come on Adele, I didn't mean – it's just going to take some extra work, that's all. Let's get some lunch. We'll have a chat about the rôle.' He touched her elbow patronisingly.

'Forget it,' she snapped, flicking his hand away. 'I'm not hungry. I'll stay and rehearse the bits I've missed. I've obviously got a lot of work to do.'

She turned and flounced up to the stage, ignoring Jessica's sneer as she pushed past her on the narrow wooden staircase. Jamie lingered behind and met her at the top.

'Do you want me to stay? We could go through our pas de deux.'

'Don't worry about me. Go and get some lunch with the others.'

He touched her arm. 'You mustn't let Jessica get to you. You're a better dancer than she is.' Concerned, his gaze fell down her leotard. 'You're sweating.'

'I got lost in the woods, I was running.'

'You've laddered your tights.' Gently, he touched the hole, caressing her thigh with tiny circles of his fingertip. His smile was full of care.

'Don't touch me,' she whispered, looking down at his hand.

58

He flinched, hurt by her sudden coldness. She was filled with remorse as he ran to catch up with the others, but she needed to be alone.

With only the music for company, Adele stood still in the middle of the empty stage. Usually, musical notes were her friends, the impetus for her movements. But today it seemed her friends had deserted her. As the solo violin heralded the beginning of her theme, she could barely identify the melody she had learnt so thoroughly during the first week's rehearsals. Now that she had seen Jessica moulding her body so effortlessly to the challenging musical score, it seemed pointless to carry on fighting with herself. Jessica might have been designed for the rôle. She would go and see Rafique, tell him she couldn't do it.

'Use your anger.'

She looked up just as the auditorium lights went out. With a loud clank, the stage lights bloomed, and for a moment she was blinded.

'Rafique!' she shouted above the music, shielding her eyes and trying to focus on the tall, shadowy figure. 'I need to talk to you.'

'Dance!' he shouted back. 'Anger is powerful, Adele, use its energy. Show me what you're feeling.'

Tentatively, she obeyed. What he said made sense; anger, hurt and frustration were boiling furiously inside her. If she could harness that energy, use it to fuel her movements, her interpretation might begin to have some force.

Thinking of Richard's lack of faith in her, she rose on to pointe, one leg high at her side. The intensity within her body flowed in a wave over her limbs, and she felt herself gaining control. She held her balance for longer than usual, waiting until she was ready to move on before guiding her toe accurately into its next position. As she thought of Jessica's laughter, the internal barriers that had been holding her back slowly gave way; her legs rose higher than normal, her feet were quicker and surer, her arms were lighter than air. As she thought of Jamie, pressing his face between Jessica's legs, body shaking in time with hers, she attempted the extra pirouettes that Jessica had added. With a startled cry, she tripped off balance.

She knelt to unfasten her pointe shoes, flexing her feet a couple of times to make sure she hadn't twisted anything, before stomping to the side of the stage. Switching off the tape recorder, she glared into the audience. 'It's no good,' she snapped at the darkness, hands on her hips. 'I can't do it.'

'Come here.' The chandeliers illuminated again, and she abandoned the stage and joined Rafique in front of one of the huge mirrors. 'Tell me what you're feeling.'

She blinked rapidly, unnerved by the latent power in his eyes. 'I'm frustrated, angry with myself. Envious, too, of Jessica. She makes it look so easy.'

'Tell me what you're feeling in here.' He pressed his fingers to her breast. Her heartbeat echoed against his hand.

'I feel trapped. I know I can do this rôle, but I – I'm afraid to let go.'

'You weren't afraid to let go this morning.' His fingers moved upwards, spreading over the swell of her breast. 'You weren't afraid when you knelt and took me in your mouth, were you?'

'No.'

'No, what?'

'No, Master.'

'You weren't afraid last night, when I licked your sweet pussy until you came?'

'No, Master.' The words shivered in her throat.

He grabbed her shoulders and turned her to the mirror. He was standing so close, she could feel the

60

bulge of his penis between her buttocks. 'What do you see?'

She looked from his reflection to her own. She didn't much like the person who stared back at her.

'I'll tell you what I see.' A warm hand stroked the back of her neck. 'I see a young woman who doesn't realise the effect she has on men, doesn't realise the power of her own body.' Fingers trailed over her shoulders, hooking once again beneath the straps of her leotard. 'Look at those breasts,' he murmured, pulling her leotard down to her waist, 'they're wonderful.' Reaching around her, he squeezed her mounds of flesh together, her wide, soft areolae peering out between his dark fingers and thumbs. 'Wonderful,' he reiterated into her neck, his breath hot on her skin. Adele was unsure whether he was still talking to her, or to himself.

She looked anxiously towards the door. 'What are you doing?'

He pinched her nipples hard, and the agony ached in the core of her being. 'I'm enjoying your body.' Dropping to his knees, he pulled her leotard and tights down over her hips, lifting each foot in turn to help her out of her damp practice clothes. He flung them aside, then smoothed his hands back up the front of her legs to her belly. Lost in fascination at the sight of his fingers cradling her stomach, she jumped as he pulled himself into her and kissed the smooth skin at the top of her cleft.

'Don't,' she begged, as he softly spread her buttocks and pressed his lips between them. 'Oh no!' Mortified, her voice trailed away as his tongue flicked at the sensitive skin around her anus.

Rafique rose to his feet. 'What's the matter? Are you worried what it tastes like, down there?' One finger teased down her spine and poked gently inside her bottom. 'You taste beautiful, Adele. Every part of your body is beautiful.'

In the mirror, she watched as his touch crept around her waist and into the soft curls of her pubic hair. A foot hooked around her ankle and opened her legs. A warm fingertip discovered her moistness, tracing the delicate edges of her labia. 'Look at your beautiful pussy.'

Her voice was hoarse. 'Someone might come in.'

He ignored her. 'Look at your sex lips. The way they kiss my skin. The way they part for me, the way my finger slides so easily inside you.' Mesmerised by the sight in the mirror, his head peered over her shoulder, and his dark hair tickled her cheek. With every breath he moaned softly into her neck, in time with his finger as it moved in and out of her pliant flesh.

His thumb pressed around her tender clitoris, and as if he had flicked a switch, her resistance dissolved. With a deep sigh she raised her arms, resting one hand in his thick, soft hair, the other touching her neck as it rolled in ecstasy. Her back and hips arched sharply as he squeezed her breast and dipped into her sex.

'Look,' he uttered, under his breath. 'Look at yourself.' She looked. The woman in the mirror, with her half-closed eyes, was barely recognisable.

'Now, dance.'

Adele whimpered as his tall frame disappeared from the reflection. She turned, watched him searching for something. 'Put this on,' he commanded as he pushed Nadia's white practice dress into her trembling fingers.

Adele stared open-mouthed at Rafique. Practice dresses were worn over leotards and tights. Made from soft, almost transparent gauze, they allowed the dancers to check the lines of their bodies while getting accustomed to the feel of a skirt.

'I can't dance in that,' she whispered. 'The others will be coming back from lunch any minute now.'

'Good. You need to get used to them looking at your body. Your costume will be much more revealing than this.' Snatching the wisp of material he slipped it over her head, pressing his palms against the sides of her breasts as they were covered. Then he kissed her, forcing his tongue on to hers with such urgency that she lost the will to protest. He grabbed her hand and pulled her on to the stage.

'Dance,' he commanded, crouching at the tape recorder. 'Remember how you looked in the mirror. Show me how it feels to be such a beautiful woman.'

As the music filtered into her consciousness, he slowly walked to the centre of the stage, kneeling in place of Jamie. The look in his ravenous, black eyes spurred her body into action. Now, the violin was part of her, its mysterious force emanated from her soul, vibrated through her veins and oozed from her pores. The luscious, seductive notes entwined around her limbs and guided her as she began to whirl about the stage.

Suddenly, she didn't have to think about the steps. The choreography, which had been so difficult to remember, flowed naturally from within her. She was no longer rehearsing but performing, and it felt easy. She had become the physical manifestation of the music's power. Her body was an instrument, and she was in control of it.

As she jumped, she felt every muscle in her long legs contracting. She seemed to soar, covering the stage with a single leap. Without her pointe shoes, she was intensely aware of the feel of the floor beneath her bare feet, and the strength she used to lever herself from the cool, unyielding stage amazed her. The air whizzed audibly as she spun in furiously fast pirouettes. Her fingers reached for the wings. Her neck arched.

And then, before she knew it, she was in front of the Master. Relishing the delicious pull of her tendons, she lowered her face towards his and slowly swung her leg up behind her into an arabesque. Even without a mirror, she knew her line was perfect. The muscles of her spine and buttock ached sharply as she pushed her leg further than it had ever gone before, until her toe was high above her head. She opened her mouth over his, and her rapid breath mingled with Rafique's as he tilted his head backwards. Rotating her hip in its socket she brought her leg to the side, clutching his wide hands when he offered them as Jamie had done to Jessica. Straightening her torso, she swivelled her leg until it was in front of her face, her calf muscle juddering with pressure as she brought her toe down and hooked her knee over Rafique's shoulder. Levering her body against his strong grasp, she pushed on the thigh of her supporting leg until her pussy was an inch away from his mouth. Following the choreography, she began to shudder.

'Oh, God,' Rafique murmured beneath her. He unlaced his fingers from hers and for a moment she poised off-balance, before his support returned at her buttocks. Violently, he crushed his lips to her dress. His breath was humid through the gauze as he gulped at her sex, attempting to envelop her mound with his mouth. 'Oh, God,' he pleaded, and he pulled at her until her knee gave way. His arms shook as he lowered her to the floor, still with her leg clasped to his shoulder. 'Look what you do to me.' His eyes burned with an extraordinary mix of admiration and rage as he unfastened his trousers and unfurled his proud penis once again. 'Look what you've done.'

He forced her shoulders down on to the stage. Kneeling above her, he watched her face as he slowly ruffled the material covering her thighs until her pussy was exposed. His gaze drifted over her breasts before stopping between her legs. He sighed loudly as he inspected her open slit.

'Not here,' she begged feebly, feeling suddenly vulnerable. She lifted her fingers towards his face. 'The others –'

With a ferocity that stunned her, he grabbed her slender wrists and slammed them to the floor. She struggled valiantly, but it was no use. He was far bigger and stronger than she, and it was impossible to escape him. 'Do you think I could stop now?' he hissed. 'You did this. It's your fault if the others come back and find me fucking you.'

Trapping her as much with his eyes as his body, he lowered his hips. The music paused dramatically as the head of his penis nudged between the succulent lips of her sex. Looking down at her, he smiled knowingly while impaling Adele upon his thick erection. With his full length inside her, her body relented. Fear of discovery melted into abandon and she pulled at his shoulder blade with her heel, urging him deeper still.

'You see,' he leered. 'You can't stop it either.'

Her throat arched as he withdrew to his tip and then plunged into the core of her. The muscles of her sex clenched, attempting to hold him still and slow the unrelenting, unbearable pleasure that blazed inside. There was nothing she could do, and yet she felt in command, watching his face contort in agonising ecstasy above her. In the far distance the music began again, a torrential rhythm which Rafique absorbed as his thrusts grew increasingly rapid and irregular. Their bodies went into spasm. Adele cried out as her clitoris burned against his flesh, desire searing her every pore. Her scream mingled with his low, satisfied moan, and he collapsed on top of her as they came.

She fought for air as his weight compressed her lungs. His neck was damp on her face, his sweat sharply masculine in her nostrils. Inside Adele, his penis pulsed.

'Thank you.' Her words were barely distinguishable beneath the music's fire.

'Thank you, Master,' he corrected. 'Never forget that I am in control.'

'No, Master,' she agreed.

Chapter Four

'*D*on't you ever learn?'

Nadia grinned and slipped inside the door. She was holding Carmen's tiny fingers in her own.

'You two are incorrigible,' Adele tutted disapprovingly. 'Do you want to get us into trouble again?'

'Yes!' Carmen exclaimed, taking a small run up and launching herself through the air. She landed face down on the bed, giggling uncontrollably. 'I love trouble!' Flipping on to her back, she slid the palms of her hands over her tight belly and between her thighs until only her narrow wrists were visible.

'It wasn't exactly a harsh punishment, was it?' Nadia stepped further into Adele's bedroom and slumped into the armchair. 'Having your supper delivered by a gorgeous Mediterranean stud.' She threw her arms above her head and smiled dreamily. 'Now that's what I call room service.'

Adele felt suddenly cold, despite the evening's humidity. The warm droplets scattered over her skin from the bath turned to ice, and she shivered and pulled her towel tighter around her breasts.

'The Master. Rafique, he came to your room as well?'

'He brought my dinner on a tray. Carmen's too. It was ages after you left, though. I was nearly asleep. If he hadn't been so totally yummy, I'd have told him where to stick his supper.'

'Did he – what did he say to you?'

Nadia looked puzzled at Adele's unease. 'He told us we were privileged guests in his house and should behave as such.'

'And?'

'And what?'

Warmth began to slowly seep back over Adele's body. She had no idea why jealousy crept into her mind at the thought of Carmen and Nadia receiving the same punishment she had so enjoyed. But there it was, a spark of possessiveness, smouldering inside her like a lit fuse. Despite the other worries crowding her mind, what she wanted more than anything was to believe that Rafique's ministrations were solely for her. For the first time in her adult life, her reticence with men – with this man – was being eclipsed by something fierce and uncompromising. She wanted Rafique.

'Is that what he said to you?' Nadia asked.

Unstoppable, a secretive smile lurked on Adele's face, and she bit her lip to hide it from her friends. 'Pretty much.' She moved to the balcony. The sun glowed orange on her fresh, clean skin and she closed her eyes, bathing in its splendour.

'We're going to the pub,' Carmen announced.'

'Which pub?'

'We passed it on the way here, it's about a mile down the road. Want to come?'

Adele recognised the challenge in Carmen's voice. She turned to find gentle mockery in her friends' eyes, they were fully expecting a refusal. 'I could do with a cold beer.'

Carmen raised her dramatic eyebrows. 'What's this? Not afraid to break the rules any more?'

Adele smiled naughtily. 'Like you said, being punished by Rafique isn't too bad.'

'Get dressed then,' Nadia urged. 'And wear something nice. We'll see if we can find some local talent.'

The air in the corridor was surprisingly cool on Jessica's face. She looked to either end of the long passage, neither window was open. Outside, the slowly dying sun was bequeathing an impenetrable humidity to the night. The atmosphere in her bedroom was stifling, and yet, just beyond her heavy door an inexplicable breeze swept the corridor. She shuddered as its chill curled around her ankles.

'Did you hear it too?'

'Oh my God!' She jumped as Jamie's face appeared from behind a dark doorway, and clutched dramatically at her breast.

'I'm sorry, Jessica.' His body emerged into the gloom. 'I thought I heard voices.'

'I did too.' Jessica shivered violently. 'It's so cold out here. Come into my room, have a drink with me.'

'I – I was going to find Adele, see if she wanted to go for a walk in the grounds.'

Masking her annoyance, Jessica gave Jamie a sincere, sweet smile and tilted her head to one side. 'I wouldn't bother. Adele will be tucked up in bed by now, darning her pointe shoes and dreaming of swans and fairies. Come on.' Denying him the chance of any further protest, she darted across the corridor, grabbing his wrist in her long fingers. 'I feel like getting drunk, and I hate drinking alone.'

With a satisfying pop, Jessica opened the chilled Chardonnay. She poured two glasses and held one out to Jamie. He had his back to her, and was closely studying one of the long portraits that dominated the room. Glad of the opportunity to study him, she sipped her wine in silence.

He was even more attractive than he had been five years ago, if that were possible. She had wanted him then, and now, just having him in her bedroom made the downy hairs prickle at the back of her neck. His tall, lean frame was covered in just the right amount of well-toned flesh, as if a sculptor had carefully followed the pattern marked 'perfection' when chiselling Jamie's muscles. His shoulders were broad, his legs long, his buttocks so tight, he seemed to be clenching them beneath his faded jeans. With his wild blonde mane and majestic, powerful body, he reminded Jessica of a lion, lazily lethal. He would pounce on her before the night was out – the wine and her outfit would see to that.

As his gaze moved around the room, he slowly turned to face her. She moved towards him and offered a glass, keeping hold of the stem after he had accepted it. Quizzically, he looked from her hand to her face and she answered his silent question with a wicked smile. Teasing, she waited until the moment became uncomfortable before relinquishing her grip and stalking away from him. Her narrow hips swung slightly as she imagined his eyes on her long legs, moving up from her delicate ankles, over the tautness of her calves, along the backs of her thighs and on to the pertness of her bottom. She was glad she'd chosen her short, pale blue dress, it matched the pastel iciness of her eyes, and left nothing to the imagination. She had selected it for Alexei's benefit, but this was even better.

A tiny dent appeared in her self-satisfaction when she turned to find Jamie engrossed in another of the room's dark portraits. She slumped on to the wooden pew at the foot of the bed, crossing her legs so that her skimpy dress rode high up her thighs. She sighed, loudly.

'How do you sleep at night?' Jamie mused, almost to himself.

Unsure of exactly what he was asking, Jessica shrugged in silence.

'I've never seen anything like it.' He walked slowly towards her, his eyes on the ceiling, his boots loud on the bare floorboards. 'It's so dark in here.'

She nodded and murmured in agreement. Her bedroom was incredibly gloomy. Its theme was a purple so deep it was almost black. The bed, the chairs, the walls, even the ceiling – all were clothed in this unrelenting shade. Not even the paintings alleviated the darkness, being so covered in centuries of grime that it took close scrutiny to make out their subjects at all. Still, she had had no trouble sleeping on the first night.

She attempted a wan, sorrowful smile. 'I didn't get a wink last night, I'm exhausted.'

'I'm not surprised, it's so stuffy in here. You don't even have a window.'

She shook her head forlornly. 'I suppose you've got one, being at the front of the house?'

'I've got a balcony, too.'

'Can I see?' She jumped to her feet.

'Well, I'm not sure if –'

Ignoring his hesitancy, she fled, grabbing the wine bottle on the way.

'Oh, this is much better.' Jamie's room was a luscious, regal green. Jessica flounced out on to the balcony, leaning over the parapet until she felt her dress rise behind her, exposing, she hoped, a glimpse of the G-string riding up her bare arse. Turning her back on the view, she looked up at Jamie as he joined her. 'I think I could sleep in here.'

The hint was lost on him, his attention already drawn elsewhere. Jessica rolled her eyes frustratedly and followed his gaze.

'Is that Adele?'

On the edge of the wood, three figures were running.

Carmen, in a skimpy dress of burnt orange, Nadia, her black dress flapping around her pale, muscular thighs, and Adele. Her wavy golden hair caught the fading sunlight. Her short-sleeved, green silk dress matched the splendour of Jamie's room, its deep hue matched Jessica's mood, too, as she filled with envy. In the stillness of the evening, the sound of her laughter easily reached the balcony.

'She's so beautiful,' Jamie whispered, seemingly oblivious of Jessica's presence.

'I thought gentlemen preferred blondes,' she laughed.

'I wonder if she knows how lovely she is.'

Jessica could feel her heart blackening. 'I didn't realise she was quite so friendly with those two. It would explain a lot.' She waited for the words to sink in through Jamie's annoying wistfulness.

'What are you talking about?'

'Carmen and Nadia. They swing both ways.' She curled her lip in disgust. 'They like women as well as men,' she reiterated, in case any doubt remained. She nodded towards the three figures as they disappeared up the path which led to the gates. 'They're probably off for a lesbian threesome in the woods.'

Jamie drained his glass and walked back indoors. He sat on the edge of the bed, his head in his hands.

'That would explain why she's never kept a boyfriend for very long.' Jessica crouched at Jamie's feet and refilled his glass. 'And why she's so pathetic around men. Of course, it all makes sense now. Who would have believed it, Adele King, a dyke!'

'Has it ever occurred to you that she hasn't met the right man, yet?'

'Sorry?'

'I haven't stayed with any of my girlfriends for very long. Does that mean I'm gay?'

'No! I didn't –'

'No. It means I wasn't in love with them. It means we

71

had nothing in common. It means I was fooling myself that I could be happy, when all the time I wanted someone else.'

'I'm sorry,' she huffed indignantly. The sound of backfiring plans was deafening in her ears. 'You seemed upset. I was just trying to help.'

'I'm not upset.' He ran his fingers through his hair, his curls bouncing back into shape as he combed them. 'If you must know, I'm feeling incredibly horny and frustrated.'

I know the feeling, she thought. She crossed her hands at her chest, and flicked at the spaghetti straps of her dress. 'Well, that's something I *can* help you with.' With a shimmy of her narrow shoulders, the pale blue fabric slid from her breasts. She swung her weight on to one hip, her pale nipples stiffening as Jamie slowly looked up.

'Unbelievable.'

Jessica's pussy twitched helplessly as she stood before him, snared in his eyes. Now she knew how a gazelle felt, heart pounding, time slowing, the moment before the lion's pounce. 'Thank you,' she smirked.

'I've never known a woman with an ego so out of control.' Jamie stood, pushing her away. 'I think you've got the wrong idea, Jessica.'

'Huh?'

'Haven't you noticed? I like Adele. I can't think of anyone but her. The idea of Adele with another woman . . .' His words drifted longingly towards the balcony. 'I'll be the one who doesn't get any sleep tonight.'

Her mouth gaped in the shock of rejection. This had never, ever happened before. 'So you want me to leave?' Her voice was thin and high with indignation.

'Please.'

Jessica's jaw hardened. 'Fine.' Once again, she

72

retrieved her old friend, the Chardonnay, and slammed the door behind her.

Following Alexei's instructions, she counted the doors as she walked towards the end of the corridor. Hesitating, she began to pull at the straps of her dress, then changed her mind. She pressed the cold bottle to each nipple in turn, watching her areolae pucker into leathery points. Licking her lips, she knocked five times, as arranged.

Alexei's chest was also bare, and glistening with sweat. He carried a dumbell in one thick hand, and a nasty leer on his wide lips. His thick hair was stuck to his forehead with perspiration.

Jessica smiled, lifting a finger to his shining torso. 'You look hot.'

He opened the door wider. His gaze lingered over her naked breasts. 'So do you.'

The regulars at The White Rose were clearly unprepared for the invasion of three young women into their all-male domain. Adele, as taken aback as they were, stood frozen as the door creaked shut behind them. Her entire body blushed under the appreciative gaze of a couple of dozen pairs of eyes, and she wished she'd worn jeans and a T-shirt. Her dress, which had felt so light and cool on the long, hot walk to the pub, now seemed far too flimsy. Its simple, scoop-necked bodice and its long, slightly flared skirt showed nothing, and yet it suddenly seemed to cling tenaciously, revealing every curve as if it was made of rubber. Looking around at the clientele, she suspected that their femininity would have elicited just as much interest had they been dressed as nuns.

Carmen and Nadia did not seem deterred. With unabashed confidence, Nadia strode towards the bar. There, the only other woman in the pub nodded a curt but suspicious welcome. Her shoulders were as broad, her chin as angular as any man's, the only hint of femininity was the brassy blonde, heavily lacquered bouffant perched precariously on top of her head.

Adele watched with envy as Carmen hovered expectantly at a small table in the corner, smiling cheekily and blinking through her thick auburn fringe. Sure enough, the seats were vacated, and Carmen beckoned triumphantly to Adele.

Gratefully, Adele sat with her back to the pub. Nadia joined Carmen on the cushioned pew opposite her, bringing three bottles of beer. Incredulous, Adele saw that her friends were glowing, basking in the attention.

'Are you two afraid of anything?'

Nadia's brow furrowed. 'What is there to be afraid of?'

Adele leaned across the table. 'All these men, staring at us. Doesn't it make you feel uncomfortable?'

'Actually,' Nadia grinned, fidgeting in her seat, 'I find it exciting. But then, I've always enjoyed being the centre of attention.'

'I'm not afraid of men,' Carmen whispered, excitement darting in her eyes. 'It's men who are afraid of us.'

'What on earth for?'

'We've got what they want.'

'And they can't have it,' Nadia added, a giggle like a jackhammer reverberating around the tiny pub.

Adele took a swig of her icy beer. A droplet trickled out of the corner of her mouth, and she looked around self-consciously as she wiped it away. 'I don't think any man's ever been afraid of me.'

'Rubbish,' Carmen scoffed. 'There are men in the company who are afraid to talk to you. You're beautiful. You intimidate them.'

'Jamie couldn't take his eyes off you in rehearsal today,' Nadia interrupted, changing the subject. 'How's it going, with him?'

'It isn't. I – I've got other things to worry about at the moment.'

A derisory laugh hacked in Nadia's throat, its force making her breasts bounce beneath the low-cut neck of her dress. 'Other things?' she coughed. 'The delectable Jamie Butler has chosen you to share his bed, and you're worried about "other things"! You must have something pretty serious on your mind.'

'I have.' Pins and needles of guilt pricked her conscience as she thought of Rafique, pinning her to the stage. She had barely had time to struggle back into her practise clothes before the others had returned from lunch. Jamie had still looked hurt.

'Care to elaborate?' Carmen urged.

'Oh, you know, the rôle. I'm finding it difficult.' She took another sip. Mixed with her guilt, the lager tasted bitter. 'I shouldn't think Jamie's too enamoured with me at the moment, anyway. I was pretty off-hand with him when he offered to miss lunch and rehearse with me.'

'You're mad.' Nadia shook her head slowly. 'You must be. There's no other explanation.'

'I like rehearsing with Jamie,' Carmen sighed. 'He's such a good partner.'

'So is Alexei.' One of Nadia's eyebrows flickered suggestively.

So is Rafique, Adele smiled to herself.

'Can we buy you girls some more beers?'

Adele turned in her seat. If she hadn't seen them with her own eyes, she would have presumed the two young men to be caricatures, stereotypes invented by some London advertising executive promoting life in the English countryside. Their ruddy cheeks were as shiny and plump as apples, their thick blonde hair as golden as straw, their arms like branches beneath their rolled up shirt sleeves. Knobbly fingers gripped pints of something dark and rich as soil. Their grins were wide and friendly, their eyes shining with youth.

'No, thanks,' Adele muttered.

'Yes, please,' Nadia contradicted.

They lumbered to the bar. 'Don't encourage them,' Adele reprimanded.

'Why not?' Nadia shrugged disinterestedly. 'We can have some fun with these two.'

Adele's eyes widened as nine bottles of beer appeared on the table.

'I'm Ian,' said the older of the two, dragging a chair up between Adele and Carmen. 'This is my brother, Robert.'

Robert joined the party, his thighs so heavy they touched both Adele and Nadia's knees as he sat between them.

'What are three lovely lasses doing in Rantree village, then?'

Adele looked to her friends, but Robert's accent was so broad, his words so stilted, that neither had understood him.

'We're staying at the Manor.' She cursed as she felt her cheeks heating up. This afternoon, she had lain on the stage while a man she barely knew fucked her, and now, just talking to this pleasantly friendly young man was embarrassing. 'We're dancers. There's a party on Saturday, and we're performing a ballet for the guests.'

'That'll be Rafique's birthday,' Ian nodded. 'Always has a big party.'

'You know him, then?'

'He comes in here from time to time. He's all right, for a foreigner. Don't know how he lives in that place though.'

'What do you mean?'

'Didn't you know?' Ian grinned evilly. 'It's haunted by a wicked demon.' His eyes twinkled mischievously. 'Isn't that right, Joe?'

A hush descended on the pub, and for a moment the girls lost the spotlight. Slowly, the lone figure hunched over the bar straightened up. 'That's right,' he muttered, without turning round.

'Joe's the stable lad at Rantree.' Ian's stumpy fingers flickered over the table. 'He's seen the demon,' he mocked, his voice low and tremulous. 'Isn't that right, Joe?'

'You can laugh all you like, Ian, but I've seen things and heard noises that would curdle your blood.'

'Ask him if he wants to join us,' Adele whispered, her shyness smothered by a morbid curiosity to meet the man who lived in the explicitly wallpapered shed.

'Joe? He always drinks alone.' Ian tapped the side of his nose. 'Does most things alone, if you know what I mean, according to his shyness with the lasses.' Ian leaned across the table. Resting on his huge forearms, he whispered. 'He's eighteen, I reckon, and never been with a woman.' He winked at Adele. She fervently hoped that poor Joe hadn't heard.

'Ask him over,' Nadia grinned. Adele caught her admiring Joe's behind, and she rolled her eyes. Already, she could tell, Nadia was savouring the thought that she could be the one to deflower this beautifully proportioned young man.

'Joe! These ladies have invited you to join them. It'd be rude to decline.'

Reluctantly, Joe turned to face them. Carmen blasphemed quietly in Spanish and Nadia muttered her agreement. Adele's lips parted. Rafique had been right when he described Joe as 'wild'. His dark eyes had a savage, untrusting hesitancy which reminded Adele of the stallions she had seen in the wood. He had a long, strong nose with flaring nostrils, and a heavy forelock of chestnut hair. Easily discernible beneath his soiled white shirt and tight jodphurs, was a body as sinewy and powerful as any horse's.

'I don't want to seem rude, Miss,' he blustered, looking imploringly at each woman in turn as if they held his future in their hands, 'but I prefer my own company.'

'That's all right, Joe,' Nadia waved, dismissing him.

Adele suspected she was anxious to get another look at his handsome hind quarters.

'Told you.' Adele and Carmen both flinched as Ian slapped his weighty hands down on their thighs. 'Although we have a problem now, ladies. I'm not too good at maths.'

Adele looked down to where his hand gripped her knee. 'Maths?'

He leered across the table at his brother. 'How to divide three ripe, juicy peaches between two hungry lads.'

Nadia sprayed the air with beer as she snorted.

It was lucky the gates opened for them, because by the time they arrived back at the Manor they were laughing so hard, they didn't have the energy to climb. Carmen and Nadia, as drunk on the thrill of leading the brothers on as from the alcohol, didn't comment on their easy re-entry to the grounds. But Adele's heart began to pound as she watched the gates close again behind them. There was obviously a camera at the entrance to the Manor, as she had suspected. The Master would know she had broken the rules again, and she would be punished.

Carmen grabbed her hand and interrupted her thoughts. Adele was glad as the path was steep and the darkness impenetrable. She held her free hand in front of her face but couldn't make out its shape. When the other two started to gather speed, building into a run, she had no choice but to cling on and run with them, out of control, screaming with the dangerous thrill coursing through her veins.

They carried on running until they reached the house. Breathless, they collapsed on to the cold granite step and leaned against the door, beneath the dim light of the lantern.

'We could have injured ourselves, running like that.'

'Sometimes it's fun to do things you shouldn't. It's like I always say, go with the flow.'

Adele looked across at Nadia. Her fingers were lost in Carmen's hair, their lips pressed together. As she was about to stand up, Adele was halted by Carmen's hand reaching out and landing on her thigh. Astounded, she watched her friend's tiny fingers drawing swirling circles on the silk of her dress. Then Carmen turned, and before she knew it, her own lips were pressed to her friend's.

Carried on the same wave of abandon that had sent her careening down the hill, Adele gave in to the urgency of her mouth, twisting her tongue with Carmen's. The feeling of a woman's soft lips on her own was everything she had imagined; wildly exciting, completely natural, so different from a man's kiss.

'Let's do something we shouldn't,' she ventured, when they parted for air. 'Let's explore.'

'Wow.' Carmen succinctly summed up their feelings. Tentatively, they crept further inside the tower, drawn by the bizarre sight that met them.

Adele stood open-mouthed, slowly turning, letting the details seep gradually into her mind so as not to overload her already crowded thoughts. 'Wow,' she repeated, unable to think of any other word which was as apt.

One wall of the octagonal room was filled by the heavy oak door. On each of the other seven, harnesses waited expectantly. Some were simple contraptions, like those on the two windowed walls, couplings of leather wrist and ankle restraints, fastened with chains to either side of the window frames. Others were more elaborate, involving metal cuffs, spiked collars and straps sporting phallic protrusions. Hanging from hooks on the wall were masks of rubber, blindfolds, gags, gloves and corsets. A pair of black, thigh length boots stood, eerily empty, in the middle of the room. Beside them, an umbrella stand was crammed full of evil-looking whips, and beside them, a child's toy trunk crouched enticingly. Compelled to look inside, Adele lifted its heavy lid.

They were toys, but not for children. Inside, each on its own red satin cushion, were sexual playthings of all colours, shapes and sizes. Adele could only guess at the purpose of the less obvious ones. Picking up one of the more innocuous, phallic-shaped toys, she turned its base. With a low hum, it began to vibrate. Clasping it in her palm, she felt the reverberations echo up her arm and she wondered how it would feel, pressed against her sex.

Adele looked up at the sound of Carmen's gasp. She and Nadia were standing at a tall, narrow chest of drawers next to one of the windows. Delving inside, they lifted up piece after piece of flimsy underwear: slivers of lace, with slits in all the wrong places; fishnet leotards; red, fluffy bras; shiny black suspender belts; rubber stockings; leather G-strings.

'I would love to see you in this.' Nadia held up a gaudy, red satin body.

Carmen snatched at it eagerly. 'OK, but only if you'll wear this.' Metal clanked as she pulled out an awesomely complicated contraption from the drawer, a web of thin, soft leather straps joined by thin chains. The garment, if it was one, didn't seem to make any sense, and the pair fell into yet another giggling fit.

'What about Adele?' Nadia gasped, when she had recovered.

Carmen knelt and opened the bottom drawer. 'There's one still in its box.' She held it out towards Adele. 'Come on, it's no fun unless we all do it.'

Her friends had drunk more than she had that evening, but still Adele felt tipsy with excitement as they admired each other.

Carmen's red outfit clashed tackily with her hair. The underwired bra scooped low beneath the gentle mounds of her breasts, pushing them upwards and giving them extra fullness. Her nipples peeked provocatively over the edge of the satin. The legs were cut so dramatically high that wisps of pubic hair escaped beneath the elastic at her crotch. As she raised her arms and spun for her audience, Adele realised the reason for the high cut: at her hips, the body tapered into a thin, red string, separating Carmen's taut buttocks. She looked cheap and gaudy, conversely, she also looked beautiful, like a butterfly trapped in a case, the bright frame clashing with the subtlety of its wings.

Nadia had managed to untangle the mess of leather and metal, and wore it with barely disguised relish. A wide collar circled the pale length of her neck, from which three soft leather straps straddled her torso; one pulled tight on the outside of each breast, one down her cleavage. They were linked by loops of fine silver chain, and beneath the strands her breasts perched heavily. The central strap stopped at a metal ring above the dark hair of her mound; there, twin chains imprisoned her pussy, gently distorting her labia so they resembled pursed lips. As Carmen had done, Nadia turned around for the others. Behind her, the chains rose together up her cleft to another ring, before parting in the small of her back to join the two side straps.

Attention turned to Adele. Her pulse quickened in anticipation of their question.

'You look lovely, Adele, but –'

'It's not very revealing.'

'It is if I do this.' Watching their faces, Adele arched her back ever so slightly. As her breasts pushed forwards, the slits in the black satin cups of the bra, which had been invisible before, widened to expose slivers of her breasts. Her nipples, already hardening at her friends' delighted reactions, poked eagerly from the caress of the material. She opened her legs and they looked down at her crotch. As with the bra, the concealed fold in the knickers parted, revealing a snatch of dark

golden hair and, she knew, the lips of her sex, plump
with arousal. She turned her back. As she did so, she felt
the warmth of the material part from front to back, and
her cleft became open to inspection too.

'Wow,' Carmen breathed, reverting to single syllables
once more.

'You look amazing,' Nadia concurred. 'Why don't you
try those boots on? They'd look fantastic on you.'

She had never worn stilettoes, worried about the strain
they would put on her ankles, knees and spine. But, with
a sigh of satisfaction, Adele realised the time for being
sensible was over. Common sense had certainly never
felt as good as this.

She slipped easily into the long, leather boots and
zipped them up from the ankles. They were the perfect
size, not only at the feet but in the way they snugly
sheathed her thighs. Their heels added five inches to her
height, and she savoured the feeling of towering above
her friends.

'What shall we do now?' Carmen asked, her eyes
widening as she peered into the trunk.

Inspired by her sudden growth in height, Adele
selected a short whip from the collection, and brought it
cracking to the floor, inches from Carmen's naked arse.
'You'll do what I say,' she snapped.

Carmen looked at Nadia, then back to Adele. Shock
slowly turned into a grin of delight. 'All right, Adele.
Tell us what to do.'

She thought for a moment, her gaze traversing the
room, her mind weighing up the many and varied
options. With the end of her whip, she pointed at Nadia.

'You. Put Carmen into that harness.'

Nadia practically jumped with glee. Smiling unstoppably, she grabbed Carmen's slender wrist and pushed
her roughly against one of the walls. Adele watched
Carmen's nipples rise as Nadia clipped her hands into a
pair of fur-lined, metal cuffs above her head. Kneeling at

her feet, Nadia spread her ankles and fastened them similarly. Finally, she lifted the spiked collar from its hook on the wall, and fastened it around Carmen's neck. Then she stood back, looking expectantly at Adele. 'What now?'

Adele looked deep into Carmen's eyes. Within their azure blue, a fire burned brightly, the same fire that sizzled in her soul, whenever she thought of Rafique. She knew just what Carmen would enjoy. 'Lick her nipples.'

Nadia rested her hands on Carmen's shoulders, but Adele flicked them away with the whip. 'Don't touch her unless I tell you to. Just use your tongue.'

Chastised, Nadia clasped her hands behind her back. Bending her torso, she teased the crimson tips of Carmen's breasts into stiff, wet peaks of pleasure.

'Now suck.' Adele trailed a finger down the furrow of Nadia's spine. Hooking beneath the metal ring where the chains joined and then parted, she tugged on them gently, pulling them higher between Nadia's quivering, alabaster cheeks.

Carmen and Nadia moaned in unison. Adele felt her own pussy beginning to dampen the satin of her knickers at the sight of Nadia's wide lips on Carmen's pouting nipple. Drunk on her position as dominatrix, she felt dizzy and clear-headed all at once; empowered, and yet weak with a lust that was out of control.

'Bend over.' She turned Nadia to the side so that Carmen could see, and pushed her head down until it was level with her thighs. Running the leather-bound handle of the whip along a tautly stretched hamstring, she looked at Carmen before allowing her eyes to feast on Nadia's chained sex lips. Her heart pounding furiously, she pressed a hand on Nadia's lower back until her head hung inches from the floor. As her shoulders lowered, the chains parted, and the secret, scarlet folds of her pussy gradually spread.

Adele's breathing deepened. Her hand shook as she reached for Nadia's sex. Since their first night at the Manor, she had dreamt about discovering the silken, curling edges of another woman's inner labia. It was fascinating, incredible, to be peering so closely into the core of Nadia's being, her crisp black curls a dramatic contrast to her own. Enticed by the moistness oozing from Nadia's slit, Adele gently slipped a finger inside her.

Nadia's spine shuddered and she groaned with relief. Amazed at the sensation of the hot, ridged flesh clasping at her own skin, Adele let out a low sigh. Carmen joined in with an envious whimper.

'Let me touch her,' she begged, pulling helplessly at her cuffs.

Adele slid in and out of Nadia a few times more, teasing Carmen, before removing her finger. Looking down at her tiny, shackled friend, she pushed her gleaming finger between Carmen's open lips. Closing her eyes in delight, Carmen suckled on Adele's skin, feeding from the taste of female arousal. She whimpered in despair again as Adele removed her hand; Adele silenced her with a kiss as deep and long as Carmen's had been, earlier.

Leaving her friend gasping, Adele stalked back to the trunk. Her hips swayed as she walked, and she felt power in her seductive movements, power in the vibrator's weight as she retrieved it. Turning it on, she slid its tip into her open mouth, taunting Carmen. Then she paused, holding the smooth, plastic rod at the entrance to Nadia's vagina.

Slowly, she pushed the vibrator between Nadia's waiting lips. Transfixed by the sight of her friend's secret flesh eagerly swallowing the buzzing stem, she held it still. Adele had always frozen with nerves when her boyfriends had lowered their faces to her sex, worried that the view was too hairy, too wet and dark to be pretty. But Nadia's sex was beautiful; the tiny flower of her anus, the soft, black curls, the tender pinkness of her clitoris, the interminable succulence of her lips as they clasped around the rod. Never again, she thought to herself. Never again would she be nervous of exposing her sex to a man's inspection. She had never seen anything so enticing.

Nadia groaned and pushed herself back towards Adele's hand. Suddenly, Adele knew what it felt like to be a man, and she pushed the phallus deep into her friend. She began to slide in and out, with long, expansive strokes; with every thrust, her desire became more masculine. She wanted to plunder Nadia's trembling body, to force it into violent orgasm with the hardness of the tool between her fingers. Her arm quickened into a rapid jerk, and she heard the tension in Nadia's throat as she began to fall towards her climax. Adele withdrew the false penis and as she pressed it remorselessly against the shining tip of her clit, Nadia's voice rose from protest into pleasure. Her legs shuddered uncontrollably, and she fell to her knees.

'Please,' Carmen begged from her unwilling position of spectatorship.

Adele nodded and without offering her a moment for recovery, she pulled at the straps across Nadia's damp back. 'Lick her pussy,' she commanded.

Gratefully, Carmen sighed as Nadia knelt between her legs. Hooking her fingers beneath the tight, shiny red strip at her crotch, Nadia revealed the deeply sensuous auburn of Carmen's pubic hair. Her legs were spread so wide that Adele could clearly see the gap where her clitoris jutted angrily. Involuntarily, she leant forward to watch as the tip of Nadia's long tongue lapped between her pussy lips, and up on to the shining, scarlet nub.

'Don't you ever learn?'

85

All three jumped at the sound of Foster's voice at the open door. 'Get your clothes and go!' he raged.

In a panic, Adele and Nadia fumbled with Carmen's harness. They grabbed their dresses and shoes where they lay discarded on the floor. Adele watched in dismay as her friends disappeared, leaving her to totter slowly to the door, suddenly unsteady beneath Foster's venomous gaze.

'Not you,' he spat. 'The Master will deal with you. Yet again,' he added, spinning on his heels and slamming the door in her face.

'If I didn't know you better, Adele, I'd suspect you did this on purpose.' Behind her, the Master lifted his hands on to her shoulders. 'I'd suspect you were beginning to enjoy my punishments, perhaps even to crave them. Am I right, Adele?'

'No, Master.'

'The trouble is, Adele, I've been lenient so far. Too lenient. But tonight, you have overstepped the mark. You will have to face up to the consequences. Is that clear?'

She shivered nervously. 'Yes, Master.'

His footsteps moved around until he stood in front of her. 'You went out of bounds, left the Manor, and invaded my playroom.' He picked disdainfully at the strap of her bra. 'On top of all that, you dared to use my toys.' Viciously, he clasped her face. 'Now, you will learn that these toys can be used for punishment, as well as pleasure.' He backed away. 'Put your hands on your hips.'

She obeyed. His eyes fell as her nipples poked between the slits in her bra.

'You look like a slut.' His lip curled as if the word tasted bitter. 'There's something very exciting about seeing a beautiful woman, a shy woman, dressed like a slut.' His eyes lifted lazily to hers. 'Does it excite you, Adele?'

'No, Master.'

He turned his back and walked to the door. 'I think you're lying. If I find out you're lying to me, you'll pay for it later.'

Adele gulped, trying to swallow her rising excitement and terror. 'I'm telling the truth, Master.'

'We'll see.' He flicked a switch and the lights went out. He flicked another, and a bright spotlight illuminated Adele from above. Like a nocturnal animal, she blinked confusedly. 'I can't see a thing,' she muttered to herself.

'No, but I can see everything.' A faint creak followed two loud clicks, and Adele assumed he was opening the metallic silver briefcase he'd arrived with. More clicks, followed by a whir and a flash. 'Be honest with me, Adele, and I'll be gentle.' Another flash, and Adele gasped as she realised he was taking photos. 'Lie to me and you won't believe my cruelty.' He moved to the edge of the circle of light. Adele saw her miniature reflection in the camera's lens, and behind it, the dim outline of the Master. 'I'll ask you again. Does it excite you, to dress as a wanton slut?'

Her pulse began to quicken. She didn't know quite how to play this game. She did know that the Master had been right about her craving his touch. She hoped another lie would be like a spark to his touchpaper. 'No, Master.'

'Sit down.' Her panties gaped behind her. The chair's wooden seat was startlingly cold on her buttocks. 'Open your legs.' Tentatively, she parted her knees. 'Wider!'

Gradually, she spread her thighs. The camera clicked, its tiny motor whirred at every stage until the fold in her knickers parted. Rafique paused and the sudden silence unnerved Adele.

'Look at your pussy.'

Obediently, she bowed her head. Dark, golden curls, wet with dew, spilled through the gap. Looking up again, she found Rafique storming towards her. Unceremoniously, he stooped and wiped a finger between her open labia. He sniffed his skin and tasted her arousal on his tongue as if it was a rich delicacy.

'You're wet,' he accused. 'You're telling me you're not excited, and yet your beautiful cunt is soaking wet. Do you know what that tells me?'

'No, Master.' Her voice was a hushed whisper.

'It tells me you're a liar. You like being a slut.' He knelt and pushed his face between her legs until she felt his breath inside her. 'My beautiful slut, to do what I want with.'

He stuck out his tongue. Adele inched her bottom forward, squirming desperately towards his mouth, but just as she felt the tip of his tongue on her sex, he sat back on his heels, out of reach.

'No, no, no,' he tutted, taunting her with his dark eyes. 'You're forgetting why you're here. Punishment, not pleasure.' He retreated back into the darkness, out of sight. 'Touch yourself.'

'What?' Her voice seemed to come from somewhere far away.

'Touch yourself, slut. I want to see you touch your breasts.'

Simultaneously mortified and delirious with excitement, Adele lowered her chin and lifted her hands. She began to circle the soft brown tips of her breasts with tremulous forefingers. Her areolae felt smoother than the finest silk, more tender than her inner flesh. The sensation was addictive. Gradually, her touch increased in pressure until minute crinkles appeared in the darkening skin surrounding her nipples. As her pleasure deepened, its source became indistinguishable. Fingertips, breast tips; the energy flowed in an infinite loop, radiating in warm waves until it encompassed her entire being.

She widened her circles of pleasure, spreading her hands across her breasts. The satin of her bra was smooth and sensuous on her palms. In contrast, her nipples ached stiffly, and she pinched them between her fingers and thumbs. Unable to stifle a tiny grunt of delight, she pinched again, harder, until the pain shivered down her spine and her pelvis involuntarily arched.

Raising her head, she found her tiny image in the camera's glass eye. She began to roll her hips suggestively. Now, the click of the shutter was barely audible beneath her heavy sighing.

'Touch your pussy.' Rafique's voice was devoid of emotion, but its hoarseness told Adele of his longing. Sliding one hand up beneath her warm hair, she began to stroke her neck. The other hand dropped between her legs. With a boldness that shocked her, she kept her eyes fastened to the lens as she caressed her inner lips. For a moment, her mind clouded as a finger slipped inside her moist vagina, then, with startling clarity, she realised what she had to do. It was Rafique's turn to taste punishment. She would drive him wild.

A second finger joined the first. Adele tilted her hips, allowing herself deeper entry. Glad of her ballet training, she opened her thighs until they were flat, spreading her pussy lips wide open for the camera. Her head fell back, and she moaned as she imagined the sight of her fingers, sliding easily in and out of her succulent, secret flesh, just as her fingers had slid in and out of Nadia.

As if she had taken a furtive dip into the juicy filling of a pie, she pulled out her fingers and rolled her tongue seductively over their shining wet tips. Sucking them deep inside her mouth, she half-closed her eyes and allowed a faint smile to raise the corners of her lips. Not long now, she guessed, and he would give in. He would have to.

Her free hand pushed its way down her body, over her breast, belly and mound, to the screaming nub of her

clitoris. A twitch fluttered in her inner thighs as she
tweaked its yielding hardness. She rolled it between her
fingers, her gasps muffled by her full mouth. It seemed
to grow beneath her touch, and as she pressed around it
and flickered over its raw tip, it swelled and stiffened
until it dominated her whole body.

Her sex screamed with frustration as her own fingers
deserted her. Orgasm was so near, another touch would
have sent her trembling, but her need for Rafique was
overwhelming. Convinced that he, too, needed only a
tiny push before he lost control, she stood up. She took a
step towards him, turned, and lowered herself on to all
fours.

Her guts twisted nervously at the brazenness of her
position. Images from Joe's magazine flickered into her
mind. She realised that she must look just like those
women; she also realised that it was exhilarating to
display herself wantonly for the Master, offering her sex
as if she was an animal. That was how she felt; like a
primitive, slavering, wild creature, with hunger her
driving force.

She arched her lower back. He would see her dangling
breasts, see her scarlet clit, engorged with blood. He
would see her anus, the slick, open lips of her pussy.
Adele closed her eyes and swallowed hard, attempting
to push her heart back down her throat. She heard the
Master stand, and his footsteps quickly approached. She
had won.

Pain seared her skin as the whip flailed across her
arse. The shock of it brought up a yelp from deep inside
her belly. Her hair fell on to her shoulders as her head
jerked backwards.

'How dare you.' The calm monotone of his voice was
petrifying. 'How dare you assume that I am as weak as
you are.' His feet moved round until he stood by her
bowed head. 'It's all very well, dominating your friends
in your high heeled boots and your slutty underwear,

but we both know who is really in control.' He squatted on his heels and raised her chin with the handle of the whip. 'Say it.'

'You're in control, Master.'

'You broke the rules on purpose.'

'Yes, Master.'

'You lied to me.'

'Yes.'

Leaning forward on his hands, he brought his face so close to hers that she opened her mouth in anticipation of a kiss. But instead of his lips, she only felt his breath on her skin. He enunciated his words deliberately, as if she might not understand. 'When I fuck you, if I fuck you, it will be my decision, not yours. It will be for my pleasure. Not yours. Do you understand, slut?'

'Yes, Master.'

He yanked roughly at her wrist, pulling her to her feet. In her stiletto heels she equalled his height, but the strength of his presence towered above her as he dragged her to the window. Avidly, she watched as one wrist, then the other, was buckled into a soft leather cuff. Heavy chains attached the restraints to the window frame's top corners. Her ankle chains were wider apart and much longer, and they coiled at the pointed toes of her boots before joining hoops at the base of the wall. She stood so close to the glass, her breath clouded one of its tiny panes. Beyond the circle of steam, she was vaguely aware of looking down into the woods. In the distance, a faint light flickered through the black trees.

Rafique reached around Adele to smooth her hair away from her face. 'Now, to choose my weapons.'

'Weapons?' She strained her neck. Behind her, he crouched over the gaping jaw of the trunk.

'My instruments of torture.' His gaze flickered among the choices. The spotlight reflected on the gloss of his raven-coloured hair. Out of sight, his hands picked up one toy after the other, and he muttered distractedly in

French as he evaluated and then discarded each one. At last, he straightened up. His eyes darkened with glee.

'This for your pussy.' A huge, shiny black phallus rose menacingly from his fingers, realistically moulded and unnaturally massive. 'And this,' he smiled, 'for your arse.' Much smaller than the first, it nonetheless looked far too big to fit inside her tiny, sensitive hole. Adele felt her forehead erupting with sweat.

Her neck began to ache and she turned back, watching in the window's reflection as Rafique moved closer behind her. Carefully putting down his toys he slowly unbuttoned his white shirt and dropped it to the floor. Hair snaked in a narrow path from his belly, spreading like black ivy over his wide chest. The sight of his bare torso, so fiercely masculine, made her insides ache.

Gathering his 'weapons', Rafique approached Adele, his captive prey. A hand reached underneath her armpit and cupped the lower curve of her left breast. Her heartbeat grew so fast, it echoed in her ears.

'Don't be frightened,' he soothed. 'I'm not going to hurt you.' His lips pressed into her hair. 'I'm just going to drive you insane.'

That's what I'm afraid of, she thought. Standing there, pinned wide open like a creature caught in his trap, every nerve ending jangled in anticipation. Her body hummed loudly enough to break glass; her clitoris throbbed. If she didn't come soon, she suspected, she could easily, willingly, drift into insanity.

Adele jumped as he hooked an arm across her waist and effortlessly pulled her hips backwards. The chains at her ankles unravelled and stretched taut, and her torso tilted downwards until her forehead and hard nipples touched the cold glass. Her weight hung from her wrists, and she held the window frame to relieve the pressure. Behind her, her lower back arched sharply, and she shuddered as she waited for her ordeal of pleasure to start.

Its gentle hum belied its size. Soothed by the soft purr, Adele sighed as her tender pussy lips were nudged wider apart, and the vibrator's head peered inside her. Its buzz was relaxing, and a creeping warmth spread along her backbone from beneath Rafique's fingers. Exerting gentle force on her lower back, he silently encouraged her to deepen the arch of her spine. As she did so, her hamstrings pulling sharply, the vibrator edged further in. Lubricated by the strength of her desire, the humming, smooth hardness slid deeper and deeper, its gradual, inexorable progress stretching the inner walls of her sex delightfully. She let out a long, grumbling moan of relief as its synthetic strength filled her completely.

Rafique's hot palm left her lower back and a second later, the vibrations increased in intensity. Adele gasped for air as the phallus reverberated deep inside her sex, up through her belly and into her throat. Her breath began to rasp as the Master held still and the purring grew louder again, until it sounded to Adele like a distant roar. The backs of her legs trembled as the rod was withdrawn to the opening of her slick pussy, before plunging so far inside her, it nosed against the neck of her womb.

Astounded that its width and length were sheathed within her, Adele let out an anguished cry of ecstasy. The vibrator began to slide in and out, and the friction as it rubbed the hyper-sensitive walls of her sex was almost unbearable. She tugged feebly at the chains that bound her wrists, desperate to pull the huge, buzzing stem from her body and fling it through the window. At the same time she craved it deeper, and as the Master thrust once again she pushed back hard against him.

Immediately, the vibrator was withdrawn. Adele's inner muscles contracted, clutching at the sudden emptiness, and she moaned her frustration in a strange, nonsensical language which seemed to emanate from her sub-conscious.

Rafique replied in French. Adele's mind was too jumbled to even try and translate, but she could tell he was angry at her attempted interference. She cursed her lack of control. Had she stayed still, he might have continued to fuck her. Her quivering body might have found release. Now, her ordeal was certain to climb another level.

Sure enough, the now familiar hum was silenced, and another took its place. This one had a harsher tone, a tinny, remorseless drone that seemed to cackle cruelly at her helplessness. She braced herself. Still, it was a shock when something cold and slimy touched the skin around her anus.

Her whole being shuddered in time with the violent vibrations at her arsehole. The teasing and stretching of her pussy had been hard enough to bear, but judging by the shock waves skidding beneath her skin, this was going to be impossible to endure. She longed for something to clench between her teeth as the well-oiled tip gingerly poked inside her. Spasms twitched between her cheeks and she involuntarily tried to eject her invader, but the Master slowly increased the pressure, waiting for a second of relaxation before sliding the stumpy phallus up to the hilt. Secured by its plug, it shook independently inside her while the Master slid his hands up to her breasts. Adele began to cry as he rolled her nipples and her imprisoned body swung uncontrollably between pleasure and pain, ecstasy and despair. Trying to fight the intolerable feelings flooding her senses, she bit down hard on her lip.

Then, once again, Adele was deprived of the incredible ecstasy that had filled her up. She panted like a dog, suddenly aware that she had been holding her breath. Behind her, a faint rustling told her Rafique was getting to the floor. She prayed that whatever was to follow, it would come quickly. Her body was about to explode.

Rafique slid on his back between her legs. Emerging beneath her, he sat up against the wall, his face inches away from hers. He turned the first vibrator around and around in his long hands, brandishing it along with a wicked smile. One more turn and it was on, buzzing remorselessly inside her mind. Adele looked down at him imploringly.

'Please,' she begged, as he raised the phallus between her legs. 'Please don't . . .'

'Don't you want to come? Don't you want to feel this on your lovely clit?'

'No!' She squirmed with the agony of the pleasure as the plastic knob vibrated against the raw tip of her clitoris. Rocking her hips from side to side, she tried to dodge away, but Rafique reached up and pinched her dangling nipple so hard, she froze.

'Keep still, you beautiful slut. I want to watch you come.'

Adele surrendered. The energy needed to fight wasn't there, and she succumbed to the Master's complete domination. Trapped, hands and legs fettered, there was nothing she could do except wait for the orgasm to rack her poor, exhausted body.

It built interminably. He slid the shaking rod up and down between her pouting labia, briefly touching her clitoris with each forward pull. He teased and pressed the vibrator's head all around the nub of her sex, making her frayed nerve endings scream. He rolled the phallus from side to side, over the tiny hump of her clit. All the while he looked up into her eyes, studying her soul, waiting for her reaction. Her breathing grew shallow and irregular, and he sat forwards expectantly.

The shift in his weight brought the vibrator hard against a magical, infinitesimal spot that Adele had never discovered before. As if he had attached electrodes to her, Adele's body jerked spasmodically. A charge electrified her soul, and tears filled her eyes. Unable to move, unable to do anything, she hung transfixed as wave after wave of intense power surged through her veins. She thought she heard herself scream as her tears spilled on to the Master's delighted face. Heat burned her sex, and she realised that never before had she experienced an orgasm so deep, so consuming. Despite being tied like a slave, she felt free: the Master had unleashed the beast inside her, and its hunger was sated.

Rafique lowered the vibrator and brought it to a halt. He caressed Adele's flushed cheek, traced around her open lips.

'That was incredible.' His voice was full of awe. 'You look so beautiful when you come. So beautiful.'

Shuffling between her legs, he kissed her swollen pussy on the way. Then he stood close behind her, and she felt his long erection press at her cleft.

'No more,' she begged breathlessly. 'I don't think I can take any more.'

'You will have to take some more, because I haven't finished with you yet.' He unzipped his trousers. They were soft against the backs of her thighs as they fell. 'You will have to take this.'

Without further warning, his penis plunged inside her hot, flooded vagina. Adele sobbed as he filled her. Her first orgasm had not yet subsided, and she needed time to recover from its overwhelming effect on her mind and body. It was too soon, too much for her to endure.

Then, inexorable as the Master's deep thrusts, her body once again transformed with animalistic passion. One of the Master's hands pressed at her tight stomach, but she was drenched in sweat and his palm slid up to her breast, which he squeezed greedily. His other hand reached around her hips and twitched between her legs, searching for her raw and tender clit. Adele moaned as he found it and pushed herself against his rhythm, forcing Rafique to slam further inside her. He must have been aroused by her desperation, because his pumping became urgent and frenzied, matching her unrestrained fervour. Suspended in her harness Adele was ravenous again, and her pussy gulped greedily at her Master's prick, wanting to devour its pulsating strength, trying to satisfy the new hunger rumbling inside her. Her head jerked back violently as another orgasm shook her.

Fighting for breath, she tried to give voice to her terror, but her mouth could only gape soundlessly at the terrible reflection in the dark window. Where her face should have been, a demon looked back at her; a demon with wild, staring eyes, a cruel, twisted leer and a matted tangle of hair. The vision opened its mouth wide, and its laughter echoed eerily, deep within Adele's tormented soul. She blinked, and it was gone.

She blinked again, and the room tilted worryingly. The floor rolled like a small boat riding a wave. Adele murmured and pulled on her ties, suddenly aware of aches all over her body.

The Master sighed, reluctant to free the creature he had trapped. Adele smelt his sharp, masculine odour as he leant over her spent body and unbuckled her hands and feet. The heady scent made her head spin again.

Adele turned and rested gratefully in his arms. The Master's heart was pounding as frantically as her own.

'Did you see it too?' she whispered into his neck. 'Did you see the succubus?'

He pulled away, steadying her shoulders as she swayed. He looked far into her eyes, and smiled. 'Yes.' He kissed her open mouth. 'I saw the succubus tonight.'

Chapter Five

*T*he music woke her. Blinking sleepily, Adele rolled on to her back and stared up into the golden canopy above her head, trying to work out why rehearsals had started without her. Confused, she picked up her watch. Seven o'clock. Class wasn't until nine.

Her mind reluctantly dragged itself into full consciousness, and she realised with relief that the music drifting on the breeze through the balcony doors was not coming from the theatre, but from another of the bedrooms.

With a tremendous effort, Adele swung her aching limbs out of bed and scuffed on to the balcony. Gingerly, she eased her body awake, rolling her neck, hunching her shoulders, flexing her ankles. For a moment, she wondered what she had done during yesterday's rehearsals that had left her so stiff, then she remembered. It wasn't ballet that had pushed her body to new extremes, but sex. She smiled incredulously at the memory of the previous evening, but her smile quickly faded at the thought of the ghostly vision that had confronted her. She had no doubt that it was the succubus she had seen, but why had the hideous demon laughed at her so menacingly? What was the meaning behind that evil leer?

For the first time since their arrival at the Manor, Adele felt an overpowering desire to be with Jamie. Rafique was incredible, but the way she reacted when she was with him was slightly scary. She longed for Jamie's arms to wrap her in their warmth, longed to see his cobalt eyes, full of unquestioning friendship. She longed for something more, too, but this morning all she needed was the familiarity of his smile. Wrapping her bath-robe tightly around her, she set off down the corridor in search of comfort.

She paused outside the neighbouring bedroom, Alexei's room. The heavy door was ajar. Inside, the music rose and fell in the whirling harmonies of Adele's second solo. Puzzled, she wondered why the notoriously lazy Russian was up so early. And why was his door open? Was he purposely trying to wake the others? Hesitantly, she pushed at the door.

Alexei's thick limbs were sprawled across the wide bed. One hand rested on his bare chest, the other was hidden beneath the royal blue sheet which covered the rest of his body. Adele took a step inside the room, strangely entranced by the unmistakeable jerk beneath the covers. Looking up, she flinched guiltily as his penetrating gaze met hers. His wide lips curled into an arrogant sneer.

'Adele. What a coincidence. I was just thinking about you.' With a flourish, he pulled back the sheet. Adele tried valiantly not to look, but the expression in his slate grey eyes was unnerving, and she gave in. Failing in her attempt to appear nonchalant, her eyes widened as she watched his fingers pull and push at his rigid member. It was red and angrily stiff, and just like the rest of his body, not long, but thick and meaty. The skin stretched taut where he tugged his penis away from his balls; heavy and hairy, and more befitting a wolf than a man, they sat between his open legs, twin sacks of unbridled machismo. Alexei managed to make a threat out of nudity.

The sight of his come, spurting in white droplets over his ridged stomach, woke Adele like a slap in the face. She turned to leave but he must have sprinted, because before she could think he was behind her. Over her shoulder, his hand pushed at the door so forcefully that she jumped as it slammed. Turning beneath his arm, her mouth went dry at the nearness of his powerful body.

'I – I want to go, Alexei.'

'But I don't want you to.' His eyes followed his fingers as they trailed lazily over her face. Adele shuddered; he was acting as if he owned her. 'I was expecting a visitor this morning, but this is better,' he smiled, looking at her mouth. 'Much, much better.'

'Alexei –' Her protest was swallowed in fear as he reached beside her hip and locked the door. He dangled the key in front of her eyes before hiding it in his palm. 'What do you want from me?'

He murmured in Russian, teasing her with his eyes. 'Breakfast,' he translated, as she huffed impatiently. 'I want breakfast in bed.'

'What?' Her forehead creased with confusion. In explanation, Alexei hooked a finger in the belt of her robe and pulled at the loose knot until it fell open. He grunted with unrestrained delight as the fluffy white towelling parted, revealing the contrasting outfit beneath; cami-knickers and a camisole top, in a dark grey satin which matched Alexei's eyes. A gift from Rafique, the flimsy underwear had been waiting on Adele's pillow when she had eventually returned to her room, very early that morning. A sensuous contrast to the tatty, faded T-shirts she normally wore to bed, the sight obviously stimulated Alexei's appetite. 'Breakfast,' he repeated, cupping her mound in his hot, grasping fingers. 'I like to eat pussy for breakfast.'

Ignoring her shock, Alexei returned to the bed. His narrow, tight buttocks stretched and his semi-turgid penis dangled between his legs as he leaned over and rearranged the pillows, preparing the table for his meal. Adele watched in dismay, not because she felt trapped, but because she didn't have the will to escape. She despised Alexei's arrogance, his selfish, chauvinistic assumptions. She should have felt indignant, disgusted by his domineering attitude. But all she felt was that she wanted, needed, to feel his mouth devouring her pussy. His touch had reawakened the beast in her.

In a dream, she moved towards the bed, dropping her bath-robe on the way. His chunky neck propped up against the pillows, Alexei smiled possessively as he looked her up and down. Adele felt goosebumps stippling her skin.

'Come here.' He patted the deep blue bed. 'I'm getting hungry.'

She climbed on to the high mattress and straddled his waist. Behind her, his cock nudged for entry at her cleft. Reaching up, Alexei slipped the straps of Adele's camisole from her shoulders and down to her elbows. He grinned at her breasts, displayed in front of him like ripe, plump fruit.

'Oh, yes,' he sighed in approval, his hands moving behind her and pulling her towards him. His stomach rippled and tensed as his head strained forward and his lips met a wide, pouting areola. Opening his mouth, he sucked on as much of her soft breast as he could, flickering his tongue rapidly, teasingly, over her nipple. His breath was hot and damp on her skin. Slowly, he brought his lips together, grazing her with his teeth. Adele whimpered in delight at the faint, wonderful pain.

'You're not as shy as I thought.' His eyes travelled up her cleavage to her face.

'You don't know anything about me.' With a push, she forced his head back on to the pillow and shuffled up his body. 'You don't know me at all.' Positioning her knees against his armpits, she pushed her pelvis forward. Carried away with the force that was rushing through her body, Adele pulled aside the curtain of her knickers. Delighted, she saw Alexei's mouth gape speechlessly. Her pulse pounded in her sex as she lowered herself on to his open lips.

He hadn't lied about his hunger. Ravenously, he gulped at Adele's pussy, opening her labia with a lap of his tongue before darting inside to taste her honey. Pressing forcefully against her swollen, fleshy lips, the stubble on his chin scratched her, and she retaliated by grinding the mouth of her sex down on to his face and making him struggle for oxygen. Pushing his head hard into the pillow, he gasped desperately.

Adele sat back on her heels. Her pussy kissed wetly at his hard stomach. She twisted her hair in her hands, piling it on top of her head and arching her back. Her breasts jutted proudly. 'What's the matter, Alexei? Lost your appetite?'

He licked his lips salaciously, tasting the juice that was smeared all over his mouth and chin. 'You little bitch,' he murmured admiringly. 'I'll show you how hungry I am.' With a twist of his pelvis, Adele fell from his body. In a blur of movement, she was lying across the bed, pinioned beneath Alexei's weight. He leaned so far over her that his thick brown fringe brushed across her forehead. 'I haven't started, yet,' he warned.

He slid between her legs until he knelt beside the bed. Grabbing roughly at her ankles, he pulled her pussy to his mouth and pushed her thighs apart. Underneath her, Adele's satin knickers rode up into her cleft. She closed her eyes as Alexei tugged at the strip that barely covered her sex, and dived towards her clitoris.

He knew just what to do; plenty of practice, Adele suspected. He nibbled and suckled, pulling her bud into a peak of pleasure that made her neck roll. His fingers and thumbs dug painfully into the tenderness of her inner thighs, and his chin poked at her vulva. Adele felt a tremor cross her hips, and she hooked her legs over his broad shoulders, eager to feel the tremor build into an eruption. As her body shook into a climax, her hips lifted high off the bed and her arms flung backwards, reaching for something, anything, to cling on to. Unsuccessful, she abandoned her body to the rushing, unstoppable wave of sticky, molten lava, and allowed herself to be carried on its seething tide.

She sat up. Slowly, Alexei's eyes lifted from her pussy to meet hers. He wiped a finger across his shining top lip and dipped it into the corner of his mouth. 'Delicious. The loveliest cunt I ever tasted.' He raised an eyebrow as Adele flinched. 'What's the matter? Don't you like that word?'

'Not really.'

'Cunt. It's a wonderful word. A powerful word for the most powerful part of a woman. One of the first English words I learnt,' he smiled, rubbing his clammy palms into her thighs like an oily salesman. 'And you have a beautiful cunt.'

Adele tried to stand, but his heavy hands would not allow it. 'Where do you think you're going? I'm still hungry.' She brushed ineffectually at his stumpy fingers. His face transformed with anger. 'You're not going anywhere until I've had my fill.' He crushed her inner thighs between his fingers as if he was crumpling paper. His voice was low, and trembled with the force of his threat. 'I'm going to fuck you, Adele. I'm going to fuck you so hard –'

'Let's dance.'

'What?'

Adele's eyes narrowed as the music changed pace, and the fierce rhythm of her solo was replaced by a langorous, tempting melody. 'This is our pas de deux.'

She escaped his grasp by rolling over the bed, got to her feet at the other side and pulled up her top. 'Let's dance.'

Adele saw his expression change again as Alexei realised the possibilities for this impromptu rehearsal. Their choreography was intensely passionate; dressed as they were, the sensuality of their movements would be more than an overtone. Now, when they touched, she would feel his naked power on her soft skin, his penis, unfettered by the usual jock-strap, would rub hard against her body. Their costumes, or lack of them, could have been designed for their roles.

Moving into the centre of the spacious room, they began to fit their bodies to the lilting rhythm. Alexei's strong fingers clasped around Adele's waist and he lifted her high above his head. He brought her down, her body twisted in his grasp and she arched back dramatically over his hands until her fingertips brushed the floor behind her. Moving his feet into a lunge, Alexei leant over her, and she felt his prick nudge at her sex. Following the choreography, he made sure she was on balance before drifting away. She ran after him, catching him by the wrist and pressing his fingers to her breast – a part of their pas de deux which normally filled her with dread. Today though, it was different. As Adele had expected, Alexei took the opportunity of their privacy to stray from what had been set. He abandoned the next sequence, preferring instead to knead Adele's pliant flesh. His fingers slid over the shiny fabric, squeezing and moulding until her nipple brushed stiffly beneath the flimsy material. As he watched his hand, his breathing grew deep. Lowering his face, he kissed her neck. Adele smiled to herself.

Turning away, she rejoined the choreography, stretching her leg into a languid arabesque. Alexei met her, hooking his arms around her uplifted thigh and her waist, sweeping her off the floor and effortlessly swinging her body over his bended knee. Adele folded her other leg beneath her, and felt the usual pull in the muscles of her spine; unusually, she also felt Alexei's palm slide from her waist to her breast. He straightened up and she unfurled her bent leg until her toe touched the floor. Carefully putting her down, Alexei's other hand inched along her extended thigh, into the silk of her knickers, into the silk of her sex. Adele gasped as a stubby finger slid easily inside her wet vagina.

Again, she pulled away from him, determined to make him follow the pas de deux up to a certain point. It was almost impossible to steady her resolve; at every opportunity, his insatiable touch slid over and under her lingerie, teasing her nipples, brushing against her engorged clitoris, fingering her damp labia as if he was grasping at slices of succulent fruit. The sensuality of Richard's choreography became apparent to Adele again, as it had done when she had danced for Rafique. She was no longer performing steps, linking chains of movement, drawing pleasing patterns with her fingertips and toes, she was performing sex. Her body was an instrument of lust, the shapes her limbs made in the warm air were simply expressions of a desire that would not be denied. She wanted so badly to lie down on the thick rug, to spread her pussy wide open and let Alexei plunder her ferociously. But she fought the urge, focusing instead on the chair in the corner, on the elasticated ballet belt and the sweat-streaked T-shirt that hung from its wide back.

At last, he sat down. During the climax of their duet, Alexei was supposed to be dozing while the succubus ravaged his prone body, stealing his life force to supplement her wicked power. Adele, preparing to pounce, whirled around the armchair, taking care not to hit the furniture with her flailing legs, and rehearsing her plan repeatedly in her head. Alexei was so strong, she would have to be quick.

She knelt astride Alexei's thighs. Whipping his belt

from the back of the chair, she fastened his wrist to the chair's wooden arm with a deftness that surprised and delighted her. She paused for a moment to savour Alexei's amazement, before snatching at the grimy T-shirt and using that to tie his other hand.

'Oh, I see,' he nodded, after a minute's uncertainty.

'What do you see, Alexei?'

'You like to play kinky games,' he winked. 'I always knew it. I always knew that beneath that quiet, timid facade, Adele King was a kinky little bitch.'

'Oh, did you?' She pulled aside her knickers again. 'You're so clever, Alexei. You probably knew I would do this, too.' Splaying her sex lips with the fingers of one hand, Adele eased herself on to the tip of his rearing prick, swallowing only its purple plum inside her. 'And you must have known I would do this.' Summoning all her strength, Adele slammed her body down, impaling her flesh on his, slapping her buttocks against his bare thighs. Like a ventriloquist's dummy, Alexei's jaw dropped woodenly. Thighs quivering, Adele raised herself up again until only an inch or two of him remained inside her. Alexei looked down, and Adele shared his view. Where they joined beneath her triangle of golden curls, Alexei's penis strained for release, lubricated with arousal. Adele paused and Alexei waited, eyes fixed to her pussy. Slowly, she lowered her sex on to his lap until his thick rod was sheathed inside her again, stretching her with his width. Adele began to slide up and down, watching Alexei's knuckles turn white as he gripped the chair. She clutched voraciously with her pussy, and his throat emitted an unearthly, gutteral growl. She quickened her pace until her hips juddered and jerked above his and he rolled his eyes deliriously. He was close to coming and so was she, but instead of lengthening the strokes of her inner flesh against his pulsing stem, she stopped them altogether. Leaning forward, she gripped Alexei's face with mean fingers and pressed her lips to his ear. 'You're clever, Alexei. But you can't possibly have known I would do this.'

Adele raised herself up, unsheathing his fat penis until it swung between her legs, alone and weeping from its single eye. Dismounting, she walked slowly to the door, collecting the key and her robe on the way.

'Adele?' She turned. There was no sign of gloating any more. Alexei looked lost, afraid. 'You can't leave me like this.'

'I can do whatever I like, Alexei.' Her eyes lingered over his swollen member. Her pussy ached sharply, but above the ache was a shimmer of satisfaction. 'You're a bully, Alexei. You need to be taught a lesson.'

'But – I need to come!' Exasperated, his accent suddenly thickened.

'So do I. But it's worth missing one, second-rate orgasm to see you like this.'

Unlocking the door, Adele's face glowed in the heat of her smile.

'Well, well. What have we here?' Jessica pulled on her cigarette and exhaled into Adele's face. 'Didn't you get enough with the lesbians, last night?'

'How did you – ?'

'I spent the evening with Jamie.' Jessica circled Adele menacingly, like a boxer psyching up her opponent. 'He was very interested to learn about your dalliance with Carmen and Nadia.' Jessica arched an eyebrow. 'He'll be enthralled when I give him the latest instalment.' She leant conspiratorially close, mean eyes glittering. 'You're a dark horse, Adele. I never knew you had it in you.'

Adele wafted ineffectually at the haze of acrid smoke. 'Nothing happened between me and Alexei,' she coughed.

'Of course not. You probably went to his bedroom to practise, didn't you?' She held up her cigarette and raised her eyes, listening to the music. 'That's your pas de deux, isn't it?' She looked at her watch. 'Now, that's what I call dedication, unscheduled morning rehearsals. I can understand it from you, Adele, but how did you manage to get Alexei up, so early?' Jessica pushed at the door. Alexei glanced up. With one freed hand, he was unbuckling the other. His penis glowered furiously in his lap.

'It's not what it looks like. I – I was teaching him a lesson.' Adele's voice faltered as she realised how feeble her words sounded.

'I believe you,' Jessica sneered, looking down at Adele's dishevelled lingerie. 'But I doubt that Jamie will be so understanding. Pity, I think he really liked you.' She pushed her cigarette between Adele's open lips. 'Now, if you'll excuse me, I think I ought to rehearse with Alexei, pick up where you left off. I am your understudy, after all.'

With a flick of her long blonde hair, she slammed the door.

She saw it in his black face, looming on the horizon like a thick grey cloud. She sensed it in his silence, heavy in her head like the oppressive air before a storm. She felt it in her bones, the same way animals sense the impending crash of thunder. Any moment now, lightning would split the sky. Richard was about to explode.

The fact that Adele had danced well yesterday, after her private tuition with Rafique, made it far worse. Richard had grudgingly congratulated Adele, admitting that her body seemed looser and that her interpretation was beginning to show promise. Expectant of further progress, he had started today's rehearsal with Adele's second solo. Obviously astounded by her complete regression, he had not yet said a word. Adele's heart pounded furiously as she danced, in anticipation of the inevitable outburst.

It would have been far easier to rehearse in front of an

audience of strangers. With every movement, Adele was confronted by someone she would rather avoid. A diagonal series of leaps from upstage to down, and she met Carmen and Nadia, whispering in the recess of the front wing. A chain of rapid spins from one side of the proscenium arch to the other, and Jamie's admiring gaze filled her with guilt. Further upstage, Alexei limbered up in the wings, flexing his heavy thighs as if preparing for a fight. And behind Adele, as tenacious as a shadow, was Jessica, mirroring every turn.

The music changed, and as if it was an act of retribution, Alexei appeared at her side. They moved into their pas de deux. Unlike that morning, when Alexei's grip had been passionate, reverent even, his grasp was now harsh and unyielding. When he partnered Adele, he did so with such force that she was thrown rather than lifted, caught rather than lowered. Instead of letting her use her natural speed in pirouettes, he grappled at her waist, engineering her into dizzying quickness. He denied her his support, and Adele had to fight to find her own balance. He was no longer a partner, but an enemy; this wasn't a duet, but a battle.

Alexei slumped into the armchair at the back of the stage and feigned sleep. Adele circled him, falling off pointe as she tried and failed to regain her equilibrium. His erratic, aggressive handling had unnerved her. Her limbs seemed ungainly, her arms heavy, her pointes too tiny to balance upon. She would have been relieved to be able to stand still for a moment, had she not been faced with Alexei's leer. Holding on to the arms of the chair, she swung one leg into a high arabesque, struggling to avoid his eyes as her head lowered towards his.

'I've got an erection,' he whispered. 'Want to sit on it again?' Alexei brought his foot up behind Adele's supporting knee. Her leg buckled, and with a gasp of dismay she fell on to his lap. 'What's the matter, succubus?'

Alexei grabbed her wrists as she struggled to her feet. 'Lost your appetite?'

Richard turned off the cassette. His heavy footsteps climbed the stairs to the stage. 'What the hell's going on?' The restrained calmness of his voice was even more scary than his usual deep boom. 'Alexei, you're partnering like a first year student, and Adele . . .' He looked from one to the other, like a teacher with the school's notorious troublemakers. His black gaze took in Alexei's possessive grip on her hand, and Adele winced as she saw him drawing his own conclusions. 'I'm sorry to interrupt whatever's going on between you two, but it seems to have escaped your notice that we are rehearsing, here.'

The others emerged like curious mice from the wings. Guiltily, Adele looked up just as Jamie's mind caught up with Richard's. In his eyes, there was a bitterness she didn't recognise as he looked at Alexei, then at Adele, then at the floor. Behind Adele, Jessica let out a derisive, delighted snort.

'We'll take a break for five minutes.' Richard huffed and retreated from the stage. On his way, he was met by Rafique. Adele started at the sound of his voice.

'If I may interrupt for a moment.' He held up a hand. A white tape dangled from his long fingers like a flattened snake. 'The costumes I'm having made are being finished today. I need to be sure they will fit perfectly. If I could ask you to check each other's measurements, it would be a great help.'

He offered the tape to Carmen, and waited with his notebook while she and Nadia measured each other. Moving upstage, his eyes barely flickered in recognition as he passed the tape to Adele.

She stood still, immoveable with embarrassment. Behind her, Alexei's breath was quick on her neck. In front of her, pen poised, Rafique waited for her to take his measurements. It was a simple request, yet she

110

couldn't comply. She was reluctant to look at Alexei, let alone touch him. Her gaze darted around the stage, searching for an ally, allowing the silence to grow increasingly uncomfortable. The others looked back: Carmen and Nadia egging her on; Jamie puzzled; Jessica sneering. Silently, Adele begged with Rafique, hoping he would read the situation. But how could he? With a slight shudder, she realised that she had no choice. There was no way to avoid this without causing a scene. She took a deep breath and turned to face Alexei.

He grinned and raised his arms to shoulder height. Adele leant into his torso, the smell of his sweat pungent in her nostrils as she passed the tape around his back. 'Forty-four,' she read, her voice cracking. She lowered the tape to his waist. 'Thirty-two.' She turned to Rafique, praying there was no need to measure Alexei's hips.

Rafique nodded and Alexei snatched the tape from her fingers. Flicking at her wrists with the backs of his hands, he made her raise her arms. Adele looked away as he pressed his body unnecessarily close, tightening the tape around her chest. 'Breasts, thirty-four,' he announced loudly. Her breath caught as his fingers brushed over her nipples. 'Waist, twenty-four.' He dropped his touch. 'Hips, thirty-four.' His hands withdrew but Adele could still feel his eyes, burning her skin. 'Anything else, Rafique? Inside leg?'

Adele looked anxiously at the Master. He shook his head, but her relief was immediately swamped in desperate disappointment. 'Adele's costume is a little unusual, and I need an unusual measurement. If you could put the end of the tape against her navel, and pass it to me between her legs – '

Unable to restrain his delight, Alexei followed Rafique's instructions, stooping to pass the narrow plastic strip to Rafique between Adele's inner thighs. Behind her, the Master pressed his fingers into the small of her back, in front of her, Alexei pulled at the tape until it dug into her cleft, slicing between the lips of her pussy and forcing them apart. The edges of the thin band were sharp where they cut into her delicate flesh, and Adele's breath caught in her throat, humiliated at the thought of the others, watching her suspended between pleasure and pain.

'You beautiful bitch,' Alexei mumbled, so that only she could hear. 'It's you that needs to be taught a lesson. No one treats me like you did this morning.'

Adele reluctantly met his eyes. There was disdain in his expression, but there was something else too, something crackling brightly at the edges of his dark grey irises. Stunned, she realised he was desperately aroused. Her behaviour that morning had awakened a fresh, fierce lust within Alexei, just as the Master had unfurled her own desire so that she could marvel at its deep colours. She returned Alexei's stare; now it was his turn to flinch from the ferocity of her eyes. He was stronger than her in every way. He could knock her to the floor with a flick of his hand. She was trapped by his fingers where he tugged viciously, splitting her sex with the tape, holding her on a tightrope of delicious torture. And yet, she was in control. She had shocked, intrigued and conquered Alexei, and he wanted her. If the situation hadn't been so awkward, Adele might have revelled in it.

'Alexei.' Behind her, Rafique pulled impatiently on the band that split her body. 'Alexei! Let go!' Reluctantly, Alexei released his grip. Adele turned away from him, watching the Master as he moved across the stage. Jessica's outstretched hand met his, and with a smile of pure delight aimed in Adele's direction, she moved her fingers over Jamie's waiting body. Over her shoulder, Jamie looked at Adele. His lips were parted, his eyes clouded with disappointment. Any satisfaction Adele might have enjoyed at the effect she had had on Alexei was obliterated by the despair on Jamie's handsome face.

Beneath his halo of golden curls, he looked like a fallen angel.

Jessica handed over the tape with a flourish. 'Don't forget the most important bit,' she smirked, opening her legs. Jamie rolled his eyes.

'That won't be necessary,' Rafique said. 'You're only the understudy. You don't need a costume.'

Jessica put her hands on her narrow, boyish hips. 'So, what happens if Adele gets injured?' she demanded. 'Her costume will be much too big for me.'

'Oh. I hadn't thought of that.' Rafique turned to Richard. 'Should I have another costume made, just in case?'

Adele felt her cheeks reddening violently. Alexei was so near, she could feel the hard lump beneath his jock-strap, straining against her buttock. As Richard began to speak, Alexei's voice caressed the nape of her neck. 'Do you feel that, bitch?' he whispered. 'Do you want it?' He squeezed her other cheek in his strong fingers. 'Whether you want it or not, you're going to get it later. I said I would fuck you, and I will.'

Suddenly, Adele snapped. Her mind cleared and she whirled around, slapping Alexei's face with such force that the sharp sound echoed around the small stage.

Richard broke the stunned silence that followed. 'Would one of you care to tell me what's going on?'

'I'll handle this.' Rafique lunged towards Adele and pulled at her wrist. 'Please continue with the rehearsal, Richard. I think Miss King and I need a little chat.'

Adele was glad of the auditorium's darkness, and of the music's loudness. One hid her tears, the other disguised her sobs as she cried softly in Rafique's arms. On stage, Jessica danced in her place once again, but Adele was too upset to really notice. Drowning in a torrent of emotion, she struggled to make sense as her words got tangled up with sorrow and shame.

113

'Calm down.' Tenderly, Rafique dabbed at her tear-streaked face with a soft handkerchief. He led her into the back row of the stalls, and sat down beside her. 'Take a few deep breaths.' He waited while she did. 'Now, what's the matter?'

Adele peered into the gloom. She could barely discern Rafique's dark eyes. 'I don't know what's wrong with me. I can't stop myself, and now ... now Jessica's going to ruin everything.'

She began to shiver uncontrollably. Rafique shrugged off his jacket, and draped it around her shoulders. 'What are you talking about?'

Guilty, she stared into her lap. 'I went into Alexei's room this morning.'

'And?'

'He locked me in, and ... well, you can imagine what happened.'

'No, I can't. Tell me, Adele. Tell me what he did to you.' There was unmistakeable eagerness in his rich voice, as easily discernible as his concern.

Adele gulped and blinked nervously, several times. Her own voice was barely audible. 'He went down on me.'

'He did this against your will?'

'No! No –' Shame washed her soul and stained her mind. 'I wanted him to do it,' she admitted. 'I enjoyed it.'

'Then what's the problem?' She bowed her head, but Rafique raised her chin with cool, insistent fingers. 'Why are you so upset?'

'Jessica was on her way to see Alexei. She caught me.' Her shoulders began to shake again. 'She's going to tell Jamie. She was with him last night. She told him about me and Carmen and Nadia. God knows how she found out. What's he going to think of me?'

Rafique's touch left her. Sitting back in his seat, he pretended to watch the rehearsal. Adele watched him. In the light from the stage, she could see that his eyes were glazed, and for some reason, his strong jaw was set in resignation. When he spoke again, his voice had changed. 'Are you in love with Jamie?'

Adele looked towards the stage. Jamie's lithe body bent and swayed, manoeuvring Carmen's tiny frame easily around his own. His curly hair shone beneath the strong lights, and his blue eyes pierced the gloom of the auditorium. A pang of remorse and longing hit her in the guts. 'Maybe. I thought I was. I just don't know any more.'

Rafique's eyes remained fixed on some non-existent, distant point. 'Why did you go to Alexei's room, if it's Jamie you want?'

'I don't know.' She searched her mind for an explanation, but only found more questions. 'I don't understand it. This morning I couldn't stop myself. There was nothing between Alexei and me, and yet I felt so powerful, so alive. It's the same when you touch me.'

Suddenly animated again, Rafique shifted in his seat, turning his whole body towards her. 'What do you mean?'

'I like Jamie. I always have done. I hoped that maybe this week, being away from home, staying in the Manor, dancing with him ... I thought it might be the start of things between us. I thought this rôle might be good for me, give me some confidence. But I can't concentrate on anything. The ballet, Jamie –' She hung her head. 'I can't stop thinking about you.'

Rafique brushed the back of his hand against her cheek. 'And what do you think, when you think of me?'

'I've never met anyone like you. I love the way you make me feel.'

'And how is that?' he urged, determined, it seemed, to unravel the mess of her emotions.

'You make me feel like a woman,' she whispered.

'A beautiful woman.'

'The things you say, the way you touch me . . . I'm not in control of myself any more. I think about sex all the time and I don't feel awake unless you're inside me. When I'm with you, it's as if I'm someone else. It's as if there's someone else in here,' she touched her forehead, 'someone I have no control over. Oh, God,' she sighed. 'What's happening to me? I've changed since I've been here. I can't think straight any more.'

'You mustn't worry.' His fingers moved around her neck, curling in the delicate wisps of hair that had escaped from her chignon. 'Let yourself go, Adele. There's no time for guilt in this life, and there's no reason to be afraid of anyone or anything. You're a strong, talented, beautiful young woman. If you want Alexei, take him. If you want Carmen, or Nadia, or both of them, then take them too. If Jamie loves you, he won't judge you.'

Adele shook her head sadly. 'I wish I could believe you, but Jessica can be very persuasive.'

'I'll take care of Jessica.'

'You would do that for me?' she gasped, wondering what he meant, but knowing that he meant it.

'I'm your Master, Adele. I give rewards as well as punishments. Talking of which, you have transgressed again.' Warmth rippled down Adele's spine in anticipation of what was coming. 'You realise I will have to chastise you, for visiting Alexei's room?'

'Yes. Yes, Master.'

'Stand up.'

Panicked, she did a double take between the stage and Rafique. 'Not here. Not now, surely?'

'Yes, Adele.' He gripped her thigh determinedly. 'Here. Now.'

'No,' she pleaded, but his hand had already slipped on to her breast. Beneath the soft drape of his jacket he skilfully rolled a nipple, swiftly manipulating it into stiffness. Adele sighed with the helplessness of it all, and

116

as he began work on the tip of her other breast, her body relented. Her mind was a fog of concern, and only a few metres away, her colleagues danced on obliviously; but in spite of this, the slightest touch from Rafique and she forgot everything. Perhaps, she mused, perhaps it wasn't in spite of, but because of these things that she welcomed the Master's touch. When she was in his hands, under his control, she no longer had to think. She could leave Adele King behind with her shyness and her worries, and she could be the other woman. The woman who craved fingertips, tongues and hot, hard flesh. The woman whose body sung on a single note of perfect pleasure. The woman she had always wanted to be.

The Master slid his hand between her legs. She was damp from the strenuousness of the morning's class and rehearsal. She was also damp inside, and the Master discovered it too as he hooked a finger beneath the crotch of her black leotard. It was wet where her tights hugged her naked flesh. The Master's face hovered close to hers and Adele sensed delighted urgency in his quickening breath.

'You're wet.' He touched his lips to hers, and she felt them move when he spoke. 'You want this, don't you Adele? You want me to punish you?'

'Yes, Master.'

His tongue darted into her open mouth. She strained to grasp it, to trap it within a deep kiss, but like an insect, it was gone almost before she could react. Rafique stood and pulled her behind the high-backed seating. Barely giving her time to check that she was hidden from view of the stage, he pushed his jacket from her shoulders and snatched at her leotard, unpeeling it from her body until it crumpled at her feet. The rise and fall of her naked breasts was rapid beneath the Master's glare.

'You want this. Your friends are only separated from you by a few rows of seats and some music, which could stop at any time.' He knelt and rolled down her tights, his face inches from her aching pussy. 'They might see you, or hear you, but you want it anyway.' Reaching between her thighs, his finger slid between her labia, sliding easily on the dew that sprung from deep inside her and lined her sex like silk. 'You want this punishment as much as I do.' Standing again, he rubbed his finger over her mouth, coating Adele with her own faint musk lipstick. 'Tell me you want it.'

'I want it. I want you,' she agreed. 'I don't care about the others.' She dipped her head and sucked the tip of his retreating finger. 'You can do what you want to me, I don't care.'

'The problem is, Adele, I don't know what to do with you. I've punished you several times, and still you have a blatant disregard for the rules. What to do with such a naughty girl?'

Adele looked up into his face. Standing so close, his masculinity was overpowering, addictive. She reached out for him, wanting to be a part of him, wanting his body to be a part of hers again. He clamped his fingers around her wrist on its way to his neck.

Twisting her arm behind her back, he pushed her upper body into a deep bow. Hampered by her leotard and tights she stumbled, but Rafique caught her around the waist, releasing her arm and allowing Adele to place her hands on the floor. On all fours, she trembled with nervous energy as he knelt behind her.

His touch was smooth as he fondled her exposed buttocks, rubbing his palms into her tautly stretched muscles. 'You have a fantastic arse,' he muttered. 'Truly fantastic. Such a shame I have to hurt it, but I must –'

The music grew louder. A crash of cymbals muffled Adele's startled cry and Rafique's grunt of effort as he brought his hand smarting across her bare cheeks. A shock of pain stung Adele's vulnerable body. He slapped again, and inexplicably, the pain dissolved into sticky,

118

warm sexual excitement that swirled and spilled inside her, seeping from her pores and welling in her wide eyes. The Master spanked and spanked, throwing all his force into the flat of his hand, and as Adele's buttocks turned raw her sex grew heavy with arousal. Bracing herself, she steadied her shaking arms against the onslaught, tilting her lower back upwards to meet his hand, seeking contact, seeking the extraordinary thrill of the Master's welcome cruelty.

Then the music paused, and so did the Master. Adele heard a zip whizzing open and she spread her aching knees a little wider apart, showing Rafique the crimson beauty of her sex which must surely match the redness of her arse. He moaned in appreciation and Adele tensed herself for the invasion of his penis. It didn't happen, yet his moans grew regular, and then the crease of her bottom was dripping with something hot and slimy.

'Fantastic,' he repeated, working his semen into Adele's tightly closed anus. 'Such a tight, ripe arse, waiting to be buggered, wanting to be buggered.'

Without any further preparation, the Master's penis prodded for entry. Spreading her quivering cheeks with eager fingers he forced an inch, then another inside her. Eased by his own secretions, his pulsing length quickly filled her until Adele thought she would scream in terror of the pleasure. It scared her to feel so good, so open, so dirty. It was unnatural. Her body was not designed to withstand such indescribable, agonising rapture. And yet, like a drug, she wanted more.

With unbearable deliberation, the Master slowly pushed and withdrew, pushed and withdrew, stretching her grasping anus, letting Adele become accustomed to the fullness of his prick inside her secret passage. The tip of his rod seemed to touch the base of her brain, and her elbows collapsed as intense joy swept through her senses. She made fists. Her fingernails dug painfully into her palms and she bit down on the knuckles of one hand, moaning into her skin. Behind her, the Master began to thrust more violently, and as he pumped himself deeper inside her, her nipples rubbed against the harshness of the carpet. The ballet's music rose again, and as it did Rafique matched its relentless rhythm, driving further into Adele's helpless body, piercing her to the core. His hands slid over her shoulder blades and clutched at her shoulders, gaining greater purchase for the final effort, and with a tremendous shudder he emptied himself of passion. Falling over her doubled-up body, Rafique enclosed her in his grateful arms and muttered into her back while his penis throbbed.

Tears overflowed from Adele's tightly closed eyes, staining her cheeks once again with their heat. This time, they weren't tears of sadness or confusion, but of wonder and relief.

'Oh God, oh no,' she moaned, as their bodies parted. Like a fish gasping for air, Adele's sphincter expanded and contracted spasmodically, confused by the sudden emptiness. Rolling on to her back, Adele caressed her tender, grazed nipples with one hand, dropping the other to her sex. 'Rafique,' she breathed, 'Master, please ...'

It was too late. His penis was already hidden beneath the well-cut folds of his trousers. 'It's time to get back to work.' He offered his hand to help her up.

'I don't want to work.' She accepted his hand, and watched like a child as he unrolled her tights and leotard up over her trembling limbs. 'I want to be with you.'

'You've got rehearsals. And anyway, I'm going to be busy this afternoon.' He kissed her flushed cheek. 'I think it's time Jessica met the Master.'

Chapter Six

Making her annoyance plainly obvious, Jessica relinquished her domination of the stage. Scuffing her brand new pointe shoes loudly as she retreated, she began once again to mirror Adele's movements as she finally rejoined the rehearsal. Jessica noticed that her cheeks were even more flushed than usual.

Adele was always blushing. Life seemed to embarrass her. She was certainly mortified by her new rôle; the tension in her body showed her discomfort with the succubus's overtly raunchy choreography. Jessica would never understand why Rafique had chosen Adele instead of her to play the part. If he was such an avid balletomane, how could he make such an error of casting? Never mind, she consoled herself. By the end of the week, the part of the succubus would be hers. Along with the affections of Rafique, with any luck.

Jamie was a different matter. For some reason, a reason which would always remain a mystery to Jessica, men seemed to go all serious when they were with Adele. At company parties, they would crowd around her, fawning like courtiers with their reticent queen. When she was given a soloist rôle, the wings would be full with admirers, from the fresh young adolescent corps boys to the coarse, beer-bellied stagehands. And now Jamie Butler, barely settled back into the company, insisted he couldn't think of anyone else. It was absurd. Certainly, she was attractive, but too curvaceous to be a ballerina. She was a good dancer too, Jessica had to admit that, although Adele was nowhere near as technically proficient as she was. Thanks to her gymnastics training when she was young, Jessica could whip out five pirouettes, hold her balances impossibly long and raise her legs unfeasibly high. Adele, on the other hand, preferred to stick with her usual, boring triple pirouettes, to control her balances rather than risk losing the thread of the music. How pedantic. How predictable. How safe. Sure, it annoyed the conductor when Jessica delayed the music, and on more than one occasion she had had to shout at him during performances. If he wasn't going to watch her, she had said, he might as well go home. But Adele's insistence that the music was her guiding force was boring. To Jessica, the music was simply the accompaniment to her pyrotechnics.

Jamie and Carmen joined Adele centre stage, and Jessica half-heartedly marked the steps behind the threesome as they rehearsed their pas de trois. She seethed as she watched Adele in the most pathetic interpretation of a sex demon she had ever seen. Jamie was wasted on her, last night's humiliation still tasted bitter.

The rapid pizzicato of the violin reminded Jessica of the last time she had been usurped. Paul had been intense and tediously dull, but then any young man who had dedicated his life to the violin was never going to be normal. He had been extremely attractive, though, and she had wanted him from the day he'd joined their orchestra. He had seemed interested, shunning his fellow musicians and choosing to socialise with the dancers instead. He appeared everywhere they went. He even used to watch rehearsals, staring dreamily through the studio windows. Eventually, he had invited Jessica for a coffee. Her sex still twitched excitedly at the memory of his pale grey eyes, looking wistfully across the table at her.

'I hope you don't mind,' he had simpered, 'but I wanted to ask your advice about Adele. She seems so shy whenever I speak to her. Is she seeing someone?'

Jessica's intimation that Adele was indeed seeing someone, a butch dyke called George, did not have the desired effect. Paul had plucked on Adele's strings for a couple of months before returning to his native Canada. It had made Jessica nauseous, the sight of him beaming up on to the stage whenever Adele was dancing.

And now, Alexei. Alexei was a pig, Jessica knew that – a misogynist, chauvinist, horny pig. The male equivalent of her, in fact. She had never failed to please him before, but that morning, when she had continued where Adele had left off, he had closed his eyes for the first time. Had he imagined that Jessica was someone else, as she had done with Alexei, several times before?

It wasn't fair. Jessica was uncrowned queen of the National Ballet. She didn't care too much about Alexei, but Jamie was worth a little effort. She may have lost her chances with him, but that didn't mean she would sit back and let Adele have an easy ride. Jamie was the serious, sensitive type. The thought of his beloved, humping with the randy Russian, was bound to cool his passion. As she danced, she planned the moment she would tell Jamie, and a sneer raised one corner of her mouth.

Jessica watched distractedly as the slimy lizard, Foster, darted through the auditorium. Richard stooped to speak to him and a moment later, the music paused yet again. Glad of the rest, she waited while Foster slithered up on to the stage.

'Miss Sharpe,' he hissed. 'If you would kindly follow me.'

'What for?' she snapped, avoiding his pale eyes and looking to Richard for reassurance. She didn't want to go anywhere with the strange, chalk-skinned butler.

'The Master wishes to take your measurements for a costume.' Foster rubbed his hands. 'If you will please accompany me, Miss Sharpe.'

'With pleasure.' She pushed between Adele and Jamie, and sauntered to the stairs.

'Don't be long,' Richard warned.

'Don't hold your breath.' She grabbed her tracksuit top from her bag. 'Once Rafique gets a load of my measurements, he's going to want to see more,' she teased, loud enough for Adele to hear. No doubt she was blushing, Jessica thought, as she turned her back and followed the butler through the auditorium.

Out of the theatre, Jessica whistled to cover the uncomfortable silence as Foster led her towards the main hallway. Ignoring the central staircase, they passed under its slope and carried on to the end of the corridor. Producing a key from his waistcoat pocket, he unlocked a tiny door within a huge frame, an opening barely wide enough for his overly broad but bony shoulders. Jessica stepped into the gloom behind him, and waited while he locked up again. It took a moment for her eyes to adjust.

There were no windows in the turret. The steep, spiral staircase was lit only by dripping candles, high up on the granite walls. The light from their faint flames barely reached their feet, and Jessica struggled to keep her footing as she climbed the steps behind Foster. The stone slabs which rose towards the unknown were badly worn, dipping with the gradual erosion of centuries of feet. There wasn't even a banister. Jessica's fingers scanned the cold walls for support.

Looking down, she bumped her head on Foster's behind when he stopped. Coughing in annoyance, he knocked twice. The door opened immediately.

Jessica's eyes widened as she stepped into the octagonal room. The windows were narrow slits in the grey, bare stonework, and they shed measly slivers of sunlight on the dark floorboards. The room was eerily cold, grey and completely empty, apart from the monstrous contraption hanging from the middle of the ceiling, high above their heads.

Four heavy, industrial sized hooks, which looked like they belonged in a shipyard, were clipped on to iron hoops in the wood panelling at the top of the turret. From each hoop a length of steel chain, with links as thick as Jessica's wrist, stretched to her waistline. There, the chains ended at more hoops, two on each side of a worn leather stretcher. Indendations marked its dark brown surface, and it swayed ever so slightly, ever so menacingly, in the breeze that forced its way through the mean gaps in the walls which passed for windows. Attached to one end of the strange bed, one on each corner, was a pair of metal struts. Both had dry, frayed leather collars hanging open from their metal spines, and wooden foot-rests at their bases. At the opposite end, leather handcuffs dangled idly from the other corners. It looked like a cross between an instrument of torture, and a medieval gynaecology table.

Jessica attempted a smile, but it didn't work. Something like the beginning of a constipated grimace inched across her face as she turned to Rafique. 'Why, er, what . . . ?' His faint, confident leer unnerved her. 'Are you going to measure me, then?'

He ran his long, dark fingers through his glossy hair. As usual, he looked immaculate. Black hair swept back from his well-designed face, blue shirt tucked into his well-designed trousers. He blinked slowly. 'I think you realise, Jessica, that you're not here for a costume fitting.'

'No. Right.' Jessica took a deep breath, and tried again for a smile. This time it came, as her nervousness dissolved into stunned excitement. As she had suspected, Rafique wanted her. He had brought her up into the turret to fuck her. She liked a man who knew what he wanted, and took it. That was her philosophy on life, precisely.

'I've brought you up here for another reason entirely.' He turned his back on her, and slowly walked away. Reaching one of the tower's eight walls, he turned and leaned against the stonework, playing with her eyes the way an actor might play with the camera. 'Do you know what that reason is, Jessica?'

She nodded slowly. 'I can guess.'

'Can you?' He raised one eyebrow. 'You can probably guess what I'm going to ask you to do next, then.'

Jessica scanned his dark eyes, but she was unable to tell anything from his look. His body language said a lot, though. He was waiting. Waiting for her to make a move, to control the situation.

She walked towards him, unzipped her tracksuit top and dropped it to the floor. His eyes stayed on hers. She knelt and unfastened her pointe shoes, then stood again and peeled off her legwarmers, pale pink leotard and tights. It surprised her that his attention still remained focused on her eyes, despite the fact that she was now completely naked. 'Did I guess correctly?' She folded her arms across her pert breasts, feeling suddenly vulnerable beneath his glare. At the same time, an incredible wave of arousal washed her body.

Rafique looked at her in silence for a long, long time. Then he moved his eyes slightly, a movement so infinitesimal that Jessica couldn't decide whether he was still looking at her, or at some distant point just over her shoulder. 'Did she guess correctly?'

'No, Master.' Jessica jumped. Caught in the web of Rafique's sexual tension, she had completely forgotten about Foster. As he approached, snaking across the floor, his sneer made her shudder. 'Miss Sharpe,' he grinned, 'I think you misunderstand. The Master brought you here to punish you, not to . . .' He looked her up and down, and chuckled to himself.

Jessica turned to Rafique, distaste twisting her mouth. 'What's he talking about?'

Rafique was silent.

'You broke the Master's rules.' Foster's breath was cold on her neck. 'You must be punished.'

'He's insane.' Jessica leaned away from the butler as if he was a bad smell. 'I haven't done anything wrong.'

Rafique pulled one of Jessica's hands away from her chest and walked her back into the centre of the room. 'You were with Jamie last night, and Alexei this morning.' His voice was so smooth, Jessica wanted to melt it all over her body and then ask him to lick it off. 'It is against the house rules to fraternise in each other's rooms. Foster is right. You must be punished.'

'Foster's lying. I haven't been in anyone's room.'

'That's not what you told Adele.'

Jessica wrenched her hand away from Rafique's, anger sizzling inside her. 'Adele told you I'd broken the rules? The bitch. I don't suppose she told you that she was in Alexei's room this morning, before me?'

'She did, and she has already been punished. I've threatened to take her out of the ballet if she transgresses again.' Patronisingly, he patted her hip. 'But I have something different in mind for you, Jessica.' He winked.

Jessica's mouth opened and closed. She had been right, after all. He did want to fuck her. It was a kinky way of approaching it, but she liked his style. Men were usually so unimaginative.

Rafique smoothed his palm over the bed. 'Lie down.'

Jessica's hands shook as she hoisted herself up on to the strange hammock. With any other man, her natural reaction would have been to refuse, to tease him into distraction then to command him to pleasure her. But Rafique was different. She could not resist, even if she had wanted to. She was not in control here, and it felt strangely thrilling.

The leather was cold on her skin, and Jessica's back arched with the shock as she lay down. With firm, businesslike fingers, Rafique took each of her hands in turn and buckled them into soft leather cuffs above her head. Moving to where her knees dangled over the end of the short bed, he pulled at her legs until her arms straightened and she felt her bottom on the hard edge. He spread her legs, his warm palms pushing against her inner thighs, and he buckled her calves into the leg restraints. The foot-rests were hard and cool. Her pussy was hot, spread open wantonly for Rafique's satisfaction. Jessica raised her head, looking down past her stiff nipples, past the triangle of pale curls that pointed the way to her sex, and into his eyes. 'I think I'm going to enjoy this punishment.'

'I'm sure you will. Although you will try not to.'

'What?' She twisted her head as he walked round to her side. Slowly, like a painter revealing a masterpiece to an expectant audience, Rafique unbuttoned his shirt. Jessica felt an involuntary twitch in one eyebrow as enticing wisps of black hair were revealed, then his dark nipples, then his taut stomach. He was in fantastic shape for a middle-aged man. His caramel skin was as delicious as his voice, appearing darker where it was covered with trails of hair. Jessica sighed with the pure masculinity of him. She couldn't wait to feel that hard, hairy chest, pressing down on to hers. 'What?' she repeated, no longer aware of what she was asking.

Instead of answering, Rafique dropped his shirt over Jessica's face. The little amount of light in the tower was extinguished, and her vision filled with the azure blue of the cotton. It smelled of him, of his faint, spicy cologne, of his musky, exotic maleness. She breathed in deeply.

Two sets of footsteps circled the bed. One came to rest

between her open legs, the other she couldn't tell where. Foster, she concluded, would be staying to watch. The dirty old man. If Rafique hadn't been so stunningly desirable, she might have protested.

Without warning, a finger wiped between her damp labia. It slid easily in her dew.

'You're wet,' Rafique announced.

'Yes,' she whispered.

'You're such a slut, Jessica.' His voice was loaded with sensual disdain.

'Yes,' she agreed.

More footsteps, then a cold finger slipped inside her. She gasped, shocked by the sudden sensation. Her buttocks clenched beneath her.

'You won't tell Jamie about Adele and Alexei, will you?'

Jessica tensed. Her emotions tripped over themselves. Deep inside her belly, a fire burned, lit by the finger probing inside her. But at its flickering edges, ice glittered coldly. What did Adele have to do with this? 'I – I –'

'Jamie doesn't need to know.' Another finger pushed inside her tight vagina.

'What has Adele been saying?'

Rafique's fingers pushed in and out between her swollen, fleshy lips. Jessica squirmed with discomfort and pleasure. 'You upset her, this morning.'

Her head rolled beneath Rafique's shirt as another finger invaded her clutching sex. 'Adele isn't all sweetness and light, you know,' she gasped.

'Oh, I know.'

'Why should you care what she thinks?'

'I've gone to a lot of trouble to arrange this performance. If your behaviour affects her dancing, then it affects me. Now, are you going to tell Jamie, or not?'

A piercing beam of light flashed behind her eyelids.

129

His thumb grazed against her tender clitoris and she cried out in panic as pleasure wrapped her body.

'Well?'

Her breathing was deafening, echoing around beneath her blindfold, but above the rush of oxygen she heard a zip being unfastened. There was a rustle of material, and then something hard and hot was perched between her legs. It rubbed and rubbed remorselessly, and her clitoris stung with longing.

'Well?' he said again. 'What's it to be, Jessica? This . . . ?' He pressed the head of his penis hard against her pouting pussy, '. . . or this?' He was gone. There was nothing there but fierce, throbbing, anxious desire.

'I won't tell him.' Jessica pushed against the foot-rests and thrust her pelvis up towards him. 'Please,' she begged, 'I won't tell, if that's what you want. Just do it, please.'

'Do you promise?' The head of his penis poked inside her. 'Do you swear it?'

'I swear, I promise. I'll do anything, just do it –'

Her voice finished in a gurgle as he stabbed her with his flesh. He wasn't as long as she had expected – in her experience, tall men were usually well-proportioned down below, where it mattered – and his balls felt loose and baggy as they banged against her, but his fingers were skilful at manipulating her clitoris. He grunted like an animal, too, but Jessica was too far gone to care. She beat him to orgasm, her limbs twisting helplessly beneath his dextrous touch. He carried on relentlessly, and by the time he came, his body pumping desperately into hers, he had brought her to a second, rabid climax. As she howled for mercy, her anguished voice was drowned out by a terrible, maniacal laugh. The high-pitched, screaming cackle echoed in the empty tower, and chilled her bubbling passion. It was horrible. Not the sort of noise she would have expected to hear from

Rafique at all. Still, no man, however handsome, was at his most sophisticated in the throes of orgasm.

He withdrew, his laughter gradually calming down. Roughly, he unbuckled her calves and wrists, and flipped her over on to her front. Jessica's breasts flattened and she turned her neck to one side, while he fastened her back into the restraints with urgent fingers. Adjusting his shirt, he ensured her sight was still obscured. His touch was frantic, his breath irregular, and Jessica felt her body swell with pride. This was something Adele had not experienced. A real man. A man with such hunger, he hadn't bothered to stroke her pointed breasts, to kiss or fondle her. All that mattered was her sex, laid open for him between her dangling legs in the most dehumanising, humiliating, and wonderfully exhilarating position.

She moaned, still recovering from her climax, as an icy fingertip trailed over the back of her neck, between her shoulder blades, down her spine. She flinched as he reached her buttocks and ran his touch down her cleft. She had a tight arse. She knew he would appreciate it.

And he did. For what seemed like an hour, he kissed and bit her buttocks, he licked up from her damp sex to between her cheeks and he rimmed her anus with a tongue as fluent as his fingers. She gasped and writhed, pushing her pelvis up from the bed, yearning for him to grab her hips and thrust his prick inside her from behind. She felt dirty, and wanton, and possibly for the first time since she lost her virginity, she felt that circumstances were way beyond her control. The sense of willing abandon made her almost delirious. She burbled incomprehensibly as Rafique's penis, hard again, pushed inside her once more.

His grasp was cold and cruel around her waist. Her entire body trembled in his grip, the muscles at the backs of her thighs pulled sharply with the wideness of her spread legs. Deep inside, an unbearable ache rolled and spread from the sticky walls of her vagina, up through every vein and artery. Then suddenly, it stopped.

'Don't stop,' she moaned, as his short penis withdrew until only its tip paused inside her. 'Don't stop now, please, don't stop.'

There was a whip of material through the air, and Rafique's shirt was pulled away from her face. Shocked, wondering what the hell the butler was up to, Jessica lifted her head.

Her face wrinkled in stubborn disbelief. Rafique was behind her, his penis throbbing in her vagina, his hands tight around her waist. So how could he also be here, standing at her head, smiling?

The muscles of her face collapsed. It was disgusting, too foul to contemplate. 'Get him off me,' she hissed. 'You bastard. Get him off me now, or I'll scream.'

'No one will hear you.' He crouched in front of her. 'Besides, a minute ago, you were enjoying yourself. Why should it change now? What difference does it make, which one of us fucks you?'

'Was it you, the first time?' Her breath faltered and her voice came out in a whisper. She already knew the answer.

'I don't find you the least bit attractive, Jessica. But Foster does.' He stood up again and bent over to whisper in her ear. 'He hasn't had any for years. I bet he could keep going for hours.' He looked up, over her prone body, and nodded.

'No!' she screamed, as Foster rammed inside her. She tugged at her handcuffs, chafing her wrists on the ancient leather, throwing daggers at Rafique with her eyes. Foster thrust again. 'No,' she reiterated, but her voice, along with her resolve, was already weakening. Behind her, Foster reached between her legs, and pressed around the swollen button of her clitoris. Miniature shards of lightning showered her mind and flooded her limbs with electricity. She tried to fight, but her body was falling, sinking through the leather hammock, through the floor, through the earth far below and into another dimension. She was floating away, her disgust overwhelmed by the magic of Foster's clammy fingers. 'No,' she pleaded, as his penis pumped aggressively and his fingers rubbed, no longer pleading with him, but with herself. She didn't want to enjoy it. She just couldn't help herself. Her face slapped back down on to the bed in surrender. She closed her eyes in shame.

'No,' she gasped, her body quivering in contradiction.

Chapter Seven

Someone had slunk in while Adele dozed in the bath, and filled her body with helium. When she emerged from the steaming, sunken tub, she seemed to float around the bedroom. Exhaustion had drained from her tired limbs and left her feeling buoyant, her body light, and her mind empty of worry. It was, without a doubt, the most satisfying rehearsal she had ever attended.

After Jessica had been summoned by Foster, a weight had lifted from Adele's shoulders. Alexei, still smarting from her slap, had been almost subdued, and Adele, freed from tension, had danced with passion and excitement. The steps had begun to flow from her body, and both Jamie and Richard had noticed the difference. At the end, Adele had thanked Jamie for his partnering, a polite balletic tradition as sacred as saying 'break a leg' before a performance.

'That felt good, didn't it?' he suggested, rubbing the sweat from his face. He still looked slightly bewildered. No doubt he was wondering what had gone on between her and Alexei, but the hurt in his eyes had been replaced by admiration once again. 'It's coming together, all of a sudden.'

'Yes,' Adele had smiled. Fluffs from his towel had caught on his light stubble. 'It felt easier today.'

'Well done.' Richard had patted her on the bottom on her way out of the theatre. 'I don't know what Rafique said to you, but it worked.' Adele had smiled again. Richard would never believe that the place beneath his hand had been invaded during his rehearsal. She itched to tell him, it would be so gratifying to see his unshockable face change.

She didn't need a towel. The warm air curling through the balcony doors was enough to dry her skin as she stood in front of the mirror and studied herself. Really studied, remembering the things Rafique had told her. He had said she was beautiful; she still wasn't sure, but she felt it, which was a start. Her breasts were certainly pretty, full and pert, and the softness of her areolae was incredible as she hesitantly ringed them with the tips of her forefingers. She smoothed her hands into the dip of her waist and over the curve of her hips. Jessica was right, Adele's costume would never fit her, but Adele was happy to admit it. Jessica may have been the perfect shape for a ballerina, with her androgynously narrow hips and her long, spindly legs, but for once Adele was glad of her curves. She had a woman's body, a woman's arse, and Rafique liked it. For the first time in years, Adele didn't want to be Jessica. She wasn't at all sure that she would want to be Jessica ever again.

Turning her back she bowed, looking over her shoulder at her reflection, looking for the view the Master had so enjoyed that afternoon. Surrounded by tight curls, her pussy lips glistened seductively and her clitoris hid shyly. Her tiny anus showed no sign of Rafique's plundering. Lightly, Adele fingered its puckered rim, delighting in its sensitivity. It must be wonderful, she thought, to be a man. To enjoy the gentleness of a woman's flesh, to feel it contrast with hard masculinity. To stroke, and pinch, to tease and plunder the interminable softness, to feel a woman's body relenting. It must be wonderful to stretch a woman's secret tightness, to feel her pliant, living flesh close around him, to see her shudder in the throes of ecstasy. Almost as wonderful as being a woman.

She faced the mirror again. Running the tip of a finger between the curled edges of her labia, Adele wasn't surprised to find them damp – not from the bath, but from the thought of Rafique's exotically handsome face, his rich voice coating her in its soothing syrup. In her eyes, there was a steadfastness, a confidence she had never noticed before. Rafique had done that. He was the most amazing man she had ever met. Forceful and domineering, fiercely lustful, and yet, behind it all, behind the games, he seemed to care. Like a strict but dedicated teacher, he was leading her by the hand through some very unorthodox lessons. Adele sighed in gratitude, praising his efforts as she rolled her emerging bud between her fingers. She longed for her next class.

But she didn't know when that would be. By the time Adele had gone upstairs, Jessica had still not returned from wherever Foster had taken her, and she hoped that Rafique was keeping his word. Although he had set out to 'take care' of Jessica, he could easily have been side-tracked by her good looks. She knew it was irrational to want a monopoly on him, but she also knew it was intolerable to think of Jessica receiving one of his 'punishments'.

She would take her mind off the sickening thought and use up the hours until dinner with a walk. It was a glorious evening. A slight breeze caressed the tree tops, cooling their leaves as they reached for the sun. Birdsong heralded the dusk, calling for its soft curtain to settle over the Manor's grounds and lessen the heat. From her balcony, Adele could see the lake, shimmering in a haze of multi-coloured plumage. To match the splendour of the evening, she slipped on a summer dress she had hardly ever worn. It wasn't really her style, being short and flimsy and clingy, but the colour had drawn her to it in the shop. A deep, bluish purple, it didn't blend with her eyes or her hair, and the contrast was startling. Adele had packed it when she went on tour and on holiday, and had often retrieved it hopefully from her wardrobe, but had never yet found the guts to wear it. Tonight was different. Tonight, her mood matched the dramatic colour.

Pulling a clean pair of knickers from the drawer, she hesitated for a moment before returning them. There was no hope of disguising a bra beneath the thin straps of her dress, and the sensation of her breasts beneath the cotton was liberating. Why wear knickers? Why not feel the breeze kiss between her legs, feel her body, barely separated from nature? She had never gone without underwear before. The idea was enticing. And what would it matter if the breeze lifted the skirt of her dress? There would be no one outside to see. Alexei and Jamie were doing some weight training with Richard in the theatre. Carmen and Nadia were watching and no doubt salivating. Jessica was, hopefully, being put in her place.

The hallway was as cold and quiet as ever, and as she heaved at the oak door it was like stepping from death, back into life. The warmth inexplicably brought goose-bumps to her clean skin, and she smiled and stretched her arms to the sun as its heat enveloped her body. On days like these, it felt so good to be alive.

Turning left, she took the path towards a section of the woods which was much sparser and less forbidding than the part she had already explored at the other side of the Manor. The trees here were taller and spaced more widely, as if each was aloof and reluctant to touch the next. Thick rays of sunlight pooled on to the mossy carpet, and Adele took off her sandals to feel its green-ness spring beneath her toes. She could see everything.

As if she had regained her sight, she noticed each blade of grass, each leaf, each piece of bark. She marvelled at the details; tiny, dun-coloured mushrooms pushing their way through the soil, beetles with iridescent backs, the luscious brush of a red squirrel's tail as it effortlessly scaled a tree. Things which would have made her cringe were suddenly beautiful, awesome in their complexity: a spider, crouching in its intricate web; a hairy caterpillar, dangling from a leaf; a frayed and bloody bird's wing, ripped and then discarded by some sharp-toothed, ferocious creature. It was all part of the unstoppable circle of life, tiny links in nature's chain, and she was part of it. She stood in a circle of light, turning around and absorbing all the wonders of the wood's microcosm of existence. She felt as organic as the earth. She also felt the need to pee.

Putting down her shoes she crouched, holding her dress up around her hips. Heat streamed from her body into the ground, and Adele watched as her bladder emptied. It felt natural, sensual, to urinate into the dark soil, and as she relieved herself she dropped a hand between her legs. Her clitoris was stiff again, its dome poking from her bush like the mushrooms in the forest. A gasp escaped from her lips as she felt it tingle beneath her fingers. She was ready, so ready.

Barely avoiding the sodden circle of earth, she flung herself down, prostrating herself beneath the trees. Small twigs scratched her skin and through her dress, she could feel things moving; grass, perhaps, crumpling beneath her weight, or insects struggling to escape. Whatever, she didn't care. Her dress lay over her stomach, which was taut and rumbling with sexual hunger. Her knees were spread wantonly, and without a moment's hesitation, she plunged a finger between the silken lips of her pussy.

Closing her eyes, she pressed her head into the ground and raised her hips. She spread her juice around the tiny protrusion of her clitoris and felt it throb deep within her. With the lightest touch she flickered around the centre of her pleasure, brushing over its raw tip, aware of the uncontrollable jerks jumping like electric shocks from her sex and along her arm. Already, she felt an orgasm building inside her, and she held her breath as it gathered force in her belly.

If she hadn't been holding her breath, she would never have heard it. Her blood turned to ice. Too scared to open her eyes, she waited and listened, her fingers still, her heart thumping.

There it was again. Unmistakeable, deep and slow, the sound of breathing. Then, a hesitant footstep accompanied by a faint rustling. Someone was watching her.

Her body thawed a little at the thought that it could be Rafique. He would be delighted to find her masturbating, lying like a wild woman with her hair strewn across the forest floor. But what if it wasn't him? It couldn't possibly be Carmen and Nadia – they could never have approached silently. Alexei, Jamie and Richard were training. That left Jessica. If it was her, Adele thought, she would sacrifice herself to the earth and happily allow it to swallow her whole. She sat up, and turned to look.

A raucous cackle echoed through the trees, attacking Adele from every direction, and she started to her feet. Disorientated, she ran blindly forward, unsure whether she was heading towards or away from the blood-curdling laughter. Coordination deserted her, and it became impossible to simultaneously run, breathe, sweat and see the way. Stumbling, she ignored the sudden pain at her knee and scrambled onwards, desperately seeking an escape from the demonic noise reverberating through the maze of her brain. Just as she realised that she recognised the sound, the ground fell away, and she tripped down a steep bank. Everything went into slow motion as she abandoned herself to the fall.

'Miss! Are you all right?'

Adele looked up dizzily. The vision that met her was one of such natural beauty that it immediately calmed her. A gentle waterfall tumbled playfully into a clear deep pool, before trickling onwards through a gently gushing stream. Sunlight sparkled on the water, and kissed the skin of the two bathers. Half-submerged, the strong contours of their flesh rippled and glistened, and Adele found it hard to decide which was the most handsome; the horse, nostrils flaring, thick tail flicking through the water, or Joe, droplets careening over his luscious body. Both had turned as her arrival had broken their peace.

Joe waded towards Adele until the sharp ridges which pointed the way to his penis were visible above the water. Youth had so far left his chest completely smooth, but a faint trail of brown hair clung downwards from his navel. As Adele tried not to look, his dark eyes took in her bare feet, her heaving chest and the panic which must have still lingered on her face. It took him a moment to recognise her from the pub. 'Are you hurt, miss?'

'I don't think so.' Slowly, Adele gathered her senses and carefully got to her feet. 'My knee feels a bit sore, though.'

'Let me have a look.' He began to rise from the water then stopped. 'You'll have to turn your back, miss, I – I've nothing on.'

Reluctantly, she turned. The rub of a towel was followed by the rasp of material being pulled on to damp skin. Then his hand touched her shoulder. Joe averted his eyes as Adele looked up at him. He knelt at her feet and with gentle fingers, touched all around her kneecap, asking where it hurt. 'It's just a graze,' he concluded. 'No harm done. Why were you running?'

Lost in the sight of his bare torso, his muscular legs encased in tight jodhpurs and shiny black, close-fitting

140

calf-length boots, Adele had to remind herself that moments ago, she had been scared witless. 'Didn't you hear it?' She glanced over her shoulder. Beneath the grassy bank, she couldn't see the forest, only the tops of the trees looming into her vision like giants' heads peering curiously over the horizon.

'I didn't hear anything.' Joe stood, looking to the horse for confirmation. 'Neither did he, and he's got better hearing than I have.' Shyly, Joe glanced at Adele through his thick eyelashes. 'What exactly did you hear?'

'It was horrible, someone was watching me. I heard them breathing and then they laughed at me. It was awful, awful laughter. I ran and ran, but it seemed to follow me. It seemed to get louder. You really didn't hear it?'

Joe shook his head. 'It was probably the succubus.'

Adele had been dreading his saying that, even though she already knew that it was the demon who had chased her from the woods. 'You really believe she exists?'

'I've seen her.' Joe ran his fingers through his damp, chestnut hair. 'I saw her last night, up at the house.'

An almost imperceptible shudder racked Adele's neck as she remembered her own vision last night. 'What did you see?' she whispered.

'It was terrible. Terrible.' His eyes turned glassy at the memory. 'I've told the Master, he should get the Manor exorcised. It isn't right, sharing your house with evil.' Shaking his head in disbelief, Joe turned away from Adele and walked towards the stallion as he stepped out of the pool. Lazily, the handsome beast shook the water from its mane and tail. Joe bent over one of its forelegs, stroking it with a firm hand, silently bidding it to lift its foot. Fastidiously, he picked out the small pebbles that had become lodged in the horse's shoe from the bed of the pool. 'The Master's a good man,' he said, as he moved around to the horse's hind legs, 'but he's in the grip of that devil. I've seen it in his eyes.'

Adele was barely listening. Joe's arse was so splendid she longed to touch it. Trailing behind him, she wondered what he would do if she put a hand to the stretch of his jodhpurs, rimmed his anus through the pale fabric, gently poked a fingertip inside him. Slowly, she lifted her hand.

Joe straightened up and moved round to the horse's majestic head. 'I've seen it in the horses' eyes, too. The succubus can possess anyone, you know. Anyone, or anything.'

Adele moved beside him. She raised a hand to stroke the horse's beautiful, black head but it flinched and made her jump.

'He doesn't know you.' Joe soothed the animal with a strange mixture of grunting and sighing. 'You have to show respect and humility,' he advised. 'Don't make eye contact until he lets you. Tilt your head away from his.'

Adele did as she was told, looking down at Joe's boots. Gradually, a patch of skin on her cheek grew warmer as the stallion sniffed at her.

'He wants to talk to you. Slowly turn to face him, but don't raise your eyes yet. Breathe into his nostrils.'

Tentatively, Adele turned, her head bowed respectfully. She breathed out gently through her nose, watching the horse's nostrils flare. He answered her breath with his own, and for a moment they held a strange, wordless conversation.

'He likes you,' Joe assured. 'You've shown him respect, and now he respects you. You can look at him now.'

Hesitantly, Adele raised her head. Looking deep into one of the stallion's black eyes, she realised that there was recognition there, communion between human and beast. It took her breath away.

'You can touch him if you want, but do it slowly.'

With the back of her hand, she stroked one long

cheekbone. Content, the horse closed his eyes and nodded.

'That's amazing,' Adele gasped. 'Where did you learn all that?'

'I didn't have to learn it, I've always known it.' Joe caressed the horse's other cheekbone, smiling shyly over its nose at Adele. 'Ever since I was a child, I preferred horses to people. I've always been able to speak their language.'

'Are you related to Doctor Dolittle?'

Joe's thick brow furrowed. 'I never knew my family,' he said, in all earnestness. 'I was abandoned as a baby. The gypsies brought me up.'

'Oh. I'm sorry.'

'Don't be.' He moved alongside the horse, gently combing its tousled, damp mane with his fingers. 'I had a wonderful childhood. The only thing I missed out on was an education, but Rafique saw to that.'

'How?'

'He caught me trying to steal one of his horses. I was fourteen, and could barely read or write. He offered me a job as his groom, on the condition that I took lessons as well.' His chest puffed with pride. 'Within a year, I was better than the Master at algebra.'

It didn't surprise Adele. Despite his shyness, Joe had the ease of the intelligent. 'So, you're happy here? You enjoy your job?'

'I love it. The Master pays me well, I have everything I need and I get to ride the horses every day.'

'I've never ridden.' Riding was another of those pastimes, like skating and skiing, that Adele had eschewed in case of getting injured. But now, now that she felt a bond with this animal, she longed to sit astride its powerful back, to feel it move beneath her. 'Is it difficult?'

'You're a dancer, aren't you? It would be easy for you. You should already have good balance and rhythm.'

'Will you take me riding, Joe?'

He hesitated, but politeness overruled his shyness. 'Certainly, miss.'

'Joe, you can call me Adele.'

For a second, he made eye contact. 'We'll have to go back to the stables and get him tacked up, miss.' He set off with long, purposeful strides. Adele ran to catch up. She touched his forearm and he stopped.

'Aren't you going to bring ... what's his name?'

Joe looked down at her with enforced patience, as if she were a child. 'Horses don't have names, miss. And he'll only follow us if he wants to. If he doesn't, we'll ride another horse.'

In that moment, Joe forgot his bashfulness and looked right into Adele's eyes. And in that same moment, Adele knew without any doubt that she was going to take his virginity.

The barn smelled warm with straw that had been baked in the sun. There was room for ten horses, but because of the heat, they were grazing outside and every stable was empty. The stallion followed Joe and Adele inside, walking through one of the open stable doors and waiting expectantly. Joe smiled as Adele joined the horse, and it nuzzled at her neck.

'Well, I think he's decided. He wants you to ride him. I've never seen him so keen.' He patted the animal's broad back. 'He can't go if he's still wet, though. He'll catch a cold.'

Adele watched anxiously. They had passed a white mare and a young, leggy chestnut on the long walk to the stable, and both had looked up with interest. But Adele had her heart set on the stallion. She knew it was probably foolish, to want such a huge, powerful beast for her first ride, but something about the flash of its dark eyes, the way it held its proud head, reminded her of Rafique. She no longer wanted to play safe. She wanted this horse, and she wanted Joe behind her, his body close to hers.

Pronouncing him thoroughly dry, Joe proceeded to tack up. The metal buckles clanked as he lifted a wide, black leather saddle from a rack on one wall, and gently positioned it on the horse's back. The muscles in his own bare back flexed and pulled as he fastened the girth strap, and his smooth shoulders shone with perspiration. Next he held a bit to the horse's snout, letting him sniff it until he decided to open his mouth and allow himself to be harnessed. Pulling the leather halter over the horse's head, Joe made tiny adjustments to the fastenings around its ears and jaw, until he was sure it was happy. Adele watched Joe's handsome young body as he worked, and she cursed at the wastefulness of his discomfort around her. He kept sneaking glances at her, his eyes furtively flickering over the pert mounds of her breasts, which were easily discernible beneath her flimsy dress. He wanted her, and yet when she met his eyes and smiled, he blushed furiously. When she nonchalantly brushed past him in the narrow stable, and her nipples touched his back on the way, he flinched as if she had hit him. Looking down, Adele found her dress faintly streaked with his sweat, and the tips of her breasts stiff with excitement. She laughed, sure that she could see the beginning of a bulge in the crotch of Joe's jodhpurs, praying he would lose control and push her down on to the hay. Instead, he moved around the stable, putting the horse between himself and Adele for safety.

'Ready, m – m – miss,' he stammered, the colour of his cheeks deepening from red to a shade that almost matched the colour of her dress. 'Oh, hold on, though.' Joe looked perplexed. 'I haven't got a hat to give you. I never wear one, but you should.'

'You'll be sitting behind me, won't you?' Adele looked up at him, widening her eyes innocently.

145

'Well, yes, but still –'

'I trust you Joe. You won't let anything happen to me.'

'This horse has a mind of his own. Anything could happen, and I might not be able to save you.'

Adele dismissed the image of Jessica dancing in her place from her mind. Reaching up, she rested a hand on the horse's long neck. 'I trust him too.' She held Joe's gaze until he was forced to blink nervously. 'Now, give me a leg up.'

Outside, the horse stood patiently while Joe explained to Adele what she should and should not do. Then he gently cradled one of her shins and effortlessly hoisted her up into the saddle. Adele looked down at him, an excited grin on her face. It wasn't until she saw his expression, the telltale colour on his strong cheekbones, the quiver in his bottom lip, that she remembered her lack of underwear. Joe had caught a glimpse of her bare buttocks, and it had thrown him off balance. He stared up at her, his mouth open with shock.

'Come on,' Adele urged, patting the saddle behind her. She was certain he would have reneged if he dared, but his politeness was stronger than his shyness and a moment later, he hooked his boot into a stirrup and sat himself behind Adele. The saddle was just big enough for the two of them, its dip pushing their bodies together, and Adele wriggled at the feel of his torso pressing against her back. Beneath her, the horse felt so warm and strong; behind her, an equally powerful beast radiated his heat through her body. She barely listened as he instructed her.

'You can hold the reins. Like this.' He reached around her and threaded the leather straps through her fingers. 'Keep your hands relaxed. Don't pull, but hold the reins tightly enough to feel a link with his mouth. That's how you tell him where to go and what to do.' He weighed her wrists, demonstrating what he meant. 'I'll keep my feet in the stirrups because you've no shoes on. Hook your legs under mine if you feel unsteady. Whatever you do, don't press your heels into his sides, because that will make him think you want to go faster. I'll control the speed. Happy, miss?'

'Very.'

At that, Joe clicked his tongue and the horse moved into a gentle walk.

It was a strange feeling, but at the same time it felt so natural. Adele's hips tilted slightly with each stride, her body swaying with the rhythm. A tangible link flowed between her touch on the reins and the horse's soft mouth, and despite the latent power of the animal between her thighs, Adele felt on balance, in command. It was fun to be so high up, almost mesmerising to listen to the soft, rhythmic thud of the hooves on the grass, to feel the muscles flexing in the horse's sides, the hairs brushing against her legs. She sighed contentedly.

'Are you all right?' Joe asked. 'Would you like to go into a trot?'

'OK.' She would have tried showjumping, if he'd offered.

'Try and weigh yourself down in the saddle. Don't fight the rhythm, go with it.'

At some unseen signal, the stallion picked up the pace. Lifting its forelegs, it began to trot with long, elegant steps. Caught off guard, Adele bounced around jerkily before sinking into the movement's swing. Then, all of a sudden, she was in tune with the animal again. Unable to stifle a small cry as her naked clitoris rubbed against the saddle, she felt Joe tense behind her.

'What's wrong?'

'Hold on to me, Joe.'

Strong hands hesitantly slid around her waist. Joe's shoulders pressed closer to Adele's and she could feel his skin on hers. It was intoxicating, and she wanted more.

Disobeying his instructions, she gently squeezed with

her heels. As she had hoped and suspected, the horse's breath quickened, and with an arrogant flick of its black mane, it lengthened its stride into a langorous, rolling canter.

'Miss, what are you doing? I said not to –'

'It's all right, Joe, I'm not scared. Just hold me tighter.'

As the Manor loomed in the distance, Joe hooked his right arm across her taut belly. His other hand held one of hers, steering away from the house, controlling the animal with gentle pulls on the reins. Adele's consciousness honed itself into peaks of intense, tactile pleasure; the lilting motion between her legs, the breeze in her hair, the unmistakeable bulge rubbing against her cleft, the sensation of his hand, slipping upwards with every hoof beat, moving away from her waist and inexorably approaching the underside of her breast. She squeezed with the full length of her legs, harder this time. In response, the horse whinnied and shook its head, pulling at the reins, shortening and quickening its steps until it reached a gallop. Fear stung Adele's senses as the ground blurred beneath them, but on top of the alarming speed, over and above the realisation that they were no longer in control, Adele felt arousal flooding her body. Joe was gripping her firmly in the crook of his arm, but he was not thinking of safety. With his palm over her racing heart, his forefinger and thumb were advantageously positioned so that with every fall of the horse's weight, the lower swell of Adele's breast bounced on to his hand. Danger dissolved, and despite the relentless, rapid approach of the Manor's grey stonework, Adele could think of nothing but his touch.

'Whoa, there. Whoa, boy.' Joe released Adele from his forearm and squeezed on the reins with both hands, steering them away from the Manor just as they reached the building's shadow. Gradually, as if to remind them that he had a will of his own, the black stallion calmed the pace back to a walk, shaking his head and snorting excitedly before stopping altogether. Swinging himself to the ground, Joe held out his arms for Adele to do the same.

'What on earth were you doing, miss?' Running his fingers through his thick forelock, he shook his head reproachfully. 'You've no shoes, no hat. If you'd been thrown, he could have trampled you to death.'

'It was fun,' she grinned mischievously. 'What on earth were you doing?'

'Sorry, miss, I don't know –'

'Don't pretend you don't know what I'm talking about. You were touching me.'

Joe's mouth flapped soundlessly.

'You were touching me here.'

His eyes widened as she raised a hand to cup her breast. 'I – I'm sorry, miss. It's just that, you're so lovely, and I – I've never been so close to a woman before. I'm sorry. I'm so sorry.'

Adele took a step towards him, and reached for his hand. 'It's all right, Joe. I liked it.'

Amazement replaced the fright on his face. 'You did?'

In reply, Adele lifted his fingers to her breast. Stunned, Joe's hand was frozen for a moment before he swallowed loudly and his fingers softened to her shape. A gasp of surprise flew from his lips as his body took over from his mind, and a look of confused gratitude lit his eyes as he spread his touch over the sensitive swell. Watching his hand as he moulded Adele's soft flesh, he breathed in long sighs of pleasure. He squeezed and kneaded, and rimmed her engorged areola with the side of his thumb. Power surged through Adele's body as she saw his instincts take control.

'Kiss me,' she commanded. She pushed his face away as his mouth bowed to hers. 'Not there.' She pushed the fine straps from her sun-kissed shoulders and let the scoop of her dress fall beneath her breasts. 'Kiss me here.'

Adele arched her upper back. Her nipples pouted provocatively, swollen and pink, and still soft around their pointed peaks. Joe stood mesmerised for what seemed an eternity. When he spoke, he addressed the tip of one breast.

'What if someone sees?' His voice was unsteady. He gestured vaguely towards the Manor.

Adele looked at the building. The stallion had halted at the edge of the woods behind the house, but still, they would be easily visible to anyone staring from the dark windows. 'What if they do? I don't care,' she shrugged. 'Of course, if you don't want me . . .' She went to pull her dress back on.

Joe stopped her with a quick hand. 'Don't.'

'Kiss me, then.'

He had been holding on to the reins with his free hand. He let go, and the horse wandered off and began to nibble at the grass. Joe's head dipped and his handsome mouth pursed around a tender areola. Carried away on a tide of sudden greed, he pulled at Adele's soft breast, opening his lips wide, feeding on her skin. She cradled his head in her gentle hands, watching with pride as if he was her baby, suckling for milk. He switched his attention to her other breast, and Adele touched the dampness he had left with quivering fingers. Distracted by the sight of her fondling herself, Joe's mouth hovered for a moment. Adele cupped her other mound, lifting her engorged nipple towards his face to tempt him back. Then she pressed her breasts together and he darted between their dark tips, moaning quietly, unable to decide which was the sweetest. An idea as tempting as chocolate flashed across Adele's brain.

She knelt, pulling Joe with her to the ground. Shuffling her knees between his, she sat down, unzipped his jodphurs and with a small cry of delight at finding that Joe too, had no underwear on, she unleashed his penis. She felt his eyes, anxiously watching hers for a reaction.

'Beautiful,' she whispered, stroking his silken length. His hot prick tensed and reared under her touch.

She lay down and beckoned him on top of her. Following the urgent signals she gave him, he planted his hands either side of her face, and tentatively lowered his pelvis. Reaching around his forearm, Adele guided his long stem until it nestled in her cleavage. Then she pressed her breasts together, enveloping him in her twin mounds of flesh. Above her, she saw his stomach tense, and she heard him gasp. Slowly, he began to rock his body.

Adele strained her neck to watch the purple head of Joe's penis emerge at the top of her deep, exaggerated cleavage. It was long enough to reach her mouth, and she licked her lips and formed a pout to welcome its weeping tip each time he thrust. She flickered her tongue over him, making him groan and shudder above her, and she added her moans to his by pinching her nipples, hard. Arousal flooded Adele's pussy as any sign of Joe's bashfulness was swallowed up by his rampant lust, and he began to fuck her breasts. The neat sacs of his balls banged against her as he slid between her curves and he pushed harder, reaching further for her mouth with every jerk of his hips.

He came quickly and loudly, dribbling his juices over her lips and throat, spilling creamy droplets on her breasts.

'Oh God.' He slumped on to the grass beside Adele and sat up with his head in his hands. 'Oh God, oh God.'

Adele rolled over and knelt at his side, soothing him with a hand on his sweaty neck. 'What's the matter, Joe? Didn't you like that?'

Anguish creased his brow when he turned to look at her. 'What have I done? What have you done to me? It's not right, I hardly know you.'

'What does that matter?' She squeezed the hard ridge of muscle stretching from his neck to his shoulder.

'It's not right, to feel like this about you.' He looked doleful, lost.

'To feel like what, Joe?' Adele touched his open lips. Her touch wandered over the lump of his Adam's apple, over his hairless chest, over his stomach and beneath his spent penis. 'Tell me how you feel.' She delved for his balls. They felt warm and heavy. His breath faltered as she squeezed.

'I want you.' There was helplessness in his whisper. 'I want to feel you here.' Cautiously, he pressed his fingertips to Adele's dress where it covered her aching pussy.

Adele smiled in sultry invitation. 'Fuck me, then.'

Joe shook his head, but did not remove his hand. 'I can't,' he said, sadly. 'I – I – I've never been with a woman.' He lowered his chin in shame. 'I'm scared.'

'Of what?'

'Of making a fool of myself.' His voice was barely audible. 'I wouldn't know how to please you. You'd laugh at me.'

Adele started in recognition of herself, at his age. He was so handsome, and so afraid. Years of ogling models in magazines had distanced Joe from the opposite sex, put them on a pedestal way out of reach. He needed someone sympathetic to show him that women existed in three dimensions, that they were flesh and blood like him, and not just glossy pictures. He needed a teacher.

'I'll show you what to do.' She lifted his jaw and raised his gaze to hers. 'I'll show you how to make me happy.'

Adele dropped her hand on top of Joe's, lightly pressing it to her sex. His eyes locked with hers, and as she lifted her bottom from her heels, kneeling up in front of him, he knelt to face her. Eager astonishment took over his face.

'But first, you must clean up this mess.' She lowered her eyes to the patches of creamy white staining her upper body. Pulling at Joe's neck, she brought his lips to her neck. Willingly, he licked up every drop, lapping

152

over her throat, her cleavage, her pouting breasts. When he was done, Adele released him from her grasp. He stared at her, waiting expectantly.

Widening her knees, Adele took Joe's hand. She moved it beneath her dress and up the inside of her thigh. She saw his dark brows twitch as she lifted his fingers between her legs. Joe drew in an urgent breath.

Guiding his touch, she moved his fingertips along the fleshy edges of her labia. She gasped softly and blinked slowly as Joe narrowed his brown eyes in amazed concentration. Out of sight, beneath the cover of her skirt, he was discovering the interminable, inviting softness of a woman for the very first time, and it showed in a multitude of emotions on his young face.

Curiosity increased the pressure of his fingers and Adele withdrew her hand. Joe slid his palm on to her vulva, and her sex lips kissed damply at his skin. For an age, he held still, and Adele began to wonder whether he was immovable with shock.

'Touch me, Joe,' she reminded.

He jumped, and began to knead her sex as if he was squeezing an orange.

'Not like that.' Adele raised her hand to his mouth. 'Softly, like this.'

She rubbed her fingertip in the slight gap between his lips. He followed her guidance, and the faint flutter of a butterfly's wings made her thighs quiver. She poked a finger into Joe's mouth; between her legs, he followed suit, and they sighed in unison as Adele's inner flesh sucked at his. Slowly, Adele moved her finger in and out of Joe's mouth, feeling the warm wetness of his tongue as he felt the warm wetness of her pussy. A second finger joined the first, and it was Adele's turn to freeze. Her hand hovered, motionless, as Joe's fingers found some primitive, urgent rhythm. Her muscles melted in the heat spreading over her body, her neck rolled and she caught sight of Joe's penis, rearing towards her again.

Joe slid a third finger inside her, and as he did so, his thumb brushed tantalisingly against the throb of her clitoris. Adele shuddered with the impact, making Joe pause in concern.

'Did I do something wrong? Did I hurt you?'

'The place you touched just then, Joe, that's the – oh God, that's the way to make a woman happy.'

His thumb flickered around. 'There?' His face leant expectantly towards hers. 'There?'

She answered with a long, helpless groan. He found the spot, the centre from which he could hold her body in blissful suspension, and with the naive keenness of the inexperienced, he proceeded to rub her little bud ferociously. Too close to her climax to calm his pace, all Adele could do was drop one hand to his. Beneath the soft cotton of her dress, his thumb circled, his hand pumped inside her, drawing out the essence of her being. She raised her other hand to her breast, and Joe covered it with his free hand, rolling her protruding nipple, producing a line of ecstatic pain to link her areola to the epicentre of her pleasure below. Adele felt her breasts shake as she came. Fighting the urge to tightly close her eyes and fall into oblivion, she watched Joe, watching her. Breathless and unable to take any more, she eased his touch away from her trembling body.

'Was that . . . was that an orgasm?'

She nodded weakly. Confused and amazed, Joe stared at his glistening fingers. 'That was incredible. I'm so wet.' Unleashed from any self-consciousness, he sniffed his fingers. 'You smell wonderful.' He rolled his tongue over his skin. 'You taste wonderful.'

'I feel wonderful.' She caressed his burning cheek.

Slowly, Joe looked up. There was a change in his eyes now, a dark fierceness, a longing that would not be denied. 'I want to fuck you.' He pushed her hand away impatiently. 'I want to fuck you, now.'

Behind Adele, hairy lips kissed her shoulder. Curious nostrils sniffed at her skin. She laughed. 'I think he's jealous.' Getting to her feet, she kissed the horse's black snout. 'Let's go for another ride.'

'No.' Joe stood up. Adele hooked a foot into the cold metal stirrup and heaved herself up on to the stallion's back. Beneath her, Joe looked like a truculent child. 'I want to fuck you,' he whined, fiddling nervously with his angry penis.

'Let's ride, first.' Adele took her feet from the stirrups and shifted forward to make room on the saddle.

'No.'

Adele felt her heart quicken as she held the hem of her dress in her fingers. With one swift pull, it was over her head. Rolling it up, she stuffed it under the front of the saddle.

Joe seemed to lose control of his face. One eye blinked, his mouth opened and closed and his breath rushed noisily from his aquiline nose. His eyebrows alternately raised and furrowed. His gaze drifted erratically from the stripe of golden hair at her pussy, to the cleft of her buttocks, to her belly and breasts and back again.

'Come on, Joe.' Adele ran her hands over her breasts, tweaking her nipples provocatively. 'I want to go for a ride.'

Without another second's hesitation, he swung himself up behind her.

Adele held the reins again as the horse followed the path into the woods. But this time, Joe's touch wasn't hesitant. His fingers roamed all over, greedily mauling her buttocks, her spread thighs, her jutting breasts. While one hand fondled, another moved around her hip and combed her pubic hair, finding the tender nub of Adele's clitoris and making her cry out. He grabbed voraciously at her body, biting her neck, pressing his turgid prick into her cleft as if it was a warning. The horse's gentle rhythm produced an enticing rub which was obviously driving Joe insane, as it was Adele. She felt a drop of moisture in one of the dimples at the base of her spine.

It was time, she thought. She wanted him now, with his desire at boiling point. She wanted a handsome beast beneath her legs and another between. She wanted his eager passion to fill her up.

Looping the reins around her wrists, Adele leaned foward and put her arms around the horse's neck. His mane was itchy on her face but she didn't care. All she could think about, as she arched her lower back and lifted her pelvis, was that Joe would be able to see her anus, her clitoris, and her pussy, shining with dew. He would be able to see the complex delicacy of a woman's sex, and he would want to ram his simple, masculine hardness deep inside.

'Can you see that, Joe?' She tilted her hips up and down with tiny, seductive humping movements. 'Can you see my pussy? Can you see how ready I am?'

A finger slipped inside her. 'You're so wet,' he murmured incredulously.

'That's because I want you, Joe. I want you to fuck me, now. I want to ride your beautiful cock.'

Heavy hands pressed at Adele's hips, holding her still while the velvet head of his penis nudged at her open sex. Then he was inside her, his full, excruciating length buried in her soul, searing against her nerve endings. He pumped with slow, deliberate strokes, stretching her pussy muscles, making them twitch and spasm around him. He grunted and must have pressed with his legs, because the horse began once again to trot.

Adele was helpless, a prisoner to the rhythm. Her clitoris banged on the saddle, making her whimper with ecstatic pain. She could smell the horse's hair, feel its neck straining as she held on tightly. If she hadn't been anchored to Joe, she could easily have fallen from the horse. With the reins twisted around her wrists, she would have been dragged along like a limp rag doll until he stopped. But Joe held her in the vice of his fingers. He matched the horse's pace, thrusting with hunger, forcing himself further and further into the heaven of her sex. As if a phial of precious fluid had been spilled within her, Adele felt stickiness flooding her senses, overflowing from every orifice and coating Joe's penis in musk. As he held her still for the final assault, her raw clitoris rubbed against the unyielding leather. Her pleading scream mingled with Joe's agonised groan. The two sounds twisted together, and twirled like smoke up through the trees, towards the sky.

At that moment, the forest echoed with another sound; eerie, menacing and gleeful, they heard the laughter that had chased Adele into Joe's arms. Joe, Adele and the horse all froze, rigid with fear at the raucous, blood-curdling noise.

Joe slid from her pussy, and the saddle, and helped Adele down. Suddenly cold, Adele retrieved her dress and slipped it on, while Joe's eyes flicked all around, searching for the source of the ghoulish hysteria. As abruptly as it had started, it stopped, and the silence was almost as threatening.

Adele looked up at Joe. 'That's what I heard before. It's horrible.' She moved towards him. 'Hold me, Joe.'

He put his hands to her shoulders, but flinched as if she had scorched his skin. Taking a step backwards, he looked Adele up and down, his eyes filled with fearsome loathing.

'It's you,' he whispered to himself. 'Why didn't I see it before? How could I have been so stupid?'

'Joe?' Adele held out her hand. He raised his heavy arms in defence. 'Joe, what's the matter? What are you talking about?'

Treading a wide circle around her, Joe went back to the horse and re-mounted. 'I should have known. A woman like you would never want a man like me. A woman like you would never act like that, unless –'

Another peal of laughter reached them through the trees. The horse neighed and rose up on its hind legs, rolling its eyes until the whites showed.

'What do you mean, Joe? Joe! Joe!' Adele shouted after him as the stallion galloped away.

'You're possessed. It's in your eyes,' he shouted back. 'She's inside you.'

'Who is?' Adele muttered frustratedly to herself. She began to walk, heading, she hoped, out of the woods and back towards the Manor. Stepping in something wet, a shock coursed up from her foot, along her spine and into her scalp. Looking down, she realised the familiarly shaped damp patch of soil was her urine. Beside its darkness, her sandals waited where they had been discarded.

Joe's words raced feverishly around her mind. What was she possessed by? What had he seen in her eyes? What was inside her?

The succubus. Joe had seen it in Rafique, and in the horses. And now, he believed he had recognised its presence in her. Was it superstition, or was the demon really haunting her, taking her over? 'A woman like you wouldn't act like that,' he had said. Her behaviour that evening had certainly been totally out of character. Going out without underwear on, peeing on the forest floor, flaunting with danger on the stallion, taking Joe's education in her hands. But then, she hadn't been herself since she had arrived at the Manor.

Adele ran her fingers through her long, tangled hair. Something strange was happening to her, without a doubt. It frightened her, but somewhere, deep in her subconscious, far beyond rational thought, it excited her too. Perhaps that meant it was too late. Perhaps the succubus had already claimed Adele as her own. Perhaps it was useless to fight.

* * *

Peering through the narrow window slit, Rafique saw Adele emerge from the woods. A plethora of feelings struggled for supremacy in his mind. There was envy, that Joe's loss of virginity had been so undoubtedly wonderful; pride, that his protegée was progressing so quickly; sadness, too, that his teaching had been so effective that Adele was already searching for new stimuli. Self-pity took over a corner of his heart. He wanted Adele to need him, but pretty soon his rôle would be obsolete. It was going to be hard to accept.

As she approached the house, he watched her breasts, bouncing slightly beneath her dress. The sun shone through the flimsy material, outlining the perfection of her legs. He noticed the carefree flick of her head as her hair waved at him in the breeze. And he noticed the telling flush across her neck and throat. Sadness flowed inside him and he longed for another life, longed to be twenty years younger. She would have loved him, he was sure.

He turned away from one vision and sought solace in another. Yet another manic roar of laughter filled the high-ceilinged room as, for the third time, Foster pumped himself to climax in Jessica's fettered body. The poor girl no longer had the strength to protest. Humiliated, and furious that she was enjoying Foster's plundering despite herself, her eyes remained steadfastly closed. It was enough to bring a smile back to Rafique's face.

Chapter Eight

A dele watched Jamie and Carmen, dancing together. Carmen looked so tiny, a foot smaller than Jamie's six foot frame. She was strong and robust and yet fragile, doll-like in the flawless beauty of her small, olive-skinned limbs and wide blue eyes. She acted her innocence well, responding shyly to Jamie's touch as he held and caressed her, spun and lifted her in his fluid embraces, and Adele felt lost in the emotion of the music as she watched the girl's supple body yield to Jamie's hands. As the ballet unfolded in front of her eyes, Adele's arousal grew.

She could see Carmen's breasts, pert and firm beneath her white gauze night-gown, her large dark nipples pulling into peaks as she acted her love for Jamie, brushing against his gorgeous body. She could see the dark outline of Carmen's areolae distinctly beneath her flimsy costume, and she looked down at her own breasts, encased in a black chiffon dress, shocked to find her own arousal clearly stated in her pointed nipples. She looked away from the lovers' dance for a moment, fascinated by the sight of her swollen mounds of flesh, pale underneath the dark gauze of her costume, the engorged tips of her breasts chafing against the fabric as she breathed. She felt unbearably stimulated. It was incredible that the sight of another woman could create such an immediate, involuntary frisson of excitement in her body. But then she remembered. She wasn't Adele any more. She was the succubus.

Adele looked up to the ballet again, but Jamie and Carmen weren't dancing. She smiled as she saw them. In the centre of the stage they lay on a wide bed, naked, tenderly making love. Adele's mouth gaped and she licked her lips lasciviously. The couple were brazenly lost in their love, oblivious of her, oblivious of the succubus.

Jamie was lying on his back, his slim, fine limbs stretched out languidly, invitingly, his legs brushed with downy blond hair. His eyes were closed, and a silent smile of gentle pleasure raised the corners of his open lips. Carmen's compact body was astride his, her legs folded neatly on either side of his hips, her thick auburn hair flopping over her face and caressing Jamie's taut stomach as she leaned forward and decorated his smooth, tanned torso with fluttering, dainty kisses. Carmen sat up, and her expression mirrored Jamie's as her hips began to rock, gently squirming from side to side and front to back, in time with the seductive melodies of the orchestra.

Jamie looked serene, completely at peace as he lay supine beneath the caresses of Carmen's inner flesh. Led by a powerful force that pushed her, like a firm hand in the back, Adele moved to Jamie's side and stroked his hair, gently touched a fluttering eyelid and a strong cheekbone. She traced his lips, feeling his breath warm and slow on her finger. She should have felt jealous, angry, but she didn't. Normal, human emotions were fading and being replaced by something dark and animalistic. She was the succubus now, and she felt only the roots of lust gripping her cold heart as she watched

161

the two beautiful bodies entwined, lost in the persistent, primeval pulse of their pleasure. Jamie and Carmen had lost their personalities, to her they were simply two tempting arrangements of flesh, laid before her like a delicacy that she would soon devour. A torrid, potent power was invading her limbs and taking over her soul. It would not be denied.

Adele watched Carmen's body, her small, dark breasts moving provocatively as she squirmed, fluid as water, on top of Jamie. Her nipples were a rich, exotic brown flecked with crimson, the areolae still large despite their puckered stiffness, and Adele took one in her lips and tasted its delight. As she sucked greedily, Jamie's long fingers appeared in front of her eyes to tweak and pinch at the tip of Carmen's other breast, and Adele's gaze moved onwards, her attention being pulled downwards to the gentle curve of Carmen's tiny, feminine belly. In the recesses of her mind, Adele was still aware of the ballet's music, the yearning, haunting theme of the violins heralding her entrance. It was time for the succubus to take control.

Her eyes moved downwards again, and she felt a pang of hunger inside her sex as her gaze fell between Carmen's legs. Beneath a beauty spot, a neat triangle of deep auburn curls pointed to the place where the lovers' bodies united. Beyond the damp tendrils of curling hair, the lips of Carmen's vulva, tender and crimson and smooth, were clasped to Jamie's long, gently thrusting cock. Adele was transfixed by Carmen's secret flesh, the delicately pretty pussy lips sliding up and down Jamie's smooth velvet rod, wetting his skin with her glistening love juices, making the dew of desire form inside Adele. The sight was startlingly sensual, and it awoke the succubus. She knew what to do.

She was going to touch this woman all over, not for Carmen's pleasure but for her own. She was going to feast on Carmen's desire, to draw her strength from the power of this woman's imminent climax. She was going to steal her ecstasy.

In a swirl of dark colour, Adele was astride Jamie's legs, behind Carmen as she glided towards orgasm. She stroked Carmen's back, tracing the path of the tiny rivulets of perspiration snaking towards her bottom. Her hands moved to Carmen's narrow waist and over the slight flare of her hips. Cupping her sweat-shiny buttocks, she delighted in their erotic movements as Carmen's tiny body rose and fell on Jamie's proud phallus.

Moving her hands around Carmen's waist she lifted them higher until she felt the soft brush of the edges of her breasts. Adele slid her fingers over the smooth orbs, gently stroking, enjoying the wonderful sensations of the small weights cradled in her fingers. Carmen's head fell slowly back and Adele circled her erect nipples into further stiffness and then pulled lightly on their aching tips until her fingers ached too.

Carmen's narrow back was moving up and down in front of Adele, and she could see the muscles contracting and relaxing in her pliable spine, as ecstasy rippled through her body. Adele lifted her hands and rested them on Carmen's shoulders. Immediately, the heat of the glistening skin radiated into Adele's body, awakening her senses, and her touch became ultra-sensitive.

Sliding up Jamie's legs, Adele moved closer to Carmen and her swollen breasts pressed against her back, the girl's sweat immediately wetting Adele's flimsy costume and her hot skin beneath. Carmen's head rested on Adele's shoulder, and she found herself moving to her pace, gyrating her hips in a sensuous echo of Carmen's movements, which in turn were governed by the music's mesmeric power.

Adele's vulva, naked and swollen beneath her costume, was aching for contact with flesh and she pressed her hips down onto Jamie's thighs, wriggling until she felt her wetness spill on to his skin, rubbing her clitoris on his leg until peaks of pleasure began to form and spread within her hips. Recognising the deep, familiar heat at her sex she moved a hand away from Carmen's tender breasts, searching for the centre of the woman's joy. This was the place that held the key to the succubus's pleasure, the food for her dripping hunger. Both women gasped and sighed and Carmen's back arched sharply as the succubus found the treasure she craved.

Adele's fingers quivered at the fantastic sensations: the damp, wisping hairs brushing at her hand; the smooth, tender labia, clasping and kissing at Jamie's swollen prick; the smell of sex, the exotic, salty musk that wafted faintly over the bed and intoxicated its occupants; and the clitoris, the tiny stiff bud at the apex of their trio that radiated visible waves of pleasure up Adele's arm and throughout the simultaneously rippling bodies.

Adele was in control of the rhythm and all three moved in unison now. Jamie's hips rose and fell with gathering momentum. Carmen writhed as she bore down on Jamie more forcefully, her clitoris engorged with lust under Adele's circling fingers, her aching breasts fondled and kneaded by her two lovers. Adele squirmed with her, and their flesh became one as she pressed herself into Carmen's body and shared in her rising joy. The tender bud grew beneath her fingers, Adele's pointed nipples brushed roughly through her costume against Carmen's back, and her own climax hovered within her sex as she ground her dripping vulva on to Jamie's hard thigh. All three joined like a panting, lustful beast at the brink of ecstasy, poised at the edge of pleasure as the music crashed and rose to its first inevitable climax. In a moment they would come, and as they did, Adele would steal their pleasure and feast upon it. She slavered at the thought that in a second, her desire would be satiated.

But her hunger wasn't quelled, only sharpened.

Carmen and Jamie were spent, lifeless, but Adele was only just awakening. In a cackle of seething colour, she left the exhausted couple, and went in search of fresh prey.

Alexei was asleep in the armchair, his thick limbs flopping out of his old-fashioned white nightshirt. As his chest rose softly, Adele contrasted his peaceful rest with the wild, maniacal dance of the succubus, her black chiffon costume whirling and floating up around her. She leered provocatively, circling Alexei's prone body, seducing him as he slept. She spun around the chair, a demonic dream that was filtering into his unconscious mind, teasing and taunting him until she twisted herself into a frenzy and fell upon his legs. Lifting his nightgown, Adele hardened Alexei's wide, thick cock with one piercing glare and sucked its tip between her lips, relishing his taste and smell. Her mouth was an instrument, a harmony of torture and pleasure, and she licked and licked at Alexei's musky, twitching rod, making him shudder and moan but never waken. Her hold over him was so great, so powerful, she could do whatever she wanted to him, and he would never know. He would assume it all to be a wonderful, terrible dream.

Like a vampire craving the blood of a human she was ravenous, hungry for his flesh, desperate for a hit of semen to rouse her devilish energy once again. Grabbing Alexei's smooth, taut buttocks she pulled his hips to her slavering jaws and sucked him in. Her mouth clutched at his tender prick, squeezing, sucking, and her tongue grew long and wrapped itself around his rod like poison ivy, imprisoning it. She would hold it inside her lips until she had done with it, gained her pleasure.

Her head thrashed and writhed on the pulsing pole, and Alexei's face contorted in his sleep, unable to pull himself from his sharply pleasured slumber. Adele cackled gleefully as her claws pierced Alexei's tensed buttocks, and she felt beads of hot crimson appearing beneath her fingertips where she had punctured his skin. And then he was coming and she was gulping frantically at the stream of burning, salty semen that was flooding her throat and coursing through her rapidly beating heart, racing through her arteries like an injection of quicksilver.

She was finished with Alexei. He was spent, drained, his threatening cock red and shrivelled, emptied of its strength. She laughed at him, her pleasure giving her the force to float above him, regurgitating a few drops of his oily come on to his flickering eyelids, beneath which she caught a glimpse of the rolling whites of his eyes. She wiped the back of her hand across her cruel mouth. She didn't care for him any more. She had received her lifesap.

With a twist of her silently screeching body she was in another room, coiled like a serpent at the foot of the wide four-poster bed. Joe was there, with Nadia and Jessica, a chaste and peaceful threesome sleeping lovingly in each other's arms. The drapes and rugs and bedclothes were crimson and burgundy, rich and dark as her lust. Slithering through their twining limbs she made them stir, but like all her victims they wouldn't wake, they couldn't wake, until she'd fucked them dry, extracted their very essence.

She hovered above Joe for a moment, savouring the evil anticipation of her actions, ruminating over the method of her torture. Throwing her head back she laughed hysterically, her voice and mouth silver, glittering with the stain of her last prisoner. She knew what to do with these three. She would have them all at once.

She moved over each of her dozing subjects in turn, lifting their nightgowns, exposing their genitalia. She covered the women's faces; she didn't need to see their eyes roll beneath fluttering eyelids, their lips pulled back over bared teeth, their nostrils flaring at her touch. She knew well enough that they would be gripped with an agonising ecstasy that would leave them puzzled. She only needed to see Joe's cock, Nadia and Jessica's breasts, the tender lips of their sex, for that was where she would feed. Emotions gave her nothing. Sex, its smell, its taste, its force, ripping through her thrashing muscles; sex was her food.

Lowering herself, the succubus pressed her dripping vulva to Joe's open mouth. The sharp teeth which lined the lips of her sex clamped down on to his mouth, and she drank in his struggling sighs as he squirmed in his sleep beneath her. She faced his feet, reaching out with her long arms and sharp, cruel fingers to pinch and tweak at the pair of breasts flanking her on either side; Nadia's, pale and bulbous, with their dark, almost black nipples, and Jessica's, small, delicate, with their soft, pale pink areolae. The contrasting nipples immediately stiffened and engorged at the succubus's insistent touch. She pinched hard until beneath their white robes the women stirred, gurgling protestations from within their blanket of sleep.

Using her sex like a mouth, Adele sucked on Joe's parted lips, forcing him to take his breath from her ravenous cunt. Clenching her inner muscles, she unfurled his dormant tongue and pulled it up inside her, clamping down painfully on the women's nipples as Joe's slippery tongue explored her sex, the bed of her lust. She drew him up, up into her honey-soaked tunnel, lifting his heavy head from the pillow with the force of her lust, pulling his tongue from its root until the pain brought him to the brink of consciousness. With a loud slurp she let him go, giving him only a moment of respite, time enough for his head to fall back on to the pillow before she bore down on him again. His mouth was open wide and she made him take her sex between his lips, and suck and search as if he was sucking the juice from a ripe fruit through a tiny puncture in its skin. Her clitoris drew his tongue to it as if magnetised, and she bade him lick and nibble and even bite down hard upon the nub of her fierce desire. Ripples of sexual ecstasy ran like shifting sands up her spine as she gyrated her aching hips on his tongue, pushing herself further into painful pleasure until she reached her climax, drawing wave after wave of orgasm from his whimpering mouth, her juice spilling over his twisted features, her strength mounting unstoppably within her.

Insatiable, the succubus left Joe's mouth, pausing to suck his tongue, now musky with her intoxicating scent. She turned her back to his twitching feet and slid down his muscular body to his cock, engorged and purple in unknowing lust, pressing towards his taut, darkly haired belly in anticipation of her. Raising herself on all fours, she wriggled her screaming pussy into position with the purple plum of his phallus gently poking between her heavy, yearning labia. She waited, intensifying her unquenchable thirst, torturing herself. Then she relented, thrusting her hips down, her head back, her breasts forward as she impaled herself on his thick, long hardness. She writhed on his prick, letting it fill every inch of her to her womb, sliding easily with her slickness along its turgid length. She was happy for a moment, fulfilled at the sensation of his life pulsing inside her, his hips pushing him deeper, then another wave of lust overcame her again. She turned her attention to the supine female shapes on either side of her.

As she plunged and speared herself on Joe's willing cock, the succubus searched for more. She pulled at Jessica's legs, moving her glistening crotch towards her, parting her lean, muscled thighs and stroking the soft sex she exposed. As she worked, she did the same to Nadia until in each hand she kneaded a mound of yielding, wet female flesh. She inhaled deeply, the stench of sex pervading the room and filling her lungs with the nourishment she needed.

She watched the women, not their faces, which were

covered by the skirts of their nightdresses, but their pussies. She could tell all she needed to know from their crimson, weeping labia, their clutching, silken slits, their angry red clits.

She quickened the motion of her hips, her evil heart gladdening to feel Joe's pelvis push up to meet hers, forcing himself ever deeper with sharp stabs. She violated the women, thrusting two, three, then four fingers inside each vagina, delighting wickedly as she felt their pussies close around her touch. Her thumbs pressed and circled their stiff buds, making their bodies thrash with the force of their pleasure, echoed by the aching in her own sex as her clit dragged and rubbed against Joe's hot, clammy penis.

And then she was on fire. The three restless victims came in a synchronised shudder of sexual anguish. The succubus's pussy went into spasm at Joe's prick and she drank him in, her black soul feasting on the innate power of his sperm. Nadia and Jessica cried out in unison, drenching the succubus's hands with their warm flowing dew, making her roar with a lion's strength as the flames of their climaxes flickered up her arms and into her racing heart. She pulled and pulled and drew everything from them, sapped their strength, gorged herself on their open souls.

She turned. The audience, a hundred masked men and women, were writhing in their seats. As one, they had watched in awe of the succubus's raw, mesmeric power, their own sexual stimulation fired by the sight of her all-consuming energy. She laughed at them, hypnotised one and all by her astounding evil beauty. She pulled her breasts from beneath the scoop of her black dress and rubbed the juices of the two women over her own skin, showing the avid audience her teeth, taunting and snarling at them as she rubbed her wide, beautiful nipples into hard, blood-red peaks. She would have them all tonight, as they slept. No one would escape the succubus.

Adele was shivering when she woke. Every terrifying detail immediately replayed itself, and she concluded that what she had just experienced could not have been a dream. She never remembered more than a vague sense of her dreams. So what was it then? A vision? A premonition? A visitation? She pulled the bedclothes tighter around her, trying to draw some warmth into her frozen limbs. She snuggled down, willing the cocoon of sleep to enfold her once again, trying to propel her mind away from her nightmare and towards more gentle thoughts.

It was no use. Chilled to the core and wide awake, she rolled out of bed and put on her jeans and a zip-up tracksuit top. She had discovered a well-stocked library the other night, while exploring with Carmen and Nadia. She would go and find a book, and ease herself back to sleep.

The corridor's wall sconces were lit, the candles' flames dancing ineffectually and lighting meagre patches of the dark blue walls behind, but little else. Without the relief of sunshine lighting the windows at either end, the long passage reminded Adele of stories of Bedlam, with its endless miles of corridor flanked by stark rooms containing terrible madness. The Manor was just as spooky. Even if she hadn't known about the legend of the succubus, it would not have been hard to imagine insanity, dribbling and rolling its head behind the thick, oak doors. The farmers in the pub had been right, it was incomprehensible that Rafique should choose to live here.

She set off towards the stairs, but stopped almost immediately. Something was following her. She turned, but there was nothing there, so she continued along the corridor. But there it was again, unmistakeable, a second set of footsteps audible above the faint slap of her bare feet on the tiled floor. She turned once more, squinting into the empty gloom behind her. Nothing.

She walked more quickly now, fear beginning to propel her. It would have been more sensible to dash back to her room, to put on the lights and dispel her worry, but she couldn't turn back now. The corridor, stretching in front of her like a challenge, was forbidding, but nowhere near as scary as whatever was behind her.

The faint sound of laughter rose up from the icy floor, and Adele broke into a panicked run. Whatever it was that was stalking her ran as well, its footsteps synchronizing with her own. She gasped frantically for air as a rush of wind whirled along the corridor. With a flicker of protest the candles died in unison, plunging her into complete darkness. Feeling hot breath on her legs, she accelerated into a desperate, stumbling bid for the stairs. Terror bubbled like dry ice in her veins, her vision strained to make sense of the impenetrable blur and her heart beat furiously.

The floor disappeared and she found the banister just in time to stop herself tumbling down the staircase. Her feet wouldn't move quickly enough; it was the stuff of nightmares, wading through treacle while behind her, something panting, slavering, and hungry for her soul, inexorably gained on her with every second. At the bottom of the stairs, there was no time to hesitate. She flung herself towards a distant light from an open doorway, stubbing her toe in the final effort to escape from the thing, the succubus. What else could it be? She slammed the door in its face and leaned against it, her chest heaving.

For a second, the sound of chuckling stopped the flow of relief, then she turned, and saw him.

'Rafique –' She paused as she realised he wasn't alone.

'Adele, Christophe. Christophe, Adele.'

Adele smiled wanly. Wearing only a pair of jeans,

Christophe was sitting in a huge armchair. Between his open legs, Rafique, also naked to his waist, was sitting on the floor receiving a shoulder massage. 'Christophe is a wonderful masseur,' Rafique continued, although Adele could have guessed that much by the distant rapture coating his handsome features. 'I asked him to come over, in case any of you wanted massages after tomorrow's dress rehearsal.'

'How thoughtful of you.' Adele was struggling to make conversation, partly because her panic had not yet completely subsided, but mostly because Christophe was so beautiful.

For a man, it was a freakish beauty; creamy skin, wide, long-lashed green eyes, delicate features. His hands were soft, and looked like they had never been near anything dirty. His chest was completely hairless, and there was no sign of stubble on his chin. If he untied his shoulder-length, pale blonde hair, she thought, he could easily pass for a woman. A stunningly beautiful one.

'Come and join us.' Rafique smiled knowingly and motioned to the armchair at the opposite side of the fireplace. Adele gratefully sank into its arms, and forcing her gaze away from the men she stared into the core of the fire. The welcome heat seared her skin. As she sat in silence, the dance of the flames seemed to form a pattern out of chaos, and she watched the repetitive flicker and spark, mesmerised and calmed by its powerful beauty. Warmth entered her body again.

'What were you running away from?'

'I don't know,' she said, without taking her eyes from the fire. 'There was something out there, something was chasing me.'

'What were you doing out of your room? Breaking the rules again?'

'I had a nightmare. I couldn't get back to sleep, so I came to get a book.'

'Ah, well,' he said, conclusively. 'You shouldn't go

walkabout after dark, the succubus will get you.' She looked up sharply, but Rafique was smiling. Noticing the seriousness in her face, he stood up and walked to the drinks cabinet behind Christophe's chair. 'I was only joking.' He passed her a generous glass of whisky. 'It was probably one of the dogs. They like to roam about at night.'

Adele poured the drink down her throat, shuddering as the liquid fireball reached her stomach and started another blaze. 'It wasn't a dog,' she whispered. 'You were right the first time.'

'The succubus?' Rafique exchanged glances with Christophe. 'Do you really believe that?'

Adele watched as he took her glass and refilled it. Again, she swallowed it in one gulp. Unused to drinking neat spirits, she felt the whisky seeping inside her head, blurring her thoughts, diluting her reasoning. 'I don't know what to believe.' She held her glass out for another top-up. 'All I know is, something very strange is happening to me.'

Rafique poured her another drink. Then he poured two more, passed one to Christophe, and took his seat again on the floor. 'What? What's happening to you, Adele?'

Christophe began to knead his bare shoulders again. Adele watched distractedly. The contrast between Rafique's rich, dark colouring and Christophe's alabaster complexion and blonde hair was stunning. 'It's like I said this morning.' Already, that day seemed like a month ago. 'I'm not myself any more. I haven't been myself since I came to the Manor. There's something going on here, something . . .' She hesitated, the sight of Christophe's white fingers manipulating Rafique's brown neck making her lose her thread.

'Yes? Go on.'

'Something beyond my control.' She took another sip of the burning amber and bathed in its glow. 'Ever since we arrived, I haven't been able to stop thinking about . . .' she looked at Christophe, unsure about unburdening herself in front of a stranger. Then she realised she didn't care about social niceties any more. Besides, it was at least three o'clock, and two semi-naked men were hardly likely to balk at her confession. 'I can't stop thinking about sex.' Another sip, another drop of fuel to fan the flames in her belly. 'I've had more sex in the last few days than in the last two years. I've slept with two of my best friends, with a man who used to scare me rigid, and with you, I've discovered things about myself which, quite frankly, disturb me.'

'And you put all this down to the succubus?'

'What else can I put it down to? It's not me, doing these things.' She looked up. Rafique was watching her intently. Christophe was watching the progress of his hands. 'Joe thinks I'm possessed.'

Rafique laughed, not a derisory, mocking laugh, but one of gentle care, as if she was his child, admitting to some minor crime that had been eating her up with guilt. 'Joe's an intelligent lad, but he's got a rather overactive imagination. He thrives on rumour and legend. I'm afraid he's got his childhood with the gipsies to thank for that.'

'I'm not so sure you can put this down to superstition. What I did to him wasn't . . . it wasn't like me, at all.' Bemused at the memory, she shook her head. 'No wonder he was frightened. I deliberately set out to –'

'You took his virginity.'

She blinked at him through her whisky haze. 'Do you know everything about me?'

His smile faded into a wistful look. 'I wish I did.' Adele flinched from his eyes. Brushing Christophe's hands away, he came over and perched on one arm of her chair. Adele looked at Rafique's fingers as they rested on her thigh. 'Look, Adele, I don't have any answers. The only thing I can offer to help is a question.'

174

'Go on.'

'Have you enjoyed your experiences, here?' He stroked her hair. 'Have you enjoyed being with other women? Being punished? Did you enjoy it when I made you suck me in the woods? When I made you dance for me, and I fucked you on the stage? Did you enjoy it today, when I buggered you during rehearsals?'

Slightly embarrassed, Adele looked up at Christophe, but his face was emotionless. Typical Frenchman, she thought, acting so nonchalant, as if he heard this sort of thing every day.

'Adele.' Rafique put her glass down and held her hand. 'Have you done anything while you've been here, which was against your will?'

She thought for a moment, although it was difficult. Her mind was awash with alcohol. 'No,' she admitted.

'Has anything you've done here made you unhappy?'

She trawled her memory. 'Not unhappy. Just scared.'

'Of what?'

She looked into his eyes. She wanted to shelter in their rich, deep brown, to hold their cloak around her shoulders. 'Of myself,' she whispered, tears springing up.

Rafique caressed her cheek. 'There's nothing to be afraid of,' he soothed. 'I know it seems frightening, discovering all of a sudden that you don't really know yourself. But whatever's happening to you, you mustn't fight it.' Rafique looked up as Christophe joined them, kneeling at their feet. 'None of us can fight forever.'

'That's true.' Christophe's words were coated with a thick French accent. 'It is such a waste of time and energy. Don't fight it, Adele, just enjoy it.'

Adele wasn't really convinced by what they were saying, but as she sat there, and Christophe's hand drifted on to Rafique's thigh, she felt the apprehension leaving her body. Transfixed, she watched the Frenchman's fingers creep towards the soft bulge in Rafique's black trousers. His words echoed in her mind, enjoy it, enjoy it, in time with his stroking of Rafique's genitals beneath the fabric.

His other hand landed on her thigh, and gently squeezed. *'Mon dieu,'* he exclaimed. 'You are so tense!'

'Give her a massage, Christophe.'

'I think I should. A dancer cannot perform very well with muscles like this.' He clenched his hand into a fist.

'Adele? Would you like a massage? Christophe is very good.'

She could see that. An erection was already forming where his hand was working in Rafique's lap. Inexplicably, the sight aroused Adele beyond belief. 'Yes. I think I would.'

Christophe nodded to Rafique. As if it was a pre-arranged signal, he stood, taking Adele's hands, and gently lifted her to her feet. He pulled her into the centre of the rug which lay in front of the fire, and unzipped her top. Startled, Adele raised a hand to his, to stop him. She looked at Rafique.

'Haven't you ever had a massage, Adele?'

'Of course I have.'

'And do you usually keep your clothes on?'

She looked up into Christophe's pale, beautiful face, and abandoned herself to his care. 'No,' she admitted, and released his hand. His eyes smiled into hers as he opened her top, and pushed it over her shoulders and off her arms. He unbuttoned her jeans and slid them to the floor, unashamedly running both his fingers and his eyes down her legs before standing up. Feeling unsteady, Adele reached out for his support while she stepped out of the crumpled denim. He cupped her elbow. Slowly, his eyes pulled away from hers and fell to her breasts, then back again. Sleepily, as if the whisky had suddenly lurched into his brain and intoxicated him, he blinked. Then he bowed his head, and kissed her, softly, on the lips.

'You were right about her, Rafique.'

Adele looked over at him. He was admiring her breasts too, and smiling proprietorially. Adele wanted to ask what he'd said about her, but Christophe reclaimed her attention by taking her hands and pulling her to her knees. It might have been the alcohol, or tiredness, or the feeling that once again things were moving out of her control, but she felt as if she was falling through heavy syrup as she sank on to the rug. Gently positioning her limbs, Christophe silently invited her to stretch out on to her front. Turning her head away from the fire, she watched him prepare.

From behind the armchair, he retrieved a soft black briefcase, the type that businessmen use to carry their laptop computers in. But the contents of Christophe's case were far more interesting; rows of bottles, filled with oils, several smooth dildos of the purest white, and silk scarves to match. Looking down at Adele, he stood and dropped his jeans to the floor, revealing his tight-fitting white cotton shorts. By the look of the bulge beneath, Adele surmised that this wasn't going to be the same sort of massage she got from the physiotherapist at the National Ballet.

Disappearing from view, he knelt astride her hips, his knees warm where they touched her. Selecting a bottle, he poured the oil on to his palm. The exotic mixture of neroli and bergamot filtered through the humid air and went straight to her head. Like a drug hitting her brain, it brought on an immediate and intense relaxation, deepened further still when his touch landed at the base of her spine. She sighed deeply.

Like a master baker caressing the dough, Christophe pressed his palms along the length of her back. Adele could feel her tight muscles softening under his insistent touch, and as he rubbed and smoothed and kneaded, it seemed her body was both sinking into the soft rug and floating away. Leaning into her, he pushed his fingers

177

deep into her flesh, working away at the tension until it dissolved. Adele's mind drowned in whisky and pleasure, and she closed her eyes.

'She has lovely skin.' The sensual caress of Christophe's voice made her open them again. 'Her muscles are hard, which I would expect in a dancer's body, but her skin, it's so soft.'

Rafique murmured in agreement and Adele heard him stand up and move closer to them. She saw his feet approach, then his bare knees as he knelt down at her side. He too, had taken off his trousers.

'I like the way her skin smells,' he said.

Christophe's hands left her back and planted themselves on either side of her face. His mouth and nose pressed to her neck, and he breathed in deeply. 'Mmm. She smells of summer.'

'She smells of sex,' Rafique corrected.

Christophe swivelled around behind her until he faced her feet. He cupped her buttocks and pressed his thumbs deep into their fleshy mounds. 'I like her arse.' He moulded it in his strong fingers, making a twitch shudder down the backs of her thighs. 'A truly magnificent arse.'

Rafique's hand loomed over her eyes and pushed a long curl of hair away from her face. 'I fucked her in the arse this morning.'

'How did it feel?'

Adele gasped, not only with the bizarreness of the conversation going on above her, but with the motion of Christophe's hands. With every push of his body, her naked sex chafed roughly on the rug.

'It was wonderful. So tight, so forbidden. She cried out so loudly, too.'

'I love it when a woman loses control.' Christophe's hands stopped. As if he was settling down for a chat, he sat on Adele's bottom. His weight, together with the shocking heaviness of his balls resting on her through the soft cotton of his shorts, knocked the breath out of her.

'You should see Adele when she loses control.' Rafique gently traced the edge of her ear. 'She looks so beautiful when she comes.'

'There is nothing more beautiful than the sight of a woman, coming.'

For a moment, there was silence except for the sound of the flames. Then, as if they had made a decision, Christophe lifted his weight from her body. He moved between Adele and the fire. Crouching over her, he slid his fingers under her waist and hip and rolled her on to her back. Then he knelt down at her side, opposite Rafique. They looked at each other, then down at Adele.

'Pass me the scarves, Rafique.'

Adele watched him twist his body to reach over into the briefcase. With a magician's flourish he pulled out two diaphanous scarves, passing them to Christophe, then two more for himself. Tenderly, as if they were tying down a butterfly, they fastened the strips of silk to Adele's wrists and ankles, then loosely knotted the other ends to the legs of the armchairs at either end of the rug. Gently spread-eagled, Adele felt her pulse racing in her sex. Flanked by two men, one pale, one dark, both with erections as long as her hand beneath their underwear, she could only sigh in anticipation.

But then, when they had her pinned down, albeit tenuously, they turned their attention away from her and to each other. Reaching across her stomach they touched hands. Adele didn't know whether it was meant to tease her but if it was, then it worked. As she watched their heads lean closer together, she fidgeted in her fastenings. When their lips met, she blinked in disbelief. Above her, their contrasting skin tones bathed in the orange of the fire. They kissed and kissed, their mouths grabbed for each other, their tongues flickered in a frantic mating dance, their heads swayed and dipped. There were plenty of gay and bisexual men in the company, but Adele had never given them much thought. Now, she realised how entrancing it was to see such handsome men, lost in sensuality, allowing themselves to touch and taste. Her pussy flooded with dew.

But as they fell deeper into their private passion, Adele's yearning for them to touch and taste her grew overwhelming. She writhed in her bindings, and moaned faintly in exasperation.

Their faces slowly parted at the sound. 'We're forgetting ourselves, Christophe. You're supposed to be relieving Adele's tension, not increasing it.'

Christophe muttered his apologies in French, and retrieving his bottle of oil, he poured some more into his hands. Straddling her hips, he spread his palms over her belly and up to her chest. Lovingly, he oiled her breasts, squeezing them between his slippery fingers again and again until her nipples glistened stiffly. Adele looked up from her shiny skin to find both men lost in concentration, following the path of Christophe's fluent fingers.

'You didn't exaggerate,' Christophe said, without moving his eyes from her body. 'She has such lovely breasts. Such tender nipples.'

'Taste them,' Rafique suggested.

Christophe leant over her and pressed his lips to an areola. As he sucked her in, his hands never stopped working, smoothing their way along her arms. Adele trembled and arched her back up towards him, pressing her pelvis against the hardness at his groin. She felt so aroused, she could amost have cried.

'Bite her,' Rafique urged, and Christophe tentatively nibbled on the sensitive tip of her breast. Adele drew in a breath of ecstasy; he must have heard it because he bit down harder, until her body went rigid with agony. He flinched.

'I think I hurt her.'

'She likes a little pain.' Rafique bent his face to hers

and pulled on her lower lip with his teeth. 'She's dark,' he whispered, into her mouth. 'Dark inside.'

His words were cold darts in her burning skin. Dark inside. How did he know so much about her? Could he see into her soul, see how it had blackened and twisted in the last few days?

There was no time to ask him. They rearranged themselves around her body once again, Christophe kneeling between her open legs, Rafique at her hip.

'What a pretty pussy.'

'Stroke it.'

Adele braced herself. Uncontrollable spasms rippled across her skin as Christophe rubbed his oily thumbs along her labia. Once again, their concentration was intense as they both watched her sex responding to his touch. Adele could feel herself swelling under his gentle teasing, and filling with arousal. Gently, he prised her open even further, spreading her lips, and discovering their smooth inside edges with the soft pads of his thumbs. Adele whimpered, and bending her legs as much as her ankle ties would allow, she lifted her pelvis from the floor. She was desperate for something to fill not only her vagina, but the chasm in her soul.

'Pass me something to put inside her.'

Rafique selected the smallest dildo from the briefcase and passed it to Christophe. Both bent closer to watch, as Christophe slowly pushed it between her heavy lips. Slender as a finger, it slid into her easily. In answer to her feeble whimper, Rafique and Christophe sighed in admiration.

'Try this one.' Rafique selected another, this one the width of three fingers. The first was discarded, and all three held their breath as the second dildo slowly disappeared into her sex.

'Oh, God,' Christophe mumbled, his voice lost in awe.

Adele looked down her body. They were like dogs

straining at the leash, mouths open, veins throbbing in their necks, penises pushing for release from their shorts.

'This one.' There was something close to panic in his voice as Rafique offered a third dildo, this one the size of his own beautiful rod. For an eternity, Christophe held its smooth tip at the entrance to her pussy, rubbing it on her swollen labia, teasing the nerve endings surrounding her moist hole. Unable to bear it, Adele thrust her sex towards his hand just as he pushed, and the rubber phallus plunged deep, stretching the walls of her pussy.

'Aaaah!' She moaned with relief. Pushing her pelvis even higher, she watched Christophe's hand twitch between her legs as he rapidly slid the rod in and out of her.

'She's close.' Through half-shut eyelids, Adele saw Rafique kneel up and raise his hand. A whirlpool of heat ignited at her clitoris. 'Watch her come. Watch her.'

At that moment, it was as if she had ceased to exist. Hearing them talk about her like that, feeling their avid attention, had banished Adele King into the night along with her mortal fears. All that was left was a vessel of pleasure for them to drink from, and when she came, moaning and rocking her head, she could feel herself emptying into their hands.

Delirious, Adele was vaguely aware of her body being moved. The dildo slid from her pussy, her hands and feet were freed and she was manoeuvred up into a kneel. Christophe knelt in front of her, and his fingers roamed all over her face, like a blind man reading her features. Still reeling with ecstasy, Adele studied his green eyes while he studied hers.

'She's beautiful.' He touched her forehead, her cheekbones, her mouth. 'Her eyes are incredible.'

'Oh, I know,' Rafique agreed. 'Her eyes are my downfall. Every time I look at them, I want to fuck her.'

'I want to fuck her, now.'

They moved in unison. Standing, Christophe removed his shorts and knelt again. With barely time to admire his length, springing from heavy balls and thick, pale curls, she was pulled over his lap. A second later she was on top of him, her flesh engulfing him, her knees clasped around his, his hand grabbing urgently at her hips. Behind her, Rafique's naked torso pressed against her back. She began to rise and fall, pushed along by a dangerous inner rhythm, and as she did so, Rafique's hand fluttered over her shoulders, into her hair, around to her engorged nipples. Sliding down past the place where her belly brushed against Christophe's stomach, he reached into her pubic hair. Adele looked down; his fingers were spread over her pussy lips, feeling her sex, feeling Christophe plunging inside her sex. She moaned with joy and then anguish, as he took a ravenous bite at her neck.

When she looked up again, Christophe's body was tilting away from hers. He lay down on to his back and pulled her with him, stretching his legs out underneath her. Supporting herself on her trembling hands, Adele took up the relentless rhythm again, but to her surprise he stopped her, snatching at her waist and holding her tight. She looked down at him, confusion aching faintly in her brow.

The rich perfume hit her nostrils again as Rafique poured the oil down her cleft and worked it into her anus, still tender from that morning. Already full with Christophe, Adele waited apprehensively. She closed her eyes, knowing that this was going to be too much to stand, dreading the delicious torture to come. When it did, when his penis steadily eased its way into her back passage, she collapsed on to Christophe's smooth torso, leaving her hips stranded in the air. Rafique's upper body lowered on to her back. Adele was sandwiched between them, unable to move, or speak, or think, impaled on a pleasure so excruciating she wanted it to

183

stop. Inside her, their pulsing echoed in her veins. Desperate to escape the terrifying, exhilarating feeling of utter helplessness, she began to cry.

All the tension that had left her body came rushing back, although it had been jumbled and mixed, and was now barely recognisable. This was a tension that gripped the base of her neck, pulled her face into a grimace, and stopped her heart. It was intolerable, but at the same time, she craved more of it. Then the torment began in earnest. As Rafique slowly withdrew, Christophe thrust himself up from the floor; as he relaxed, Rafique pushed. Her breath strained to escape from her lungs, her vital organs had liquefied, leaving her defenceless. She was on a see-saw, rolling dramatically from pleasure to pain, pleasure to pain, until the motion blurred and the two opposites merged into one, and her whole being was consumed in it. She felt as if her blood had burst from her arteries and was swilling stickily around inside her body. She was being ripped apart, her flesh devoured; it was the closest she had ever come to the pure essence of ecstasy.

Her mind and body succumbed completely and Rafique and Christophe increased their forceful rhythm. Groaning quietly, their hands met on her shoulders as both needlessly held her down. Becoming more frantic, their thrusting synchronised and Adele shuddered violently with the shock of the two penises filling her at once, separated by a thin layer of inner flesh which seemed ready to collapse. Christophe came first, his stomach tensing beneath hers, swiftly followed by Rafique. His body curled around her and shook, while his face buried in her hair. Crushed between their sudden stillness, Adele lost the will to exist as the force of a million orgasms shot through her ravaged body. She lay there, astounded by the power surging inside her, and watched her tears falling over the edge of Christophe's smooth chest.

Eventually, as if she had braved the flame and found its cool blue core, the panic was replaced with deep calmness. The men extricated their spent, sweat-soaked bodies from hers, and lay either side of her on the rug. Adele rolled on to her side and propped her head up on her hand. Facing her, Christophe ran his fingers from the cup of her shoulder, down into the dip of her waist.

'I want her.' His hand slid on to her oily buttock. 'I want to keep her for myself. I want to fuck her every day and watch her come.'

Rafique's warm breath touched her back as he laughed. 'Dream on.'

'Please, Rafique, let me have her.'

'I can't.' He grabbed her hip and pulled her on to her back. Leaning over her, he lightly held her face and kissed her. 'She isn't mine to give. She doesn't belong to me.'

Looking up into his dark eyes, Adele was not so sure.

Sex had done the trick better than any book could have. Adele was exhausted. Rafique's body and the faltering fire kept her warm while Christophe went in search of blankets and pillows. The fragrant fog of sleep descended upon her.

'You've no need to worry about Jessica.' Adele struggled to pull herself back to consciousness, it was like trying to fight anaesthetic. She blinked determinedly. 'In fact, I don't think she'll bother you ever again.'

'What did you do to her?' Disappointment clouded Adele's mind as she imagined his prick, buried between Jessica's spindly thighs.

'I taught her a lesson she's not likely to forget. Ever.'

'Oh.' She looked away.

'I thought you would be grateful.' He turned her face back towards his. 'What's the matter?'

Hurt, her voice came out in the faintest whisper. 'I can't bear the thought of you and her.'

'You don't have to.' Adele noticed pride shining in his eyes, he was flattered by her jealousy. 'I didn't touch her, I didn't want to.' She returned his smile, her mind already sinking back into sleep. 'After all, what's the point of having servants?'

Chapter Nine

*A*dele put down her bag and looked around the small dressing room. Rafique had thought of everything. There was a wide mirror, surrounded by a delightfully old-fashioned frame of lightbulbs, and a red velvet chaise longue filled one wall. An adjoining door led to a small bathroom with a shower, toilet and basin. Outside, a tiny passageway linked the three dressing rooms to the stage, but also to a narrow staircase leading up to one of the unoccupied bedrooms on the first floor which allowed the dancers to gain access backstage without walking through the theatre. There was even a star on the door. Well, there was a first time for everything, Adele smiled to herself.

Trying to preserve the heat of her muscles after class, Adele pulled on a sweatshirt – one with the neck cut out, so that it wouldn't disturb her make-up when she took it off – and her plastic trousers. She didn't usually like them, preferring to let her body breathe rather than roast. But it was important, half an hour away from the dress rehearsal, to keep her limbs loose and warm.

Adele laid her make-up case on the dressing table and opened it up. As always, she remembered with fondness the day she'd been wandering around Portobello Road market. The battered red leather case had beckoned her to the stall where, in amazement, she had run her fingers over the gold initials that matched her own. She'd had to buy it, despite the fact that since she'd been too shy to haggle, it had cost far more than it was worth. She wondered whether she would be so timid now.

It was strange, she thought, how the usual nerves had been replaced with calm confidence. A few days ago, she had been mortified at the idea of performing for real for the first time. Dress rehearsals always filled her with more terror than performances, and this one even more so. With an audience there, it was easier to lose herself in the music, the movement and the atmosphere. But with no one watching but the choreographer, the company's directors and the other dancers, she usually felt totally open to scrutiny, too embarrassed to perform. This time was different. Despite the fact that she had not yet seen her costume, she was actually looking forward to stepping out in front of the others.

Adele sat in front of the mirror, turned on the lights and scrutinised her reflection. Time for a transformation. Her tan, although light, was not appropriate. She chose a ghostly pale foundation, patting it all over her face and blending it beneath her jawline. Instead of rouge, she used a dark grey eye-shadow to add dramatic definition to her cheekbones. The same colour was used on her eyelids. A shimmering white powder highlighted just beneath her eyebrows; these were darkened and elongated slightly with faint pencil strokes. Lashings of black mascara widened her eyes even further than normal, and fluent streaks of liquid eyeliner ran close to both her top and bottom lashes and extended a little way beyond. The soft curves of her mouth were sharpened with a dark purple lip pencil, then the outline was filled in with a matching lipstick, a colour she had not used before.

Next, she demolished her chignon. Richard had suggested she wear her hair down for the part. It made sense, how could she look wild with a perfect hairstyle? But still, she hoped it wouldn't get in her eyes. She rummaged in her bag for some hairspray, praying it would be strong enough to hold her heavy hair away from her face. Shaking her hair free she tipped her head upside down and liberally wafted the spray into her thick waves, holding her breath to try and avoid inhaling the sickly perfume.

Adele flicked her head back and gasped at her reflection. The lacquer held the roots of her hair up and away from the pale drama of her face. She looked as if she belonged in a Hammer horror film. Beneath the harsh stage lights, the effect would be quite startling.

There was something missing though, and she looked for inspiration in her make-up case. Adele smiled as she spotted a tube of silver disco glitter she had bought when she was about fourteen and had never the heart to throw away. Squeezing a thick blob of the sticky glitter on to her hands, she ran her fingers through her hair from her temples, and then again from the centre of her forehead. The silver stripes were a wild contrast against her golden hair. 'Perfect,' she said to herself.

'Fancy yourself, don't you?' Jessica looked from Adele, to the gold star on the open door.

'Say what you've got to say and go, Jessica. There's a draught.'

Jessica stepped inside, leaving the door open. She threw her bag to the floor and draped herself over the chaise longue. 'I'm not going anywhere, dear. This is my dressing room.'

Adele stood up. Turning her back to the mirror, she folded her arms and looked down into Jessica's mean eyes. 'You're not dancing. You don't need a dressing room, *dear*.'

Jessica got to her feet. She crossed the narrow room and stood in front of Adele, eyes narrowed, her mouth

189

twisted like a bad actor in a gangster movie. 'That's where you're wrong, Adele. This is my dressing room, because I'm dancing in your place.'

'What are you talking about?'

'I'm your understudy. I get to go on when you're injured.'

'But I'm not injured.'

Jessica gave Adele a knowing smile. Turning her back, she delved into her bag and found her cigarettes. 'Adele,' she smirked, pausing to light up, 'you like Jamie, don't you?'

Adele pushed at the smoke with the back of her hand. 'What are you getting at?'

'Do you think he would still like you, if he knew you'd fucked Alexei?'

'I didn't –'

'I doubt it, somehow. He thinks butter wouldn't melt in your mouth. So, I'm taking over your rôle.' Adele's brow furrowed, unable to find a link between these two statements. 'You've got a bad knee, haven't you?'

Adele shook her head. 'I haven't had any trouble with my knee since . . .' She faltered as Jessica's face leered closer.

'It just flared up again,' Jessica insisted. 'Either that, or I tell Jamie about you and Alexei.'

'Why didn't you break the news to him the other day?'

'I've been waiting for the right moment.'

A smile raised the corners of Adele's mouth. She relished the look on Jessica's face as she plucked the cigarette from her lips and crushed it on the floor. 'You don't scare me, Jessica.'

Jessica's thin mouth gaped. 'But I'm going to tell Jamie,' she reiterated slowly, as if she was talking to a child.

'Jamie said you were jealous of me. I didn't believe him, but he was right.'

'Why on earth would I be jealous of *you*?' She wrinkled her nose disdainfully.

'You tell me. Why are you so desperate to dance the lead?' Jessica didn't tell her. 'You just can't bear the thought that for once, everyone will be looking at me. Everyone. The audience, Alexei, Jamie, Rafique –'

'Rafique doesn't care about you.'

'He commissioned this ballet. Don't you think he'll want to watch it?'

Flouncing back to her seat, Jessica crossed her legs and spread her arms along the back of the chaise longue. 'Not unless I'm dancing. He's obsessed,' she tutted, faking amazement. 'He fucked me four times, yesterday. Four times.'

'Oh, really?'

There was a knock at the open door. Adele waved Foster inside.

'Your costume, Miss King.'

'Thank you, Foster.' She took the hanger from him. 'There's not much to it, is there?' Adele held the flimsy dress up. 'Who designed it?'

'I believe it was the Master, Miss King.'

'And who did he have in mind, when he was design-ing it?'

Foster hesitated, his unblinking, reptilian eyes narrow-ing. 'Well you, Miss King, of course.'

'I see. It's just that Jessica seems to think Rafique would rather see her in the lead rôle, than me.' She draped the skimpy outfit over the back of her chair.

'Is that so?' Foster tilted his head questioningly. Put-ting his hands behind his back, he stared down at Jessica with an evil shine in his dull grey eyes. 'And what makes her think that?'

'Oh, something about him being obsessed with her.' Adele leaned towards the butler, nearly laughing at the thought that she actually looked more frightening than he did. 'Apparently,' she whispered, 'he had his wicked way with her yesterday. *Four* times.'

'Is that so?' Foster looked at Adele. The iciness of his gaze thawed slightly, and they shared a surreptitious smile.

'Do you think she could have made a mistake?'

Foster bowed his head graciously. 'It's quite possible. People often mistake me for the Master.' Foster was unable to stifle a laugh. It gathered inside him, shaking in his bony shoulders before flying from his mouth like an obscenity. He turned to leave, then changed his mind and returned to stoop over a stunned Jessica. Reaching out with his knobbly, cruel fingers, he put his hand to her leotard and squeezed her small breast. Leaving her panting with indignation, he made his exit. Outside in the corridor, his giggle rose rapidly into a manic, devilish cackle, a noise Adele immediately recognised.

She waited for the shrill laughter to die down, savouring Jessica's extreme, fidgety discomfort. 'Well,' she said at last, 'do we have a deal?'

Her face rigid with fury, Jessica was unable to speak. 'Huh?' was all she could manage.

'You keep quiet about Alexei and I, and I won't tell anyone that you slept with a man in his seventies with a face like a pterodactyl. And that you begged him for more.'

Slowly, Jessica shook her head in disbelief at her defeat. 'How did you find out?'

'Rafique told me this morning. After he fucked me.' Adele resumed her seat in front of the mirror. In the reflection, she watched Jessica pick up her bag and dazedly leave the room. 'Close the door on your way out.'

With trembling fingers, Adele laid her pointe shoes on the table, and decided which ones to wear. Beneath her pale mask, her cheeks were warm with the sweet joy of revenge.

* * *

Adele paused in the wings. Standing back in the shadows, she watched the others limbering up. Chatting as usual, Carmen and Nadia practised pirouettes. Unlike Adele, their costumes were simple, stage versions of nightdresses. Nadia's had delicate straps and a pretty rouched top which flared out, Empire line style from beneath her breasts, emphasising their fullness. Carmen's was a simple slip with long sleeves and silk ribboning around the gently scooping neckline. Both were soft and light, made from almost transparent, pale cream chiffon that contrasted with Nadia's dark hair and Carmen's olive skin. They looked, if it were possible, innocent.

The men were dressed simply, too, in black tights and cream shirts. Not the flouncy type they often had to wear in some of the more traditional classical ballets; these were well cut, loose enough to dance in but clinging slightly to their well-muscled torsos. Alexei, of course, had his open to the waist. Adele nodded as she watched him, flexing his ankles in his customary non-committal warm-up and running his fingers over his chest. It was doubtful he would ever find a woman who loved him as much as he loved himself.

Jamie's blonde hair shone under the lights as he jumped, diligently working his body into warm readiness. Adele noticed the power in his thighs, the muscles pumping hard as they propelled him high into the air, his arms and shoulders soft and easy despite the effort. Her stomach felt hollow with longing. Like the succubus, her hunger for his body was sharp. A turbulent shiver rattled along her spine as she wondered how he would react to her costume. In a way, she wished she could stay there all afternoon, hiding in the wings, allowing her senses to be lulled by the rhythm of his supple limbs. But her need to see his reaction was greater. She took a deep breath, slowly let it out, and stepped on to the stage.

It was like a scene from a film. Movement slowed, heads turned, jaws dropped. The only sound was the thumping of Adele's heart in her ears. Their expressions echoed hers, as she had studied herself in the mirror. Just as her eyes had done, theirs travelled downwards, looking through her costume at her body beneath.

Like the heart of the succubus, her costume was black. The bodice was a transparent, stretchy leotard with long sleeves, which ended in sharp points hooking over her middle fingers. The neckline was high, beginning at a velvet choker around her throat. A wide band of velvet hooped around her chest, covering her areolae, while above and below the strap of fabric, the languid curves of her breasts were visible through the chiffon. Above her hipbones, the leotard was edged with more bands of velvet. These arched inwards to meet below her navel and then stretched down between her legs, barely hiding her pubic hair. The crotch narrowed into a thong between her buttocks, and stopped in the small of her back where it met the waistband of a skirt of wide, interleaved chiffon strips. When she was still, it looked like a long, flowing skirt, but she knew that when she moved, it would flare up and expose her naked behind. She couldn't even wear ballet tights, since the waistband and gusset would have been seen, ugly under the transparency of the dress. The important bits were covered, but only just, and the effect was more shocking than nudity itself.

Adele's eyes flickered from one to the other. As if they had been sitting on a train and caught a glimpse of naked sex beneath a woman's skirt, they stared and stared. Carmen and Nadia were looking at her breasts. Alexei's attention was fixed to her groin, his lips pursed in a silent whistle. Jamie was looking at her eyes.

'You look stunning.'

'Thank you.'

Carmen and Nadia fussed around her, but they

couldn't break the spell between Adele and Jamie. Their fingers caressed the velvet and stroked the airily light material of her skirt. They talked and giggled, but Adele didn't listen to a word. Stretching invisibly across the stage, there was a link between her eyes and Jamie's, a line of telepathic communication which reverberated with desire. Standing there, she felt his longing enveloping her body like a warm cloud. Dampness gathered between her legs at the thought that as they danced, he would look at the curves of her breasts, stroke her thighs, clasp her bare buttocks. Power swelled deep inside her with the knowledge that he was craving her body, as much as she was craving his.

'Well, you certainly look the part.' Richard's huge presence loomed over her. 'Now, let's see if you can dance as well as you look.'

Four hours went by as if they were four minutes. As always, Richard kept breaking the flow of the rehearsal, shouting out minute adjustments to his choreography, correcting the detail of a look or a hand. For once, he didn't correct Adele, but even if he had, it would not have broken her concentration. Despite the interruptions, her focus remained impenetrable. Her mind seemed to have become selective, shutting out all unnecessary details. Jessica vanished from her seat in the stalls, the infuriating sound of her sniffing being filtered away, along with Richard's voice. Only the power of the music reached her ears. Her body obeyed her brain, cutting fluently through the air and making the exact shapes she asked it to. Her partners, male or female, or both at once, fitted so perfectly to her movements that they might have been shadows. Adele was unaware of their features, their personalities, the effort behind their movements. Like the succubus, her single-mindedness reduced them into abstract forms, lines of movement, living, breathing curves of music. Except for Jamie.

When she danced with him, her concentration shifted on to a different plane. Adele became so intensely aware of him that it was almost as if she was him, moving within his body and feeling what he felt. With Jamie, the fluidity of their dancing unravelled itself into sharp, clear pictures: his hands, lifting her by the waist; his breath on her skin; his thigh, hooked around hers; his mouth, gasping between her legs as he knelt at her feet; his penis, a firm lump beneath his jock-strap, rubbing against her body when they were pressed together. There was more than passionate choreography between them. There was a deep, growling longing, threatening to turn into a violent, raging desire.

It wasn't until the applause died down, that she felt the sharp pain in her foot. She knelt and untied her pointe shoe. Blood was weeping from her big toe; the knuckle had rubbed raw against the rigid wall of her shoe. Her eyebrows shot upwards in surprise that the agony now throbbing in her foot had been muffled by her concentration.

'You worry me, Adele.' Richard's bald head appeared over the edge of the stage. 'Bad dress rehearsal, good performance. The others are on line for a bloody good performance, but you! You had a blinding rehearsal.'

Adele smiled gratefully. 'Don't worry, I'll be even better tomorrow.'

Richard shook his head in disbelief, searching her eyes for answers. 'What happened? You're sexy! If the succubus is watching, I reckon she could learn a few things.'

The succubus isn't watching, she thought, she's dancing. 'I've been possessed. By the rôle,' she added, aware of how strange that might sound, coming from her. 'I don't have to think about it any more, it just happens.'

He nodded suspiciously. 'You've come a long way in the last week.'

Further than you would believe, she smiled to herself.

He looked up at the other dancers as they congregated

around her on stage. 'Ten minute break, everyone, then we'll go through my notes.'

Adele ran back to her dressing room. Lifting her foot into the basin, she washed her skinned toe and wrapped it tightly in a plaster. She found an old pair of pointe shoes, on their last legs but good enough for the remainder of the rehearsal. Lifting her foot up on the chair, she bandaged her toes in the lambswool she kept for such emergencies, and carefully slid on her shoe.

Sudden warmth spread across her back beneath a strong hand. The touch slipped to her waist and squeezed. She recognised those greedy fingers.

'Alexei, I'm busy.'

'It's not Alexei.'

Adele turned as Jamie removed his hand. Confusion blurred his clear blue eyes, just as it had two days ago when she had slapped Alexei on stage. 'I – I just came to say well done. You were fantastic. Really amazing.' Bewildered by her mistake, his dull voice didn't match the enthusiasm of his words.

'Thank you.' She hoped that he could see the sincerity in her eyes underneath her heavy make-up. 'You were pretty good yourself. You're a brilliant partner. We dance well together, don't you think?'

'Yeah.' One hand made a fist and the other gently clasped around it. 'Well, I'll go. You're busy.'

She watched him leave. She called after him, but it was too late, he was already back on stage. Either that, or he was ignoring her.

'Where's Adele?'

Foster leaned over Jamie's shoulder and filled his wine glass. 'Miss King is taking supper with the Master.'

'Hmmm.'

Everyone looked at Jessica except Foster, who continued around the table.

'What do you mean, "Hmmm"?'

'Yes, Miss Sharpe. What *do* you mean?' Foster looked down his long, pointed nose at Jessica.

Her mouth opened and closed again. Anger set her jaw. 'Forget it,' she spat, looking at her plate in order to avoid Foster's glare. Jamie saw it all, and as the butler left them alone in the dining room, he wondered what the hell was going on. There was certainly something odd, tainting the atmosphere like a bad smell. Jessica had lost her ebullient confidence, and was acting very awkwardly. On the edge of her seat, she seemed to be restless, as if something was eating her up inside. Still, she wasn't behaving half as oddly as Adele. If she had been a mystery to Jamie when he'd left, five years ago, she was a total enigma now. He had hoped – or planned, if he was honest with himself – to spend his evenings at the Manor with Adele. But he had barely seen her outside rehearsals. What had she been up to? She can't have spent every night with Carmen and Nadia. Unless she didn't like men at all. Whatever she liked, it obviously wasn't him.

He toyed with his salmon en croute, wishing he could summon up an appetite. He just couldn't stop thinking about Adele. Surely he couldn't be mistaken. The rapport he felt when he partnered her – that wasn't in the choreography. The look they'd shared when she had appeared in that costume – that was more than friendship. Or had he got it all wrong?

'What about that costume?' Alexei raised a thick eyebrow suggestively.

'Adele looks stunning, whatever she wears. Don't you think so, Jamie?'

Jamie looked up. Now Carmen was acting weirdly, staring at him expectantly. 'Er, yes. Yes, she does.'

'But that costume, it's something else, huh?' Alexei winked lasciviously at Jamie.

'I didn't think it was possible.' Richard tore a piece of

French bread from his side plate and mopped up his watercress sauce. 'When she was cast, I had serious doubts. But all of a sudden, pow!' He clapped his huge hands. 'This rôle really seems to have brought her out of herself.'

'In more ways than one,' Nadia cackled, and Carmen joined in.

'I've never seen her dance like she did today.' Richard laid down his knife and fork and without asking the others for permission, he lit a cigarette. 'If she keeps it up, she'll be offered a principal's contract in no time.'

'If she keeps it up, I won't have any problem keeping it up.' Alexei beamed, obviously proud that his mastery of the English language had now extended to smutty jokes.

'I'm going to bed.' Jessica's chair screeched on the parquet floor as she pushed it away from the table.

'Don't you want dessert?' Alexei put his heavy hand on top of hers.

'I'm not hungry.' She snatched her hand away, and stalked to the door.

Richard raised his palm to his cheek and pursed his lips. 'What's got into her?'

'It's what hasn't got into her that's the problem.'

Jamie gave up on his dinner and looked across the table at Alexei. 'What do you mean?'

'Jessica and I have been – you know.' He slapped his left hand down into the crook of his right elbow, raising his fist in a typically unsubtle illustration of what he meant. 'She's been very jealous, ever since she found out about me and Adele.'

Jamie felt the blood draining from his limbs. He wanted to lie down. In the corner of his eye, he was vaguely aware of Richard sitting forward in his seat, and Nadia and Carmen exchanging glances. 'You and Adele?'

Alexei repeated his obscene gesture, satisfaction glinting in his grey eyes.

Jamie stood up. 'Excuse me. I'm very tired. I'm going to go to bed.' Somehow, he made it to the door. In a daze of disbelief, he climbed the stairs to his bedroom. Shutting the door on the world, he slumped on to the bed.

'Of course,' he muttered bitterly to himself. 'You stupid, stupid fool.'

It all made sense now. Like a detective story, all the pieces suddenly slotted into place. Her reticence when he'd asked her out. Her discomfort on the minibus on the way to the Manor; he had been sitting with her when Alexei had appeared. The electric atmosphere on stage, the day she'd slapped Alexei's face. The way she had mistaken him for Alexei when he'd followed her backstage. No wonder she'd been uncomfortable in his presence. She had liked him once, and possibly still did, but she liked Alexei more. She was with him, now.

It was so wrong. They were an incongruous pair. Alexei with his reputation, which, by all accounts, was justified. Adele with her quiet, unassuming beauty. Life was so unfair.

'So.' Richard rested his elbows on the table. He clasped his hands and balanced his sculpted chin on his knuckles. 'How long have you been fucking Adele?'

Alexei turned down the corners of his mouth and stared vacantly, as if trying to remember. 'A while,' he nodded.

Carmen could tell he was lying. 'She'd never spoken to you before we started this ballet.'

Alexei threw her a dark look. 'Excuse me, my English isn't perfect. We started seeing each other this week.' He blinked slowly and smiled at some secret memory.

'Which day, exactly?'

His eyes bored into Carmen's. 'What business is it of yours?'

'It's none of my business. It's just that I know Adele went to bed early on Tuesday night. Monday and Wednesday nights she spent with us.' She nodded towards Nadia. 'Tonight she's with Rafique. That leaves Thursday. And I seem to remember you spent last night playing poker with Richard.'

Richard snorted loudly. Alexei reached inside his mouth, picked a morsel of food from his teeth, inspected it and sucked it from his fingertip. 'All right, I slept with her once.' He paused, his mouth widening from a scowl into a sneer. 'But it was wild. And when we get back to London –'

'By the time we get back to London, Adele will be with Jamie.'

Alexei's mouth hardened once again into a frown. 'What the hell are you talking about?'

'You'd have to be blind not to notice how much they like each other.' Carmen got up and moved into Jessica's empty seat beside Alexei, delighting in taunting him. She rested her tiny fingers on his huge forearm. 'Sorry to disappoint you, Alexei, but I don't think you stand a chance. Jamie's always had a thing for Adele. They would have got together years ago, if he hadn't gone off to Munich.' She peered beneath his thick fringe, smiling incredulously at his bewildered indignation. 'Haven't you seen the way they dance together?'

His heavy brows knitted. 'If Adele likes Jamie so much, what was she doing in my bedroom?'

Carmen patted his hand and tilted her head patronisingly. 'Perhaps she was lost. We all make mistakes.'

Foster arrived, carrying a wide silver tray. Carmen and Nadia gasped as he served the four remaining diners with their dessert. White meringue swans floated on pools of chocolate sauce. On their backs, they carried slivers of fresh peach. Raspberries circled the edges of the plates, held in place with freshly whipped cream. Foster opened some dessert wine and another bottle of

201

mineral water, while the dancers murmured in admiration.

'These are beautiful,' Nadia cooed. 'Adele would love these. Is she having the same as us?'

'I believe the menu is the same. Although the Master likes to serve his meals in a slightly, shall we say, unorthodox fashion.' He turned at the door and bowed. 'I wouldn't worry about Miss King. From what I've heard, she's enjoying her meal.'

'I'm sure she is.' Richard's fork hovered above his swan, reluctant to break its neck. 'I'd happily eat dog food for a night alone with Rafique.'

Alexei looked shocked. 'Do you think she's – ? She wouldn't. He must be twenty years older than her.' His lip curled in disgust.

'He's rich. And gorgeous. I think she would.' Carmen looked across the table at Nadia. 'We think she already has.'

With a flourish of his wrist Richard put down his fork and folded his arms. 'Do I have to remind you girls that I am Queen of Gossip in this company? Come on darlings, tell all.'

Nadia didn't need any further encouragement. Her dark eyes shone, as they always did when she was fanning the flames. 'We sneaked out to the pub a couple of nights ago. When we came back, we started exploring. Foster caught us in one of the towers.' She shared a sly glance with Carmen. 'We legged it back to our bedrooms. We passed Rafique on the way, heading in the opposite direction, back towards the tower. It wasn't until we got back to our rooms that we realised Adele wasn't with us.'

'She didn't come back for two hours,' Carmen added.

Richard tutted loudly. 'The dirty stop-out. Have you two been leading her astray?'

'Not at all. It was Adele's idea to explore.' Nadia

smashed her swan with the back of her spoon, and began to devour its delicate, chocolate-stained head.

'It was Adele's idea to tie me up.' Carmen licked a drop of the rich sauce from her lips, waiting for Richard's eyes to light up.

'I beg your pardon?'

'The tower was full of raunchy costumes, toys and stuff. We were drunk. We got dressed up. Adele made Nadia tie me up.'

One of Richard's eyebrows arched dramatically. 'Adele *made* you?'

A dry laugh hacked from Nadia's throat. 'You don't argue with someone wearing thigh length boots and wielding a whip.'

Carmen savoured the silence as Richard's brain slowly assimilated this priceless information. Together with Nadia, she had been trying to find a way to shock him ever since he'd arrived at the company, parading his overt homosexuality like a challenge. 'Are you all right?' she asked, at last.

He held up a long hand. 'Give me a minute.' He closed his eyes. 'I'm trying to imagine Adele with thigh length boots and a whip.'

Alexei grunted. Carmen looked at him; his attention was far away.

Richard opened his eyes. 'I have a new found admiration for the woman. No wonder she's dancing like the succubus. She is the succubus. If I wasn't totally addicted to cock, I think I could quite fancy her.'

Alexei grunted again. Carmen smiled to herself as Nadia moved round the table into the empty seat beside her. Reaching across her, she stole Alexei's plate.

'You're not going to eat this, are you?'

He shook his head sadly. 'What a woman. She's a different person behind closed doors.'

Nadia winked at Carmen. 'Aren't we all?' she muttered, her mouth already full of meringue.

Carmen nodded. 'We all have our secrets.'

'And what are yours?'

She looked at Alexei. Holding his gaze, she wiped her finger across her plate, searching out the last morsels of chocolate and cream. Seductively curling her tongue around her fingertip, she wondered how best to answer. Deciding that actions spoke louder than words, she dropped her free hand on to Nadia's thigh. Nadia, unflinching, carried on wolfing her second dessert. Alexei's eyes followed Carmen's fingers, and he gulped.

Her skin crawled with warmth, watching Alexei's face transform. She suspected Adele had left his thoughts. His eyes were transfixed to her fingers as they traced an inexorable path up Nadia's pale leg, rumpling her soft black skirt. Nadia finished eating and sat back in her seat, opening her thighs slightly, allowing Carmen's hand to reach higher. She licked her lips and sighed with fullness; a moment later, Carmen's touch brushed over her mound, and a different sigh eased from her mouth.

Carmen bit her lip, smothering a laugh as Alexei grunted yet again. His heavily lidded eyes were full of amazement as she eased beneath the elastic of Nadia's cotton knickers.

Without a word, he slid from his seat. Ducking beneath the table, he shuffled on his knees until he was between Nadia's thighs. For a moment, he watched Carmen's hand fumbling beneath Nadia's knickers. Then, losing patience and control, he pushed her wrist away. Hooking at the waistband of her panties, he pulled them over her hips and down to her ankles. Pausing only for a moment to drink in the sight of Nadia's darkly curled sex, his head fell.

Carmen's shoulder ached where Nadia grabbed her. Looking down, she watched Alexei's thick lips sucking at Nadia, his tongue delving deep inside her friend. Her heavy breasts pushed for release beneath her T-shirt as she arched her back. Spreading her thighs, she pulled her knickers taut between her ankles, the thin white cotton stretched to breaking point. Sensing her nearness to climax, Carmen joined in. The stubble on Alexei's upper lip scratched her finger as she rolled Nadia's bud.

His face retreated as she shuddered to orgasm. Carmen noticed his attention travelling from Nadia's swollen pussy lips, up Carmen's still circling finger and along her arm, then across her shoulders and down to where her other hand was busy between her own legs. Shifting his position, he roughly snatched her hand away. In a second, her knickers too were pulled down to her ankles. Without stopping to wipe the glistening juices from his greedy mouth, he tucked in to his second helping of warm, ripe woman.

It was Carmen's turn to shudder and clutch at Nadia for help. She felt like the swan she had just eaten, marooned on the plate, her neck arching as she was drowned in hot, sticky sauce. As he ate her up, the urgent movement of his lips, tongue and teeth, blended deliciously. Tensing her buttocks she rose from the chair, reaching further into his face. She rested one hand on his strong neck, feeling the tension in his muscles. With her other hand, she slid underneath her blouse and cupped her soft breast through the lace of her bra. Nadia's fingers searched for her other breast, pinching her nipple hard as she came.

'Well, that's their secret out in the open.' Richard walked around the table. Standing behind Carmen and Nadia, he draped his long arms around their shoulders and looked down at Alexei, cowering under the table. 'Why don't you tell the girls yours?'

Like a snake, Alexei slunk back into his seat. Avoiding Richard's eyes he fidgeted, adjusting the bulge which Carmen could see quite clearly in his jeans. 'I don't know what you mean.'

'Oh, come on darling. You won't shock these two.' Trailing his fingers across the back of Carmen's neck,

Richard swaggered up to Alexei, hips swaying like a tiger on a lazy walk through the jungle.

Carmen saw Alexei's bottom lip quiver. 'Richard,' he began.

Richard pressed a finger to Alexei's mouth. He knelt at his feet. His dark hand squeezed Alexei's crotch. When he turned back to Carmen and Nadia, his eyes were dancing. 'You see, girls, you're not the only ones around here who like to swing.'

'You're not serious?' Carmen gasped, unable to keep the giggle from her voice.

'Oh yes.' He turned back to Alexei. Unzipping his jeans, he reached inside the fly. Like a conjurer, he produced a thick, bulging erection. 'Behind closed doors, our Alexei is a different person.'

Alexei looked at the women, his stony grey eyes alive with furious embarrassment and unstoppable, undeniable lust. Richard's head slowly descended into his lap. 'No, don't, Richard, please . . .'

He grunted helplessly. It seemed Richard had swallowed his voice, as well as his manhood.

Chapter Ten

'The Master requests the pleasure of your company. You are to join him for dinner in his private apartments.'

Startled, Adele jumped and lunged for the bed. Grabbing her T-shirt, she covered up her breasts. How did Foster always manage to appear without making a sound? The door creaked terribly whenever she opened it.

'The Master is waiting,' he urged, as she stood motionless.

'Oh. Right. What should I wear?'

A smirk flickered over Foster's dry lips. 'It doesn't really matter. What you've got on is fine.'

Adele looked down. Jeans and trainers. It wasn't exactly what she would have chosen for an intimate supper with Rafique. She had been about to go for a walk, planning to change for dinner, but it seemed he had other ideas. 'If you don't mind, I think I'd rather change.' She looked at Foster, hoping he would take the hint and wait outside.

'Put your T-shirt on, Miss King. The Master is waiting.'

She could see it was no use arguing. Sighing quietly,

she wondered how she was going to put her bra and top on, without giving Foster a view of her breasts. She quickly decided it was impossible. Snatching at her low-cut, lacy white bra, she fumbled with the hook and straps as quickly as she could. Foster didn't flinch, he didn't even look. His glassy, lizard's eyes remained steadfastly on her face as she pulled her tight, soft pink T-shirt over her body.

'Follow me, please.'

There was a door opposite her bedroom. Foster unlocked it and ushered Adele into the cold, dark corridor beyond. They walked for several silent minutes, descending into the belly of the house before windows announced their arrival at the back of the Manor. Going up a narrow, steep staircase lined with blazing torches, Foster knocked before opening the door and standing aside for Adele to enter.

'Enjoy your meal, Miss King.' He blinked, the first time she had seen him do so.

Her jeans were blasphemy in the splendour of that room. Even the ceiling was well-dressed. The surface was a carved honeycomb pattern of hexagons, and in every wooden frame the white rose of Yorkshire had been delicately painted. The high, oak-panelled walls also served as a picture gallery, each panel holding a portrait. There were long-haired men with pointed beards, wearing capes and slight smiles; women in beautiful, tight-bodiced gowns, their hair piled high in elaborate bouffants, eyes shining demurely; children, sewing, riding, or sitting with their dogs. All stared down enviously at the table.

Stretching the length of the room from the door to the red velvet-curtained windows, the table was so laden with food that its highly polished surface was barely visible. Ornate, silver candelabras perched between the plates, their delicate lights flickering on the sumptuous feast. Hunger growled in Adele's stomach as her eyes greedily moved from one dish to the next, like a child in a sweet shop wanting everything. Slowly, she walked along the length of the table, passing ten chairs before she came to the end. There, sitting on a high-backed, ornately carved throne, was Rafique. The tastiest dish of all, she smiled to herself, thinking she had never seen a man so well-suited to a dinner jacket. The men she knew always seemed uncomfortably aware that they were dressing up; Rafique, with his luscious skin and the opulent wave in his glossy black hair, looked like he'd been born in a tuxedo.

He held out his hand as she approached, and smiled. 'How do you feel?'

She placed her fingers in his. Her eyes fell down his long legs to his black shoes, then across the wooden floor to her scuffed trainers. 'Distinctly underdressed.' She looked up. 'I wanted to change, but Foster wouldn't let me.'

He caressed the back of her hand with his thumb. 'You look lovely.' He pulled her closer. Hooking his arms around her waist and legs, he scooped her on to his lap and kissed her. Adele closed her eyes and rested her arms on his shoulders. The now familiar scent of his after-shave filtered through to her brain. The warmth of his tongue spread over hers and as his kiss reached deeper and deeper into her soul, she felt her innards turn to liquid and flow away. One of his hands was on her neck, beneath her hair, the other eased underneath her T-shirt and up on to the curve of her breast, fingers settling around her shape as if that was where they belonged.

His face pulled away. Sighing, he slowly opened his eyes. 'Are you hungry?'

'I'm always hungry.' For you, she added silently.

He nodded. 'You do have a good appetite.' His dark eyes glittered mischievously, and Adele suspected he had read her thoughts, as usual, and was sharing her innuendo.

'I just can't stop myself. I should diet, but I haven't the willpower.'

'And why on earth would you diet?'

'Dancers aren't supposed to have hips.'

'Who says? When I go to the ballet, I want to see women.' Rafique ran his hand down her back and on to her rump. 'Real women. With curves.'

Adele shrugged. 'It's all very well having curves, but pity Jamie and Alexei. They have to lift me.'

'Pity them? They have one of the best jobs in the world.' He stood, gently sliding Adele from his lap. 'Let's eat.'

Adele drifted towards the table. She gazed longingly at the nearest bowl, piled high with king prawns doused in an oily sauce. 'Is Foster bringing plates?' she asked, noticing that there weren't any empty ones. She looked around the room for a cabinet, but there was no other furniture. 'And cutlery?'

His body pressed against her back. Reaching around her, he tenderly squeezed her breasts. 'We don't need plates,' he breathed into her hair. 'Come on.' He grabbed her hand and led her purposefully away from the table.

He pushed at a panel holding a portrait of a fey young man in hunting dress, and a doorway opened up. Inside the adjoining room, a porcelain roll-top bath held centre stage beneath a cloud of steam. A pile of white towels waited on the red tiled floor.

Slightly confused that the talk of food seemed to have been forgotten, Adele looked up at Rafique. 'I've just had a bath.'

He pulled her inside and closed the door. 'You're going to have another.'

'I'll look like a prune.'

'A peach.' Standing in front of her, he peeled her top

over her head. 'You'll look like a peach; smooth and ripe.'

Moving behind her, he unhooked her bra and pushed it from her shoulders. Realising that it was pointless protesting, and that she didn't want to anyway, Adele kicked off her trainers, unbuttoned her jeans and discarded them on to the floor. Rafique took off her knickers, palms sliding over her buttocks on the way. Then he turned her by the hips to face him, and reverently kissed her soft mound of pubic hair. 'Goodbye,' he whispered.

'Pardon?'

He didn't answer but led Adele to the bath, holding her hand as she stepped over its high side. She sank into the heat, wallowing in the perfume as it enveloped her senses. Rafique took off his jacket and hung it on the back of the door. He unhooked his cufflinks and put them in his pocket, then rolled up his shirt sleeves. Picking up a small wooden stool, he brought it to the side of the bath and perched on its worn seat.

'Stand up.'

Steam rose from her skin as the soothing water trickled off her. Adele watched his dark hands dip into the water, wetting the soap he clasped. Moving between her legs, he rubbed the slippery bar all over her groin, spreading the lather over her strip of tight curls. Putting down the soap, he produced a razor, and looked up at Adele with a lustful, longing glint in his eye.

'What are you doing?' she gasped, her body tense as she already knew the answer.

'I want to see you naked.'

'I am –'

'I want to be as close as I can to the bare, naked you. I want to see *you*. All of you.'

Carefully, he raised the blade. Gently pulling her skin taut with one hand, he swept the cold metal over her pubis.

He worked with clean, swift movements, eyes glued

to his fingers, sweeping away the hairs with a man's well-practised skill. Adele felt his breath on her as his face leaned closer, totally absorbed in his task. She shifted her stance, lifting one foot on to the side of the bath, her hands steadying herself on his shoulders. He shaved the very tops of her silky inner thighs where they curved inwards, and the inner edges of the fleshy mounds covering her sex. His fingers were deft and businesslike, never still as they mauled her tender skin to enable him to reach every fold and crease. The feeling was incredible, his eyes so close to her, his soapy fingers brushing against her swelling clitoris, opening her silky labia, but never lingering. Watching his concentration made Adele's thighs quiver.

'You're done.' His face was full of fierce admiration.

Squatting to wash off the lather, Adele looked down at herself. Her fingers delightedly, inquisitively discovered her new nakedness, shocked at the pleasure it gave her to feel smooth skin where there had been thick curls.

'It looks beautiful.' Rafique's fingers twitched hesitantly over her bare mound as she stood again, like a sculptor afraid to spoil the perfection of his own work. 'So sexy.'

Head bowed, Adele's fingers brushed over his and pressed them on to her skin. It was sexy, incredibly so. The flesh which had been hidden since puberty was unbelievably soft and like a peach, its smoothness was pleasure to the fingertips. She felt as if the essence of her womanhood had been stripped and laid bare, ready for worship from eyes, lips and penis. A different dampness from that of the bath began to well up inside her.

Rafique unfolded a wide towel, motioning for Adele to step into it. He held her tight, drying her quickly with urgent strokes. When he had finished, he gently pulled at the band holding the weight of her hair up in a pony tail. Releasing the soft waves, he ran his fingers through

212

them from her temples, combing her hair on to her shoulders. He paused for a moment, framing her face in his warm hands, his gaze very serious. Then, as if he had suddenly remembered something, he smiled. 'Come on,' he said, grabbing her wrist. 'I'm starving.'

Back in the dining room, they stood in front of his throne. 'On the table,' he motioned, the familar aggression burning in his features.

'Yes, Master.' Adele hitched herself up, shuffling backwards into the gap Rafique had cleared, until the backs of her knees fitted against the table's edge. Beneath her naked sex lips, the wooden surface was cool and hard, in contrast to her pussy which felt softer, warmer and damper than ever before.

Rafique dipped a finger into one of the silver goblets, and pushed the tip inside her mouth. The dark red wine, smooth and rich, awoke her taste buds. 'I'm not your Master any longer, Adele. There's nothing more I can teach you.'

She suckled on his skin, drawing every trace of wine from his fingertip. Looking up at him, she noticed something different in his eyes tonight; lust was there, as fierce as ever, but there was a sorrow too, a ruefulness that she couldn't explain.

'Tonight, we're equals. If there is something you want me to do, you must tell me. Tell me what you want.'

Adele smiled wistfully. For a split second she wondered what the others would think. Would they believe it if they saw her, naked on the table, her sex bare and a beautiful man offering his services? Then she banished them from her mind, along with her old self. She mourned the passing of the old Adele, but only in the same way a greedy, money-grabbing relative might grieve. She had never liked her. Now that she was gone the new Adele, the real Adele, could enjoy the spoils.

Taking a deep breath, she filled her lungs with air and

her body with anticipation. Her eyes scanned the length of the table stretching out behind her. 'I want to try everything. I want to taste it all.'

He reached for the nearest plate. Holding it in the palm of one hand, he picked up a tip of asparagus and dangled it above her waiting lips. Adele stuck out her tongue, her eyes fluttering to his to watch his reaction, intensely aware of the barely hidden agenda in her suggestive movement. Tilting her head back she sucked the firm, green tip between her lips, and chewed on its perfectly cooked texture. 'Mmmm. Another.' He lifted a second shoot. This one was dripping with butter, and a droplet of it dribbled off the asparagus and on to her lower lip. She wiped her mouth with the back of her hand.

'Let me do that.' Rafique bowed his head and sucked her lip into his mouth, gathering the butter from her skin. She wondered whether he could taste her arousal.

Having cleaned the spill he put down the plate and reached for another. Salad this time; plump tomatoes, sliced and laced with olive oil, slivers of cucumber, red, green and yellow peppers, all laid intricately on crisp radicchio leaves the colour of the wine. Patiently he fed her, seeming to relish each fresh taste as much as she did. Vinaigrette smeared her mouth and chin, sharp and oily, and again he dipped his head, licking her fastidiously like a cat cleaning itself.

'Those,' she pointed, as he pulled away and waited for instructions.

He placed the dish on her lap, shocking her with its coldness. With a faint and satisfying crack, he broke the prawn's back and peeled off its shell. Waiting expectantly, he lifted the helpless creature to Adele's open mouth.

'Oh God,' she murmured, overwhelmed by the flavours mingling on her tongue, challenging her to recognise them. There was an eastern base note; ginger, lemongrass, peanuts. Beyond that, appearing like a wicked afterthought only when her teeth dug into the succulent flesh, there was a sudden hint of fire; chillies, their heat taking her breath away.

'A drink,' she begged, and he held the goblet up to her lips. The wine did nothing to quench her thirst. Longingly, she eyed his cool mouth. 'Kiss me.'

Putting her drink back down, he rested his hands either side of her hips and leaned his body into hers. His kiss was slow, tentative, a contrast to his usual urgency, as if her mouth was a delicacy being savoured for the first time. Adele lifted her hands on to his back. Beneath his shirt, she could feel the sharp edges of his shoulder blades moving. She opened her eyes and was shocked to find his open, too. The intensity of his gaze warmed her inside more ferociously than the hottest, most potent chilli could have done.

She pushed him away. Skinning a prawn for him, she touched her greasy fingertips to his lips as he greedily ate. He took another from her, then another, sucking the juice from her fingers between mouthfuls. They took turns feeding each other until the dish was empty.

Without a word, Rafique picked the next plate; strips of smoked salmon, drizzled with zig-zags of dill-flecked mayonnaise. Chilled and sharpened with lemon juice, the rich, luxuriant taste quickly calmed the memory of the hot prawns. Gulping greedily, Adele and Rafique soon cleared that plate, too.

'Still hungry?'

'I'm just like you.' He took a gulp of wine. 'I'm always hungry.'

Adele brushed the plate out of her lap. Neither was watching and it fell to the floor, spinning loudly for a moment before it settled into silence. Spreading her legs, she pushed at Rafique's shoulders. 'Eat me, then.'

He slumped to his knees. Reverently, he rested his trembling fingers on her thighs. He gazed at the naked

215

smoothness of her pussy, his head swaying slightly like a snake in a hypnotic trance; then he fell on to her.

He licked all over her soft mound, tasting her afresh as he had done with her mouth. Moaning quietly with unrestrained pleasure, he kissed the gap where the widest part of her triangle of hair usually lay. Slowly, methodically, he moved downwards, covering every spot that had been hidden from him before, until he reached her pouting labia. Like the dishes they had devoured, her pussy lips were succulent and moist. He opened her with one lap of his tongue, and delved inside.

Adele gasped with delight, pushing food out of the way as she lowered her body on to the polished wood. Her hair spread out around her face and she lost her fingers in its softness, as Rafique pushed deeper and deeper. Her hips twitched frustratedly, hunger eating her up.

'Come here,' she moaned. 'I want to taste you.'

He joined her on the table. Standing over her prone and quivering body, he unzipped his trousers. There was nothing underneath, and Adele reached up like a drowning man, as his long, dark cock appeared.

Turning around, he splayed his legs in a wide kneel astride her hips. Like a slavering animal, Rafique's penis lowered inexorably towards her mouth. Then his taste filled her, musky, salty and warm. Adele strained her neck to pull his velvet-coated hardness further inside. As she began to suck and lick, his insistent lips pressed once again to the mouth of her sex, and wetness lapped at her like the tide slowly coming in over her body. They seemed to feed on each other for an eternity. Sometimes, Adele froze as Rafique sparked intolerable sensations deep within her, then gluttony would overcome her again and she would suck on his long prick with renewed gusto, and it would be his turn to momentarily lose his rhythm. Like wolves at a carcass they gulped ferociously, shuddering and writhing together and eagerly drinking the juices that overflowed from their ecstasy.

'More,' she pleaded as he stood, one hand clutching his trousers, the other his forehead. She knew how he felt, she was dizzy too, insane with desire. 'I'm still hungry, Rafique.'

'What do you want?' he asked, breathlessly. 'Tell me.'

'Something sweet.' She rolled on to her side, watching as he walked down the table, picking his way through the plates and around the candelabras. Finding what he was looking for he stepped down on to a chair, then to the floor. He picked up a pair of cut glass bowls, and strode back to her side.

'Fruit,' he announced, putting one of the dishes down, 'for the dancer. And chocolate,' he smiled, putting the other one on the table, 'for the woman.'

Adele dipped her finger into the sticky brown sauce and sighed loudly as it met her tongue. 'That's heaven.' Two fingers went into the bowl this time, scooping up the molten delight. Spattering its faint warmth over the downward slope of her breast, she smeared it on to her areola. 'Why don't you try some?'

His lips were already there, pursed around her chocolate-coated flesh. She watched the tender skin of her areola being pulled by the suction of his mouth, the dark stain gradually fading to reveal the paler brown beneath. When she was clean she coated the other nipple, and his lips and tongue began their voracious journey again. Watching him, hearing him, his breath quick and hurried, she felt like a Roman empress with her dedicated slave. The sensation of power flooded through her.

'Lick me all over.'

His eyes roamed along her body, deciding where to start. Impatient, Adele dangled the fingertips of one hand into the bowl, and raised her wrist to his face like a queen expecting a kiss on the back of her hand. He grabbed her and sucked each finger with half-closed eyes. Turning her palm upwards, he ran his brown-streaked tongue up the pale inside of her arm, leaning over the table to reach her shoulder. Pushing her on to her back, he softly kissed her neck before his tongue began another trail. Travelling down her cleavage to her belly, he paused to dart into the hollow of her navel, searching for some morsel she might have secreted there. Moving onwards he knelt between her dangling calves, nibbled the tender lips of her pussy and licked her inner thighs, his fingers stroking and tickling wherever his mouth had been, following on behind like the delicate, silvery track of a snail. He sucked each toe in turn, holding her ankles when they jerked at the unexpected pleasure.

'We haven't had any fruit.' Adele sunk her hand into the bowl. Like exotic fish, the cool slivers brushed slimily against her. Grabbing a handful, she dropped the mixture between her breasts and over her taut stomach. It was ice-cold, and goosebumps rippled over her skin. Rafique moved from her feet back to her side. Planting his hands either side of her shoulders, he bent and picked a crescent of peach up with his teeth. Nuzzling between her breasts, he retrieved each piece. Chunks of pear, squares of apple and melon, strawberries and raspberries were gradually cleared from her sticky skin. A mixture of saliva and fruit juice glistened on her body. Watching Rafique's dark eyes, Adele reached for another handful, and trickled its coldness on to her mound.

It was then that Rafique seemed to lose control. He stumbled to the end of the table, and knelt again between her open legs. He dived to her pussy and as he began to eat from her naked flesh, he nipped her tender skin. Snatching at a long, pink-edged piece of nectarine, he paused to warn her with mischievous eyes, wielding the fruit like the weapons he had tortured her with in the tower. Adele braced herself, but when she felt the chill slithering inside her, radiating shock waves throughout her tingling limbs, her body gave up.

The warmth of his lips quickly followed, sucking the iciness from her vagina and into his mouth. But another small, phallic intrusion was inserted between the gaping lips of her sex, and she was helpless as he pushed its coldness deep inside her. The walls of her pussy contracted but it was no use, his tongue was there to catch the fruit and tease her with it, before hooking it out and eating it. Adele propped herself up on her elbows, watching in delighted agony as he tormented her with slices of papaya, mango and orange, their surfaces as smooth and succulent as her labia.

At last he stood up. Leaning over, he took her wrists and pulled her up into a sitting position. Dropping his face to Adele's, he passed a fleshy wedge of peach from his lips to hers. It tasted vaguely of her.

'Can you taste that? Can you taste yourself?'

'Yes,' she whispered, flinching under the harshness of his glare. 'It tastes of me.'

He slowly shook his head. 'Why do you have to taste so good?' His voice was sweet, but the fury in his eyes was intensifying.

Adele stroked his cheek. 'Is something wrong?'

'No,' he snapped.

'Something's upset you.'

He winced. Blinking, he lowered his eyes. 'Don't speak. Just don't say a word.'

Bewildered, Adele watched his trousers fall to the floor. Holding her buttocks, he bowed his head and inched forward, positioning the plum of his penis between her open lips. For what seemed like several long minutes he was still, breathing hard at the sight of her pussy, helpless and naked as a new-born animal; breathing hard like a hunter, high on blood and about to make a kill. Then, with a twisted, muffled grunt of anger, he rammed himself inside Adele with such force that if he hadn't been gripping her, she would have slid backwards over the polished table.

Adele wrapped her calves around the back of his juddering thighs. Confusion blurred the sharp edges of her pleasure. The violence of Rafique's remorseless plundering was nothing new. The way he forced himself so deeply, skewering her on his hardness, bruising her inner thighs, banging hard against her engorged clitoris – that much she recognised. But something was different. The vague sense of sorrow she had detected in his eyes had metamorphosed into a rage that held his body in a vice. Every muscle and sinew in his face, arms and legs was straining, lunging frantically for the innermost depths of her sex as if the key to life was in there, and it was just out of reach. His fingers bit into her haunches, his eyes closed tightly as if he was in pain. His breath rose into a groan, he shuddered violently and with one final, gut-wrenching thrust, it was over.

He collapsed into her arms. His face rested in the slope of her shoulder, and his breath mingled warmly with her hair. Adele's hands drifted underneath his shirt and feeling his sweat, slippery on her fingers, she held him close. His penis throbbed inside her.

'I'm sorry,' he gasped

'What on earth for?'

An echo of his climax shivered down his spine. 'It wasn't supposed to be like this.'

'What wasn't?'

'Our last night together.' He lifted his head. It was hard to tell in the candlelight, but Adele thought she could see sorrow welling up in his eyes.

'We don't leave until Sunday. What about tomorrow night?'

'Tomorrow's the performance and the party. I'll have to mingle, and so will you. There won't be time for ... for us.'

'Is that why you're upset?'

His fingers stroked her throat and slowly fell to her breast. 'You're all sticky. Let's run another bath.'

For the third time that evening, Adele wallowed in the warm water. Sitting behind her, Rafique slowly, lovingly soaped her back.

'Rafique, can I ask you something?'

'Anything.'

'Why did you choose me? For the ballet, I mean.'

'That's a long story. It begins when I was a child.'

'Go on,' she urged, intrigued. There was silence for a while, as if he was deciding how to begin. 'Rafique?'

'To explain, I have to tell you about my mother. She was an amazing woman. Half Spanish, half Indian, so you can imagine how beautiful she was. But her real beauty was in her character. She was quiet and gentle but she was a free spirit, always laughing. My father was a businessman, and my mother and I would follow him wherever he went. It was a nomadic lifestyle, but we enjoyed it. We were wealthy, and although my mother didn't believe in sending me to school, she always made sure there were plenty of children around for me to play with. She was very aware of the fact that I was an only child.' Rafique put down the soap and began to rinse Adele's back. 'We were very close. I was a very happy child, up until the age of thirteen.'

'What happened then?'

'My mother died.' His voice and fingers paused. Adele turned in the bath to face him.

'I'm so sorry.'

'My father lost his mind. He refused to grieve. He moved us back to France, where he came from, and threw all his energies into building a business. He raged against the laid-back attitude my mother had had towards my education, and sent me to boarding school in England. He said I needed some discipline in my life. He shut me out, completely.

'School was utter hell. My mother had taught me a lot about people, nature, art and philosphy, but I knew nothing about maths or Latin, or English literature. I was way behind my classmates and they were as cruel as children can be. No matter how much I tried to be accepted, my accent and my dark skin made me stand out. The happy, outgoing, free-spirited little boy got bullied out of me. I left school at eighteen, a bitter, lonely and painfully shy young man.

'By then, my father had built his business into an empire. He wanted me to learn the ropes from the bottom. I wanted to be an artist, to design sets for the theatre, but I was afraid to refuse him. He sent me to India to work for the manager of his factory there.'

His eyelids flickered shyly. 'I fell in love, with the manager's daughter. She looked . . .' he paused, his eyes clouding, 'just like my mother.' He sighed deeply. 'She liked me, but I was so shy, I could barely talk to her. My self-esteem was so low, I couldn't believe such a beautiful woman would want me. On top of that, I was terribly ashamed of the way my father was exploiting the workers, using them for cheap labour. I imagined how devastated my mother would have been, to see old women and children slaving away, all for my father's profit. I had a terrible row with him, and ran away. Suraya – the girl I was in love with – begged to come with me. I desperately wanted her to, but something . . . something made me say no.' He looked up at Adele. She nodded, recognising the torment in his eyes. 'I think I was afraid to be happy.'

'I travelled around India for a year, searching for something. My mother's roots perhaps, or peace of mind. I didn't find anything except deeper loneliness and misery. I ran out of money and lost the will to live. I wanted to be with my mother. I used my last cash to buy some opium, and the last thing I remember was getting into a fight with a beggar who wanted my money. He pulled a knife on me. I tried to fight but I was weak from lack of food and illness, and he knocked me unconscious and took what little I had.'

Leaning forward between his open legs, Adele touched the scar traversing his cheekbone. 'That's where you got this from.'

'Yes.' A tear shone in the corner of his eye. 'I must have been close to death, because I saw my mother.'

Adele gasped. 'What did she say?'

'She didn't speak to me. It wasn't an out of body experience, just a dream. She was dancing in a garden, by a waterfall. She was laughing, and full of life.' He blinked, and the tear began a slow journey down his handsome, tortured face. 'That was the moment I realised that she had enjoyed her short life, and that she would have been furious to see me wasting mine.'

Adele didn't know what to say. Words could not take away the pain he was reliving, but she wanted to comfort him. Reaching for the soap, she rolled it between her hands and gently stroked the lather across his darkly haired chest. The faintest hint of a smile lifted his lips in acknowledgement.

'I woke up surrounded by women.' His smile deepened at Adele's surprise. 'At that time, India was a magnet for anyone wanting to escape conventional Western life. I was rescued by some hippies. They took me into their all-female commune, and nursed me back to health.'

'You were very lucky.'

'In more ways than one. Being the only man, I was rather spoilt. And being so shy, the women took it upon themselves to further my education.' This time, the twinkle in his eye was not a tear.

'You mean –'

'They taught me everything; to love life, to love women, to love myself.' Cupping his hands beneath the water, Rafique splashed his face. 'I stayed there for three

223

years. I would probably still be in India now, if I hadn't found out that my father was dying.'

Adele rested her hand on his thigh in sympathy as his tale turned back to tragedy. 'How on earth did you cope?'

'It was very hard. Illness had brought my father back to his senses, and he was punishing himself for neglecting me. On his death-bed, he begged for my forgiveness and made me promise to use my inheritance in the way my mother would have wanted – in the pursuit of pleasure and beauty. He left me a fortune. I came back to England.'

'I thought you would have hated England, after what happened to you at school.'

'I did. But I had made a pledge with myself, to confront all those bad memories. I enrolled at art college in London.'

'And you became an artist, like you'd always wanted.'

'Not exactly,' he laughed. 'I was hopeless. But what I lacked in skill, I made up for in appreciation. I quickly realised that my talent wasn't going to rock the world, but that my money could help. I supported everything I loved, and everything that needed my support. Films, theatres, art galleries, museums, opera companies . . .'

'And ballet companies.'

Rafique nodded. 'I love ballet. Almost as much as I love women.' He looked down at her hand on his thigh, as if he had just noticed it, and laced his fingers with hers. 'I've supported the National Ballet for the last twenty years. When David Renfell took over as director, he encouraged me to become more actively involved. It was a dream come true for me. As well as supporting the company financially, I've become a silent artistic director. David welcomes my input on everything – repertoire, casting, even set design.'

'Why do it all anonymously?'

'My father was renowned and respected as an entrepreneur, all over the world. When his business practices were revealed, the scandal shook the corporate community. Despite the fact that I made amends with all his employees after he died, the press would love to find me and dig up the dirt. I've managed to avoid them so far. I enjoy my life now, and I don't want anything to spoil it.'

'I still don't understand why you picked me, for the rôle of the succubus.'

'Come here.' He pulled on her hand, and Adele knelt on her heels between his thighs. Retrieving the soap, he worked up a soft white lather between his dark fingers and watching his hands, he spread it over her breasts. 'I recognised my younger self in you. I watched you, in class, in rehearsal, on stage, even at those corporate-hosted parties you all hate so much. I could see you had talent, but that something, deep inside, was holding you back. From the day you joined the company, I tried to find a way to help you let go.' His palms smoothed around the sides of her breasts. His thumbs reached inwards to her nipples, circling them until they peered stiffly through the soft curtain of soap. 'When the company lost its funding, I seized the chance. I wanted you to find freedom. The same freedom I found in that commune in India.'

Adele touched his neck and he looked up. 'Thank you.'

'Don't thank me. I wasn't being totally unselfish. I also wanted to fuck you.'

His fingers slid beneath her armpits and pulled her up off her heels. Again, he lubricated his hands with soap. His right hand moved over the smooth mound of her pussy, his left slipped around her back and between her buttocks. 'I wanted to fuck you, Adele. And I wanted you to admit that behind that shield you put up around yourself, you're as dirty and desperate as the rest of us.'

She flinched and gasped as a soapy finger slid inside

her anus. 'But it wasn't me doing those things. I wasn't in control. It wasn't me acting like that, it was –'

'What? The succubus?' The first knuckle of his finger poked in and out of her bottom, teasing her. 'You could have stopped me at any time, Adele. If you had said no, or pushed me away ... I didn't want to force you into anything. I was playing a game with you. You knew that, and you played along.'

Was it true? Adele thought back. 'But I saw the succubus in the window, that night in the tower. And Joe saw it, in my eyes.'

He reached between her legs. Roughly, he fingered the tender, bruised lips of her sex. Adele could feel her clitoris stiffening again as the heel of his hand rubbed against it. 'There isn't a succubus in this Manor, Adele. The succubus is in here.' A long finger poked inside her vagina and stroked its ridged walls. 'The demon lives in all of us. Some people, Alexei for instance, allow it to control them. Others, like you, are afraid of it, and try to deny it exists.' Another finger slid easily alongside the first, and his thumb pressed over her bud.

He was right. She had been afraid, but not any more. Like a snake shedding its skin, she wriggled out of her old inhibitions for once and for all. Squeezing the muscles of her vagina around his fingers, she pressed down on to Rafique, forcing him further inside her. 'I've changed,' she whispered. 'You've changed me.'

He nodded. 'You're free now. Free to be the woman you are inside. Strong, powerful, sensuous.' He rubbed against a magical place, a place where nerve endings seemed to gather and spark, just beneath the surface of her skin. The sensation drew an involuntary whimper from Adele and he looked down at his hand. 'Your pussy looks incredible like that.' He looked up again. His eyes grew limpid with desire. 'You're incredible, Adele.'

Rafique withdrew his hands. Leaning right back until his hair touched the water, he brought his knees up to his chest, then straightened them again through Adele's open legs. He urged her nearer with a pull on her hips. Dropping his gaze, he eased her over the tip of his erection, which was peering eagerly above the water. Adele heard his breath, caught in his throat as she lowered her pelvis and engulfed his hardness within her interminable, insatiable softness.

This time, she controlled the pace. Slowly, savouring every detail of his flesh, she slid up and down. The water lapped and swelled around their bodies between each gentle thrust, bathing them in warmth, as if the heat flowing between them wasn't enough. Aware of his gaze on her face, she allowed her fingers to lazily trail over his torso, brushing the dark discs of his nipples, tracing the contours of his chest, enjoying the softness of his black hair. There were silver hairs too, curling around her fingers; faint beginnings of grey at his temples as well, the first time she had noticed them. Her touch roamed all over his face, delighting in finally having the time to linger over his features. There was an ease to his good looks, a smooth, exotic opulence; a mixture of inherited genes and supreme wealth. But his eyes were something else, at once knowing and searching, secretive and honest, childishly innocent and wickedly sinful. Adele would never forget them, she decided, as she threw herself into the unending depth of his gaze.

'You're incredible,' she said.

He squeezed her against him, kissing her throat as she rose and fell. Reaching back for his hand, Adele urged it downwards. 'Touch me there.'

'Where?' He hovered over her buttock.

'You know where.'

'Tell me.' His dark eyes glittered.

Adele sighed in a show of exasperation.

'Tell me what to do.' His lips grabbed at her neck. 'I want to hear you say it, Adele.'

'Put your finger . . . up my arse.'

Immediately, delight speared her anus. It still took her breath away to feel so full, so unbearably complete, as it had the first time. She paused for a moment to allow her body to climb to a higher plane, to dive into an infinitely deeper level of sensation. Somewhere in her head, another delight flickered; the joy of telling a man exactly what she wanted, the joy of letting her thoughts out of the confines of her mind and into the open, where they could fizz and crackle.

His forbidden touch ignited a more vehement lust and, craving release, Adele moved into a more fervent pace. She pushed down on Rafique's penis with force, the water slapping, her inner thighs aching with the pain of his earlier, frantic fucking. Holding his shoulders she felt his body tremble, trapped in the throes of the ecstasy she controlled. She fed from his desperation, tensing the muscles of her sex, milking his penis until she felt the pleasure rushing from his body into hers. Her skin was on fire, coated with burning oil, and at the moment of climax she lowered herself back into the water to extinguish the searing flames.

'Are you looking forward to tomorrow, to the performance?'

Adele rolled on to her back and looked up into the burnt orange canopy above the bed. 'I never thought I would say this, but yes, I am.' She turned to look at Rafique. 'How about you?'

'No, not really.' He shifted on to his side and propped his head on his hand. 'Tomorrow's the start of a new chapter in your life. You've every reason to enjoy it. But it's different for me. Tomorrow's just another reminder that I'm getting old.'

'It's your birthday, isn't it? How old will you be?'

His fingertips brushed her cheek. 'Twenty-one years older than you.'

228

Adele did the addition. 'Forty-five?' She sucked in her breath. 'Ancient,' she laughed.

Rafique smiled, but the sadness was creeping back into his eyes, inexorable as the old age he seemed to fear.

'What's the matter, Rafique? Is something on your mind?'

'No.' He scrambled out of bed.

'What are you doing?' Adele sat up, hugging her knees and admiring his behind as he bent over the cabinet.

'I want to take a photo.' He turned, brandishing his camera. 'You'll be gone soon, and I want to remember our last night together. I want to remember the way you look after sex, all flushed and, and lovely.'

Adele winced, more at the pain in his voice than at the flash. 'I think I blinked.'

He took another, and another, moving closer to the bed until the film ran out and the motor whirred it back into its cassette. Putting the camera down on the bedside table, he lit the four candles in their miniature candelabra, and turned out the light. He sat down on the edge of the bed with his back to Adele. She shuffled across the mattress and laid a tentative hand on his back.

'Rafique, are you all right?'

She heard him swallow. He turned to look at her, and rested his gentle hand on her neck. 'I'm fine, thank you.'

'This doesn't have to be our last night together, you know.'

'I told you, there won't be time tomorrow –'

'I don't have to leave on Sunday. I could stay here, with you.'

'No you couldn't.'

'Why not?'

He pushed his fingers up into her hair. 'You've got a life to lead, Adele. A career about to take off. Did I mention that David Renfell's coming tomorrow? When

229

he sees the way you dance now, he'll offer you a promotion, I'm sure.'

'I don't want a promotion. I don't want to go home.'

'Yes you do. There's nothing for you here.'

She grabbed at his hand, pressing it beneath hers. 'You're here. I don't want to leave you.'

'I'm hardly ever here, Adele. What would you do, give up your career and follow me around, living in my shadow?' He slipped his hand out from underneath her possessive grasp. 'Besides, you're in love with Jamie.'

Adele opened her mouth, but she couldn't deny that the mention of his name triggered something inside her. Something different from the feelings she had for Rafique; a yearning as plaintive as the cry of a baby. Whatever it was she had meant to say, she left it unsaid.

He smiled. 'I think we should get some rest.'

Adele rolled over to allow Rafique back into bed. Lying in his arms, she listened to the sound of his breathing as his fingers trickled down her back, stroking her into sleep.

Exhausted with so much food, wine and sex, it didn't take long for her to drift off. Rafique curled his body around hers, cradling Adele in his arms like a fragile treasure. He stayed like that for an hour, his shoulder aching sharply. But like a monk punishing himself for his god, he couldn't let go, couldn't stop worshipping her. The sweet smell of her hair and skin made the taste in his mouth seem all the more bitter.

He hadn't meant for it to turn out this way. What had begun as lust was supposed to end as such. He didn't deserve the love of such a beautiful creature – a beautiful, young creature – and he obviously didn't have it. When he had mentioned Jamie, the truth had curled wordlessly from her lips like smoke, her silence more telling than speech.

She loved Jamie. And why wouldn't she? The fact that it made sense didn't stop it hurting.

'I love you,' he whispered to the back of her neck. He hugged her, hoping that by some miracle her body would seal with his and she would be trapped in his grasp, forever. 'I love you, Adele.'

She murmured and turned within his arms to face him. 'Did you say something?' Her voice was slurred with tiredness. 'What did you say?'

'I want to make love to you.' He felt his cheeks burning. It wasn't a lie, but it wasn't what he really wanted to tell her. 'I want to fuck you.'

She giggled dreamily. 'What's the difference?'

He pulled the sheet from her shoulder. Gathering her breast in his fingers, he dipped his mouth to the tender swell of flesh. Selfishness hoped she would translate the emotion of his kiss. Don't go, it said. Stay with me and I'll worship you every minute of every day. Say you love me.

'Oh God Rafique, that feels so good.'

She flopped on to her back, moaning as his tongue swirled over her nipple. His fingers drifted over her belly, over the wonderfully shocking smoothness of her mound and between her legs. Almost involuntarily, it seemed, the velvet of her inner thighs parted for his touch. She was wet, again, coating his skin with the delicious juice that inexplicably made his heart ache. He lifted himself over her and slid off the edge of sanity, into the eternity of her pussy. Her whole body sighed beneath him.

It was lucky, he thought, that her senses were cloaked in the confusion that lay halfway between consciousness and sleep. If she had been awake, she would have heard what his body was telling her, and it would have given him away.

Chapter Eleven

'*B*reak a leg.' Nadia grabbed Adele's shoulders and kissed the air on either side of her heavily made-up face.

'*Toi, toi, toi.*' Alexei winked and playfully slapped her backside.

'*Merde!*' Carmen squeezed her hand, giggling as always at her choice of words. Whoever had first decided that the French for 'shit' was also an appropriate good luck message, he had an avid fan in Carmen. She never seemed to tire of the joke.

'*Chukkas.*' Adele looked round as Jessica joined the huddle on the stage. Surprised to see her there, her tracksuit incongruous among their costumes, Adele was lost for words. There was something unbelievable in Jessica's eyes, warming their usual iciness; admiration and a grudging respect. 'I mean it,' Jessica insisted. 'Don't worry. You'll be brilliant.'

Adele smiled to herself. She wasn't worried.

'Break a leg.' Uncomfortably, as if they were strangers, Jamie patted her arm. The smile on his face was strained, and not echoed in his eyes.

'Thanks, everyone. Same to you.'

They drifted away, back to their own, private preparations. For a moment, Adele watched Jamie as he bounced in gentle, springy jumps. He seemed preoccupied and nervous, which puzzled her. In ballet terms, Jamie was a veteran. Why should this small audience scare him?

She shrugged inside and returned to her own warm-up. She didn't have the time or energy to worry about him. Besides getting her body ready, she had to struggle to keep her face composed until the ballet started. It was almost impossible. The sensations sparking from her crotch seemed to shoot directly to her mouth, and she was desperate to allow the grin she was hiding to spread across her face.

She fixed her eyes on a square inch of the black velvet curtain hiding the stage from the auditorium, and eased herself up on to pointe. There was a tiny but vicious pain in her toe, managing to find something to rub against despite the padding inside her pointe shoe. But above the pain, clouding her thoughts like a gas, was an almost unbearable pleasure.

She had sensed mischief in Rafique's eyes when he had brought her costume into the dressing room. 'It needed adjusting,' he had said, unable to resist a glance at her breasts as she unzipped her tracksuit top. 'It should fit more snugly now.'

'It seemed to fit pretty well, yesterday,' she had said, her fingers closing over his as he passed her the hanger.

'It wasn't perfect. It's a tiny adjustment, but I think you'll notice the difference.' He turned to go.

'Aren't you going to kiss me, for luck?'

He paused at the door, his head bowed. 'You don't need luck, Adele. Just dance the way you feel. And enjoy yourself.'

It might have been a tiny adjustment, but it had transformed her costume from layers of material encasing her body, to something that was as much a part of her body as her skin. Sewn into the satin lining of the velvet strip between her legs, a tiny, perfectly positioned ring pressed around her clitoris. The soft rubber was textured with a myriad of miniature, finger-like protrusions which tickled and rubbed with her every move. Between her naked buttocks, a plug the size of her little finger had been fastened into her thong. It was so narrow that had she been standing still, she might have been able to forget about its presence in her forbidden hole, but she was never still, and the dildo throbbed inside her like fear. Adele bit her lip to stifle a gasp, and tried a pirouette.

Richard appeared on stage, stunningly immaculate in his dinner suit. As always on a first night, he was distractedly polishing his already shiny bald head with one of his hands.

'How far off are we?'

Adele looked round at the sound of Alexei's voice. He had cracked his knuckles, flexed his feet and was obviously ready to start.

'A couple of minutes,' Richard replied.

A cyclone of nerves whirled inside Adele's spine. This was it, she thought. The moment of truth, the moment she had been waiting for since the age of sixteen. This was the chance she had dreamt about; the chance to prove herself. She was ready to grasp it.

Trying to take in some oxygen, she went through her last minute, superstitious ritual. She touched her toes. Standing up, she kicked her right leg high into the air, then her left. She rolled her neck, hearing the faint and satisfying click of her bones. Then she stepped up to the curtain, and raised the tiny flap. Peering through the peep-hole, her eye swivelled around the auditorium.

A hundred pairs of eyes looked back at her. Up in the precarious boxes, rising in the tiered seats, every one of Rafique's guests was watching the curtain, waiting expectantly. Adele scanned the stalls, looking for clues about Rafique – these were his friends, after all. But there was nothing unusual about this audience, smartly dressed in evening gowns and tuxedos and murmuring in hushed anticipation. The unusual part was that they had come to see her. As if a vacuum had appeared in her soul, her nerves were swallowed up. Even when she saw David Renfell, sitting in the middle of the front row next to Rafique, she felt nothing but a sense of command. This was her night.

'Positions please, everyone.' Richard clapped his hands and ushered them off the stage. Settling into his vantage point in the front wing, he flicked the switch that extinguished the auditorium lights, and dimmed those on the stage. 'You just can't get the staff these days,' he whispered to Adele, laughing at his multiple rôles. As well as being the choreographer, tonight he was stage manager, stagehand and musical director too. He rolled his eyes, and switched on the music.

The hum of the audience stopped. Adele drifted back, away from Richard and into the shadow that lined the wall. She absorbed the overture, watching the others.

Adele always relished that delicious, spine-tingling moment before it all started. That sense of magic to come, the silent seconds of concentration; the essence of theatre was distilled in that time. No matter how little she felt like dancing, that pre-performance minute never failed to inspire her. Tonight, when she could barely contain her desire to get on to the stage, her body trembled with excitement.

Jamie and Carmen moved upstage into the top wing. At the other side of the proscenium arch, Alexei and Nadia waited, their faces pale in the ghostly lighting. Behind them, pressed against the wall, Jessica's blonde hair was just visible.

They waited and waited. The overture seemed to stretch forever. And then, all of a sudden, Richard was turning the handle that pulled the curtain, and with a low rumble and a swish, the veil was lifted on the world of make-believe.

Carmen and Jamie drifted on to stage. Innocent young lovers, they swayed in each other's arms, demonstrating their burgeoning romance with tentative hands and shy glances. Adele watched, only vaguely aware of them. She was thinking of her entrance, shocking in its contrast. Then, before she knew it, the pas de deux was over. It was time for the succubus to appear. In a dream, she walked forward to the very edge of the wing. The lights changed, and so did her consciousness. As if she was wearing a gas mask, her field of vision narrowed and her breathing grew deafening. She hovered, teasing the audience.

'Adele.' Behind her, Richard whispered urgently.

She hesitated, her heart palpitating.

'Adele!'

She exploded on to the stage. The gasps from the audience galvanised her quaking limbs and pumped her body full of strength. She ate up the space, throwing herself violently from one gut-wrenchingly perfect position into another. Traversing the floor in a series of split leaps, arms flung back over her head, she paused to look out at the audience before spinning into her next sequence. She had them, she could feel it. Their attention was in the palm of her hand, helpless in her tenacious grip. They were prisoners, one and all, of the succubus's raw, terrible energy.

Her solo was over and she ran off stage right, passing Alexei and Nadia as they ran on. Jessica said something but Adele couldn't hear it; nothing could pierce her concentration. In a flash she was back on, dancing with Jamie.

His partnering was as sure as ever, but there was a hesitancy about him. For a second her focus threatened to blur, then she realised he was acting his fright of the succubus. To compensate, she summoned more force from a hidden part of her mind, and threw her body at his. It wasn't so much a pas de deux as a challenge, an evil, unstoppable force twisting in his hands and threatening to overpower his mortal weakness. He might have been the man but she was stronger than him. She was invincible. Abandoning himself to her, Jamie knelt, his lips raised to her pussy, and a surge of power reverberated throughout her body.

Having sapped his strength, she moved on to her next victim. In a whorl of terror, Nadia was used and thrown aside. Alexei was next, his heavy body emasculated by the succubus's insatiable greed. Then it was Jamie's turn to be ravaged once again, only this time his naïve young lover joined them in a pas de trois filled with vehement fury.

Alone on stage once more, Adele's mouth dripped with lust. Lost within the sense of power and yet totally in control, she was only aware of certain things. Desire, pulsing in her vagina and raging in her anus. Her fingers and toes ripping through the air, cracking with the breathtaking precision of a whip landing on quivering flesh. The audience, a hundred people as one, were gripped by every awe-inspiring movement; they were her doomed prisoners, clinging on to the edge of a burning cliff by their fingertips. Their skin was on fire, but they dared not let go.

Rejoicing in the purity of evil, Adele danced on. Hands and faces merged into one, each of her partners dwarfed by the magnitude of her lust. The music rushed in her veins, driving her forward, pushing her closer to the hell that was the succubus's heaven. At last she stood above them, mere mortals racked in agonising ecstasy at her feet, and she threw her head back in a silent prayer of laughter. Her fingers spread at her neck. Following the essence of sex as it trickled down into her guts, she pressed her hands over her throat, over her heaving breasts, over her stomach and on to her mound. Shaking violently, she opened her arms, palms towards the audience. Slowly, wringing every dreadful ounce of evil from her black soul, she raised her arms and lowered her head. Looking out into the dark auditorium, arms outstretched, she glowered. The music screeched to its climax. In the stunned silence that followed, her body was finally still, but her eyes blazed with a power so raw, so frightening, she felt the audience shrink away from her.

I am the succubus, she thought, as the curtain swept shut.

It was over. Back in her room, the shower rained her body in reality, washing off her make-up and rinsing the lacquer from her hair. The thrill of capturing the audience, powerful as a drug, had worn off as soon as the applause and congratulations had finished. It all felt strangely anti-climactic.

She wished she could remember more of it. Her warm-up was crystal clear in her memory, as were the kisses and hugs from the other dancers afterwards. But the performance was a vague, ethereal haze. It was as if she had walked through a time warp, losing an hour of her life.

She turned off the shower and squeezed the water from her hair. She was supposed to be hurrying downstairs, but she couldn't be bothered. She didn't even want to go to the party.

She dried her body and wrapped her hair in a towel. Whether she wanted to or not, she would have to get a move on. It was Rafique's birthday, and the dancers were his guests of honour. Everyone would be waiting.

Going back into the bedroom, she ran some mousse through her hair. Standing naked in front of the mirror, she turned on her hair dryer. Slowly, her golden waves reappeared as she teased them with the warm stream of air. Absent-mindedly, she touched her smooth pussy, still fascinated by its utter nudity. Just as the tip of her middle finger sank into her moistness, something caught her eye, and she jumped.

Switching off the dryer, she ran to the bed. There, draped across the bedspread like a woman waiting for her lover, was a dress; a long, golden, clingy sheath. Beside it was a box; inside, a pair of high-heeled, mock-snakeskin sandals perched provocatively. Laid on top of the dress was an envelope.

She opened it up. It was a note from Rafique, written in an elegant, sloping hand.

Adele,
    You already know that I think of you as talented, beautiful and sexy. Further flattery would be point-less, except that you shocked even me, tonight.
    I will never forget the way you danced. You were formidable. Now I know what the succubus would look like, should she ever decide to haunt me.
    All that remains is for me to hope that you enjoy the rest of your life, as much as I've enjoyed this week.
I remain, eternally yours,
The Master.
P.S. I hope you like the dress. I designed it myself.

So much for Rafique saying he was talentless, she thought, snatching excitedly at the long strip of satin. It slid coolly over her body, flowing like liquid pleasure over every curve. She pulled the sandals from their box and buckled the narrow straps, then stood, and tenta-tively moved back to the full length mirror.

Stunned by her reflection, she looked at herself from every angle. The dress clung seductively at her breasts and hips before dropping, heavy and straight, to her ankles. Spaghetti straps ran from the low scoop, half way down her back, criss-crossing before passing over her shoulders to the front. The neckline was low, cut into a gentle point which nestled in the delicacy of her cleavage. The fullness and shape of her breasts was obvious, unimpeded by a bra and covered only lightly in the sensual fabric. She couldn't wear knickers; the slopes of her taut belly and buttocks were also visible beneath the clutch of the dress. The dull gold sheen matched her hair perfectly, and her eyes seemed to take on a deeper shade of green in contrast. The spindly heels were low enough to walk in, but high enough to make her feel tall. Giving her freedom to move, a long slit plunged to the hem from her thigh, revealing a leg and a sexily clad foot. Her shoes, their animal print blending with the hue of her outfit, were incredibly provocative. Her high insteps arched dramatically, held only by thin bands across the toes and straps circling her ankles from the cups of leather at her heels.

She took a deep breath and snatched at her make-up bag. Putting on a brush of mascara and a shine of lipgloss, she smiled at her reflection. She tilted her head upside down, flicked it back and allowed her hair to settle into its side parting, curling over one eye.

Suddenly, she felt in the mood for a party.

The ballroom erupted in applause as Foster announced her arrival. Unsure of what was expected of her, and hoping she wasn't going to have to make a speech, she smiled shyly. The adulation was quite unnerving. It was one thing on stage, separated from the audience by the lights, the costumes, the drama; but here, she could see their faces, look into their eyes, watch their expressions. She felt naked, and intensely aware of the bareness of her breasts and sex beneath her dress.

David saved her, appearing at her side and steering her out of the spotlight and into the crowd. Adele was as tall as him in her heels.

'You know,' he said, as the clapping slowly subsided and conversation resumed, 'I'm a little angry with you, Adele.'

She accepted a glass of champagne from a white-jacketed waiter. 'Oh?'

'How long have you been in the National Ballet now?'

'Five years.'

'That's a long time to keep your talent to yourself. May I ask why someone who can dance like that, would want to keep it a secret?'

She laughed as bubbles fizzed inside her head. 'To be honest, David, I didn't know I could dance like that myself, until tonight.'

His eyes narrowed. 'Think you can do it again?'

'I know I can.'

'Good.' He slid his arm around her waist and walked her towards the buffet table. 'That ballet's a real crowd-puller, the sort of thing the critics hate and the audiences go wild for. I'm putting it into our repertoire, as part of a triple bill. How do you feel about that?'

'Well that's wonderful!'

'And how do you feel about doing Odette/Odile in *Swan Lake*? It's a big rôle, a lot to learn.'

Adele nodded. It was a big rôle, one of the most difficult for the ballerina. As well as portraying Odette, the tragic, love-lorn swan queen, there was the contrasting Act Three character of Odile, the wicked, fiery imposter, the Black Swan. 'I think I could do it, but that's a principal rôle.'

'Yes, it is.' He kissed her cheek. 'Congratulations.'

David picked up a plate and began to fill it.

'Are you hungry?'

She turned. It was Richard. 'Not really.'

'There are some people who want to meet you.'

He linked Adele's arm and paraded her across the ballroom. She felt like Audrey Hepburn with Cary Grant, all eyes following them as if they were radiating sex appeal. With a start, she realised that they probably did make a handsome couple, Richard with his powerful, dark body, and her in the golden, revealing sheath. She looked up at him and he grinned, squeezing her arm in his elbow.

'You were fantastic tonight, darling. I've learnt a lot about you in the last few days, and believe me, you're not going to get away with that shyness thing any more. You're going to be in all my ballets, from now on.' As if he was parking his prized sports car, he positioned her in front of a semi-circle of men and women. 'This is your new fan club, darling. A few of these guys have never been to the ballet before tonight.'

'No, but we'll be going again!' one of them laughed, a man with short, brown hair and perfect teeth.

'Allow me to introduce you. Adele, this is . . .'

Her concentration waned as Richard's hand wafted around the avid group. It was amazing, she thought, how her performance had affected them. She had commanded their attention from the stage, and now, memories of her sexual aggression were reflected in their eyes. The power was intoxicating.

'Can I have the ones you don't want?' Richard whispered surreptitiously.

'I hear you're dancing in *Swan Lake* next season.' An Aryan-looking man leered and offered her another glass of champagne.

'News travels fast,' she laughed.

'I'll certainly be coming to watch.'

'Me too. I never realised ballet could be so . . .'

'Sexy,' a plummy voice chipped in.

'How long have you been a ballerina?'

'You must be very fit.'

Adele sank in the sea of faces as they closed around her. The Aryan man's eyes landed like a butterfly on her breasts. A hand slid possessively around her waist then slipped, snaking over her buttock.

'Are all male dancers gay?'

'No!' she snapped, brushing the searching fingers away from her body.

'Have you got a boyfriend?'

She looked around the packed party, suddenly wanting the familiarity of a certain face. She found the dancers, clinging to Rafique as he held court. Carmen waved, and as she did, Rafique glanced up. His eyes drank in her dress, then, without acknowledging her, his attention was diverted and he looked across the room.

Adele followed Rafique's gaze and fell straight into Jamie's. Handsome in his tuxedo, a formal contrast to the usual unruliness of his hair, he was standing by the huge French windows leading out on to the lawn. He was sipping champagne and being admired by three extremely pretty young women. He smiled, a sad, forced smile, and turning his back, walked out into the night.

'Will you hold this for me, please?' She passed her glass to one of her slavering fans. 'Excuse me. I'll be right back.'

By the time Adele reached the other side of the wide ballroom and stepped outside, Jamie was nowhere to be seen. She hesitated, wondering which way he had gone, then she heard the creak of a door to her left. Her heels sank into the grass as she chased the sound.

Rounding the corner of the Manor, she realised he must have gone back into the theatre. The fire exit was heavy, designed to be opened from the inside, but adrenalin gave her the strength to pull it. The nerves that had left her alone for the performance suddenly reappeared, and with a pounding heart, she stepped back into the darkness of the wings.

The stage lights were on and he was there, staring out into the empty auditorium.

'Jamie?' He didn't jump. He didn't even look at her as she joined him on stage. 'Jamie? What are you doing here?'

243

He sighed, his breath rushing loudly as if he had been holding it in. 'I'm thinking.'

Adele's heels tapped on the lino as she walked towards him. 'What about?'

'About going back to Munich.'

'What? You've only been back in England a few weeks! I thought you wanted to stay in the National Ballet until you retired?'

'So did I. But I think I might have made a mistake.'

'I don't understand.' Adele touched his arm. His eyes remained steadfast, fixed on some invisible point in the dark distance. 'Jamie, look at me.' Very reluctantly, it seemed to Adele, he turned to meet her eyes. His expression was one she'd never seen in his happy, open face; he was forlorn, tortured. 'Jamie, what's happened to make you think like this?'

He laced his fingers on top of his head, escaping the worry in her face and resuming his stare into the blackness. 'Going to Germany was a career move.' He paused, biting his upper lip as if trying to stop the words from coming out. 'Coming back to England wasn't. In Munich I had a better wage, a company flat, seven weeks holiday, and a pension.'

Adele was confused. 'So why come home?'

'I missed England, my family, my friends. But above all, I had this ridiculous idea that as soon as I came home, the girl I had kissed, once, would fall gratefully into my arms.' He unlaced his hands, and his arms slumped down to his sides. 'I can't believe how stupid I've been.'

'Jamie?' He dropped his head back and closed his eyes, as if he was trying to shut out her voice. 'Jamie, I –'

He turned to face her, his clear blue eyes suddenly consumed with self-loathing. 'Look, Adele, there's no need to say anything. It's my fault. I've behaved like an idiot. I had this fantasy that I would come back after five years, and we would pick up where we left off. Where we left off! Listen to me! We kissed, once, at a party!' He ran his hands through his curly hair. 'It slipped my mind that life goes on. I couldn't stop thinking about you, you see, and I managed to delude myself that you felt the same. I forgot that people change, they grow up, they move on. You've certainly changed. A lot.'

She nodded almost imperceptibly to herself. 'But what does that have to do with . . . with us?'

'Adele, you don't have to pretend any more. I know why you've been avoiding me. I know all about you and Alexei.'

Her eyelids fluttered nervously. 'You know what, exactly?'

He walked away from her, to the front of the stage. 'I know you've been seeing him.' His voice was calmer now, but with a bitter tremor at the edges. 'If I was honest with myself, I didn't really expect to come home and find you alone, waiting for me. But Alexei? I don't want to sound jealous, which I am, but he just doesn't seem your type.'

Adele walked up behind him, and put her hand on his shoulder. 'And what is my type?'

'I don't know.' He hung his head. 'I don't know anything, any more.'

She pulled at him, turning him towards her. He was still a couple of inches taller than her, despite her heels, and she looked up into the wide blueness of his eyes. 'Jamie, you're right about Alexei. He isn't my type. I have slept with him though, once.' She lifted one corner of her mouth in regret. 'I won't be doing it again.'

A crease of confusion appeared in his smooth brow. 'Once?'

She nodded.

His mouth opened hesitantly, closed decisively, then opened again. 'Are you seeing anyone else?'

Her eyes glazed for a moment, then she blinked herself back into the present. She shook her head. 'There've been others. But I never stopped thinking about you, either.'

Slowly, he took a deep breath, blowing the mist from his eyes; they cleared of anger, hurt and mistrust, and refilled with love. Cautiously, as if his touch might stir remembrance of some other reason why they couldn't be together, he lifted his hands on to her shoulders. His head began to dip, stopped while he watched her mouth opening, then dipped again.

Their lips locked tenderly. Neither Adele nor Jamie moved for an eternity, transfixed by the delight of their third kiss. It might as well have been Adele's first kiss, ever. Her body fell, her soul unravelled, her thoughts flew into another dimension. The yawning chasm in her guts, which she hadn't even noticed before, was suddenly full. She was complete in her rapture.

Their kiss moved into another, then another. Parting their lips, moving fluently together in their own, intimate choreography, they shared the same breath. Warmth caressed Adele's mouth, followed by the urgency of his tongue. Her hands rested on his upper arms, feeling his muscles tense as he gripped her tighter.

After what seemed like an hour of slow exploration, they pulled apart. Jamie stared at Adele as if she was a newly discovered wonder he had to commit to memory. He reached up and brushed her lips with a fingertip.

'Touch me,' she whispered.

He paused, unsure.

'Touch me.' She guided his fingers downwards.

'Oh,' he sighed, his face racked in ecstatic agony. His touch poured lightly over her uplifted chin, over her throat and spread like oil, all over her satin-clad breast. The shape seemed to make his breath short and hurried. He dropped his eyes, watching his hand. Then he looked up, his features frozen with emotion, and he kissed her, again.

'Jamie.' Adele nearly choked on the words, they had

been in her subconscious for so long. 'Jamie, make love
to me.'

He raised an eyebrow.

'Make love to me. Now.'

'Now?'

She nodded.

He blinked, his eyes heavy with gratitude and relief.
'Shall we go to my room?'

'No, Jamie. Let's do it here.'

He gulped.

'Here, Jamie. Now. I've been waiting five years. I can't
wait any longer.' Adele pushed his hands away, and slid
the delicate straps from her shoulders. 'Make love to
me.'

'Oh,' he said, his gaze falling uncontrollably down her
body. Reaching out for her, he stroked the inward curve
of her waist. 'Oh God. You're so beautiful.' His other
hand helped her dress where it hesitated over her hips.
'I've wanted you for so long.'

At the back of the auditorium, Rafique hid in the gloom.
A lifetime ago, he had ripped off her clothes in the spot
where he stood. Now, someone else was revealing her
beauty. He watched the dark gold of her dress fall to the
floor, and slipped out of her life the same way he had
slipped in, without a sound.

BLACK LACE NEW BOOKS

Published in January

UNHALLOWED RITES
Martine Marquand
£5.99

Allegra Vitali is bored with life in her guardian's Venetian palazzo until the day sexual curiosity draws her to look at the depraved illustrations he keeps in his private chamber. She tries to deny her new passion for flesh by submitting to the life of a nun. The strange order of the Convent of Santa Agnetha provides new tests and new temptations, encouraging her to perform ritual acts with men and women who inhabit the strange, cloistered world.

ISBN 0 352 33222 0

BY ANY MEANS
Cheryl Mildenhall
£5.99

Francesca, Veronique and Taran are partners in Falconer Associates, a London-based advertising agency. The three women are good friends and they're not averse to taking their pleasure with certain male employees. When they put in a bid to win a design account for Fast Track sportswear they are pitched against the notorious Oscar Rage who will stop at nothing to get what he wants. Despite Francesca's efforts to resist Oscar's arrogant charm, she finds him impossible to ignore.

ISBN 0 352 33221 1

Published in February

MÉNAGE
Emma Holly
£5.99

When Kate finds her two male flatmates in bed with each other she is powerless to resist their offer to join them in kinky games. She's a woman who has everything: a great job; loads of friends; tons of ambition. As she embarks on a strange ménage à trois, she wants nothing more than to keep both her admirers happy but, inevitably, things become complicated. Can the three lovers live happily ever after . . . together?

ISBN 0 352 33231 X

THE SUCCUBUS
Zoe le Verdier
£5.99

Adele is a talented ballet dancer thrown into the role of the Succubus – a legendary sex-crazed demon who is thought to haunt the house of her wealthy patron, Rafique. Adele feels insecure; her every move is shadowed by Jessica Sharpe, her rival and understudy who has her eyes on Adele's boyfriend, Jamie. As Adele learns to relish her new-found success, she finds a sudden, voracious appetitie for new experiences. Can she discover the strength to conquer the other demons in her life?

ISBN 0 352 33230 1

To be published in March

THE CAPTIVATION
Natasha Rostova
£5.99

It's 1917 and war-torn Russia is teetering on the brink of the Bolshevik revolution. The Princess Katya is forced to leave her estate when a mob threatens her life. After a daring escape, she ends up in the encampment of a rebel Cossack army. The men have not seen a woman for weeks and sexual tensions are running high. The captain is a man of dark desires and he and Katya become involved in an erotic power struggle.

ISBN 0 352 33234 4

A DANGEROUS LADY
Lucinda Carrington
£5.99

Lady Katherine Gainsworth is compromised into a marriage of convenience which takes her from her English home to the Prussian Duchy of Heldenburg. Once there, she is introduced to her future in-laws but finds they have some unconventional ideas of how to welcome her into the family. Her father-in-law, the Count, is no stranger to the underworld of bawdy clubs in the principality and soon Katherine finds herself embroiled in political intrigue, jewel theft and sexual blackmail.

ISBN 0 352 33236 0

FEMININE WILES
Karina Moore
£7.99

Young American Kelly Aslett is due to fly back to the USA to claim her inheritance according to the terms of her father's will. As she prepares to fly home she falls passionately in love with French artist Luc Duras. Meanwhile, in California, Kelly's stepmother is determined to secure Kelly's inheritance for herself and enlists the help of her handsome lover and the dashing and ruthless Johnny Casigelli to assist her in her criminal deed. When Kelly finds herself held captive by Johnny, will she succumb to his masculine charms or can she use her feminine wiles to gain what's rightfully hers?

ISBN 0 352 33235 2

If you would like a complete list of plot summaries of Black Lace titles, please fill out the questionnaire overleaf or send a stamped addressed envelope to:-

Black Lace, 332 Ladbroke Grove, London W10 5AH

BLACK LACE BACKLIST

All books are priced £4.99 unless another price is given.

– – – – – – ✂ – – – – – – – – – – – – – – – – – –

Please send me the books I have ticked above.

Name   ....

Address   ....

                  ....

                  ....

             .... Post Code   ....

Send to: **Cash Sales, Black Lace Books, 332 Ladbroke Grove, London W10 5AH, UK.**

Please enclose a cheque or postal order, made payable to **Virgin Publishing Ltd**, to the value of the books you have ordered plus postage and packing costs as follows:

UK and BFPO – £1.00 for the first book, 50p for each subsequent book.

Overseas (including Republic of Ireland) – £2.00 for the first book, £1.00 each subsequent book.

If you would prefer to pay by VISA or ACCESS/MASTERCARD, please write your card number and expiry date here:

....

Please allow up to 28 days for delivery.

Signature   ....

– – – – – – ✂ – – – – – – – – – – – – – – – – – –